Montana STORM

JOSIE JADE

This a work of fiction. Names, characters, places, and incidents are the product of the author's imagination or are used fictitiously, and any resemblance to actual persons, living or dead, business establishments, events or locals is entirely coincidental.

Cover created by Deranged Doctor Designs.

A Calamittie Jane Publishing Book

MONTANA STORM: RESTING WARRIOR RANCH

Chapter 1

Jude Williams

Pain rippled along my limbs, and screams echoed off the walls of the cave. They wouldn't break me. No matter how hard they tried and how much they took it out on my body. I would resist.

Another scream echoed that caused me almost as much pain as my own injuries. Isaac. I needed to get him out. He shouldn't be a captive while I was free.

Wait…

The scream called me one more time, and I lunged at the culprit, stumbling, coming to full alertness as I struck air. My body was covered with sweat, sheets twisted around me from the way I'd tried to take down the invisible enemy.

Of course it was a fucking dream. It was always a fucking dream. Not exactly uncommon, but definitely getting old.

I sank back down onto the bed, staring at the ceiling

and letting my breath settle back to normal. If you could call waking up fighting your own worst enemies normal. Whatever this was, it was exhausting. Even with therapy, even trying to work through my own guilt along with the scars on both my mind and body, the dreams had never stopped.

Allowing my hands to curl into fists, I hauled in a deep breath. And again. It took everything in me to resist lashing out in frustration. I was *tired* of reliving those moments. Tired of feeling so out of control that I needed to compensate for it. Fucking tired of letting it hold me back, when none of it was my choice to begin with.

I stayed still as long as I could before the panic set in. The creeping instinct that told me I needed to make sure everything was the way I left it and everything was still under control.

One room at a time. I moved with methodical ease through the house, flicking the light on in each room and assessing. I knew all the details so well at this point; it only took seconds for my brain to acknowledge everything was fine. But without this, the shadows lurking in the corners of the rooms screamed at my instincts until I checked. It was easier to get it out of the way.

The whole house was quiet. No strange sounds and no echoing screams. Just the silence of the isolated countryside and the sound of my own breathing.

Soft whirring of fans and the occasional electronic grunt and beep came from the computers in my security office as I sat down. Some people might think the network of cameras I had set up all across my property—and the six-monitor setup I had in a secure room—was overkill for an ex-SEAL who lived in the middle of nowhere. And they would probably be right.

But as each image flickered up onto the screen,

showing emptiness, blowing grass and tree branches, and the occasional animal, my instincts settled. From here, if I saw something was wrong—or if I saw anything or anyone who wasn't supposed to be there—I could fix it. I had total control, and it was all I had.

I didn't like that I needed it, but it didn't change anything. Especially after a nightmare, I needed to control my environment. Everything, from which lights were on to what and who was touching me. It was the only thing keeping me from slipping too far backward and letting the memories crash into me and dictate my behavior.

Right now, it was even harder.

I glanced at the date. The anniversary of Isaac's death was getting close. Five years of guilt and wondering if there was something I could have done to keep him alive and, looking back, examining every facet of my rescue to see if we could have gotten him out too.

Those thoughts never helped, but I couldn't stop them either.

It was still early, but there was no chance I would go back to sleep now. Shadows would jump out of the corners at me, causing me to tense and verify everything before I could relax. At this point, it was better if I just stayed awake and rode out the rest of the day.

Hopefully I would make up the sleep later tonight. But a part of me knew it wasn't likely, no matter how much I wanted it.

Grant slung his bag into the back of the pickup and grinned unconsciously. It wasn't long ago he wouldn't have been able to lift something without pain. Only a few months ago, the piece of shrapnel that had been compressing his spine for years had been removed, and we were all having fun watching him relearn life without pain. Seeing him enjoy it never got old. "Still feeling okay?" I asked.

"Never better." He tapped a hand on the side of the truck. "I'm glad I can actually do things like this now and not be stuck watching all you guys have all the fun."

Liam snorted as he tossed his own bag into the back. "Fourteen hours in a truck is fun to him now. Shrapnel will really change some things, won't it?"

Grant just shook his head, smirking. Liam wasn't wrong—I was glad it wasn't me who had been tapped to drive down on the trip to Colorado, but I was equally glad Grant could feel like a part of the group again. He'd struggled with it long enough.

"Just don't let Daniel control the radio," I said. "That will make it seem like a far longer trip." Though I had a feeling Liam's teasing temperament might be the thing to drive both Grant and Daniel crazy.

"I have excellent taste in music, thank you very much." Daniel lifted his overnight bag into the bed of the truck and tossed the keys to Liam. "And you'll be asking for my music when it keeps you awake."

Liam made a face at me behind his back, but he headed for the cab of the truck as Daniel looked me up and down. "You okay? You didn't have to get up early for this."

"I was already up." He looked at me, and I knew better than to lie. But I wasn't about to open up and lay all my troubles on Daniel's shoulders before a long trip. I shrugged. "I've been better."

"Want to talk about it?"

A chuckle worked its way out of me. "Not particularly, but thanks."

He clapped me on the shoulder. "You know we're here for you no matter what, so if you want to talk about it—"

I held up a hand. "I know."

Daniel smiled. We all knew. It was part of being a Resting Warrior. And it was part of what made Daniel a good leader—he noticed things, like if we were the slightest bit off, and was willing to lend an ear if we needed it. But I knew any of the guys would do the same, if I went to them and asked.

"Keep an eye on Noah," Daniel said.

"I will." He was nowhere to be found at the moment, though I wasn't surprised. Noah had his hands full with a different, complicated situation. One of our previous clients had been dragged into some trouble, and Noah felt bound to help him and his sister. While that was going on, it was a risk to split our group, but Lucas and I would hold things down while the guys made the delivery.

"You're sure all three of you need to go?"

We rarely went anywhere overnight alone—old habits from our team days—but three was also rare.

Daniel nodded, walking with me toward the stable where Grant was already gathering the horse. "Call me paranoid, but with all this stuff about the Riders and animals going to bad places, I want us to be prepared and cautious."

I understood that. The Riders, the gang Noah was trying to pin down, had a laundry list of possible crimes to their name. Given the ranch they were taking the horse to was a client we'd never worked with before, I understood Daniel's instincts for caution. "Makes sense."

Grant led the horse out, followed by Cori, his fiancée and the local vet. "I've got it." Daniel took the bridle. "You can say goodbye."

Cori blushed, but she smiled as Grant released the

horse and turned to her instead. Grant and I were similar. He had a similar interest and...need for control. Especially in the private areas of our lives. I would never pry or overstep to ask how that was going, but the way Cori looked up at him when he pulled her in was a look I craved.

Complete trust and adoration. In a single look, I saw Cori's knowledge that Grant would never harm her. Even unintentionally. She had good reason to believe it—he'd proven he would protect her, even at the cost of his own health.

I wished I could trust myself not to hurt someone. But the walls of my bedroom had too much spackle on them from me fighting nightmare opponents for me to believe I was ready.

Behind me, Daniel shut the door to the horse trailer. "Ready?"

Grant kissed Cori quickly, running a hand through her hair before he jogged to the truck and jumped inside.

I waved. "Call me if you need something."

"Will do."

The crunch of the dirt and gravel was loud in the quiet of the morning, a small cloud of dust caught by the sun coming over the mountains.

Mara was a ways down the road, working on some repairs to one of the floral and garden beds that were her domain here at the ranch. She waved to the truck as it went by and then waved to Cori and me as well.

"Things going to be boring around here with them gone?" Cori asked, jingling her keys in her hand.

I shrugged. "Probably quieter at the very least, with Liam gone."

She laughed. "That's true. I have to get to town for an early appointment. See you around?"

"Sure thing."

"Oh." She snapped her fingers, turning back to me. "It's Wednesday. Means it's pickup day, right? Maybe I'll see you at Deja Brew, then. I'm stopping there on the way to the clinic."

I froze. It was pickup day. I hadn't forgotten—it wasn't something I would forget easily. But I didn't realize other people tracked it as closely as I did. "Maybe you will," I said. "Might as well get an early jump on it."

I let her drive off before getting into my truck and starting it up. Cori likely wouldn't mind my following her into town, but given what had happened to her, Evelyn, and even Lena, I liked to give the women in our community space.

The ride into the town was quick and easy, Garnet Bend still waking up. I parked in front of Deja Brew, the town's favorite coffee shop and bakery, owned by Lena Mitchell.

She was visible through the windows of the store, helping Cori get her coffee and making conversation with the couple of other customers in the store. Her face lit up talking to people, no doubt clear to anyone in the vicinity she was enjoying every second. She was a talented baker and businesswoman, and I could easily say Resting Warrior would be different if she hadn't befriended us early on.

Hell, it was Lena who'd convinced the town that a bunch of grumpy ex-military guys who bought a ranch and built walls around it weren't crazy or ridiculous. And just like the first time I ever laid eyes on her, she was the most beautiful woman I'd ever seen.

Her hair was a blond explosion of waves, with streaks of purple and teal all through it. Curves you could see from a mile away and a smile that made it seem like the sun was shining even when it was past sunset.

I dropped out of the truck and went inside, unable to

keep myself away, even if it was for the best. Only a couple months ago, at Harlan and Grace's wedding, I'd danced with Lena. Having her in my arms…it was everything. But that was all it could ever be.

Cori waved to me on her way out, and the last customers were served their coffee before Lena saw me. Her eyes lit up, and her cheeks turned a shade of pink I always wanted to keep there. Preferably for different reasons. But that was a fantasy I needed to keep in my head and nowhere else.

"Hey, Jude. I have the stuff ready. I'll be right back."

I couldn't keep my eyes off her as she went to the kitchen, the struggle in my mind warring back and forth. There was no one in my life I wanted more than Lena. There'd never been anyone I wanted as much as I did her. But after this morning—and every morning I woke up in the middle of a battle—it wasn't meant to be. Lena was competent and fierce. I doubted the control I both needed and craved in the bedroom was something she would be interested in.

Even if she were…if I took her home and then hurt her in my sleep? I wouldn't be able to live with myself.

She came out of the kitchen flushed, with the sound of Evelyn's laughter following her out the door. A big paper bag was in her hands—the ranch's weekly supply of bread and pastries for the communal kitchen.

"How are you today?" She swiped my card, not quite meeting my eyes.

"I'm all right," I said. There should have been more words. Everything I ever wanted to say to her seemed to be blocked behind a wall in my own mind. One I was never quite able to tear down.

"Are you sure?" Lena sucked in a tiny breath, like she hadn't meant to ask the question out loud. Her cheeks went pink all over again, and I allowed myself the torture of soaking up the image. "It's just... You seem a little down. That's all."

I smiled at her, our fingers brushing as I took back the credit card and she passed me the bag of bread. No touch should feel so significant, and yet it did. "Rough night," I said. "So I'm a little tired. I'll be okay."

"Okay," she said quietly, biting her lower lip.

That tiny movement had me thinking about her lips and all the things *I* could do with them before I could redirect those very dangerous thoughts.

"Have a good day, Lena."

Big gray eyes looked up into mine, full of hope I wasn't able to satisfy. "You too."

It was an effort to turn and walk away, more guilt building on top of my shoulders. I wasn't blind. I knew Lena wanted me as much as I did her. Maybe more. And this wasn't fair to her. I couldn't give her what she wanted or what she deserved.

She deserved to be happy and fulfilled and not pining after a man who could kill her while he was unconscious. Now I just had to figure out how to let her go.

I dropped off the baked goods at the ranch and escaped before Lucas or Noah saw me. I wasn't good company right now. Home was where I needed to be. Isolated, miserable, and alone.

Chapter 2

Lena Mitchell

I hummed into the quiet around me, the bakery long since closed and the door locked. It was easy to get lost in the sounds of baking, but now the oven was turned off and things were cooling, getting ready for the morning rush.

Usually when Evelyn was here, we played music or the radio while we worked. I used to have the same habit when I was alone too, but not anymore. Now when I was alone, if there was music, the panic started creeping up beneath my skin until I couldn't ignore it.

If music was playing and I was alone, then I couldn't hear if someone snuck up behind me. Or if someone knocked on the door. It made it so I was less aware of my surroundings, and that wasn't a thing I could handle anymore. Not after everything.

Now, I was dragging on my feet. All day, we'd been busy, on top of custom orders for people in town. We still had more to make tomorrow, my usual order for the nursing home and a couple of parties. After getting everything prepped and laid out for the morning—I was never going to be one of those bakers willing to get up at four-thirty in the morning—I was ready to curl up at home with tea and a book until I fell asleep.

I made sure the back door was locked and flipped off the lights in the kitchen, ignoring the way my heart immediately started to pound. I was a grown woman, and the fact that I was now a little afraid of the dark was not exactly one of my proudest qualities.

It didn't get better as I made my way toward the front of the shop, turning out lights as I went. I hated this feeling. It used to be there was never a time when I was afraid in Deja Brew. It was my happy place, and it felt like nothing could touch me. Now, the only place I felt truly safe was at home or at Resting Warrior.

Home had a security system—installed by Jude—and the ranch was probably the safest place for five hundred miles. And Jude was there. Jude made me feel safe. Just being around him made me feel better, though he'd looked miserable yesterday when he came in to pick up the ranch's weekly order.

Everyone had bad days. Though, I wished I were the one making his day better instead of just giving him some pastries. But it had always been that way between us. I remembered the first time he'd come into Deja Brew, and I'd been so stunned, I hadn't even been able to take his order.

I thought he was the biggest man I'd ever seen. And it still held true. Jude was well over six feet, bigger than a linebacker. Warm green eyes that crinkled with his rare smile. Not that he was grumpy. Just…reserved. It made the moments when he did smile so much better.

When I'd finally come around and was able to ask him

what he wanted to order, his voice sent me to heaven all over again. I didn't think I'd ever fully recovered from the way his voice dragged over my skin like rich honey and velvet. A dark sweetness able to wrap you up and never let you go.

Since then, we'd circled each other. I thought after the wedding something might happen, but it hadn't. It hurt more than I wanted to admit. But there wasn't much a girl could do. Two people were involved in the dance.

I flipped off the rest of the lights and locked the door behind me as quickly as I could. Bessie was just around the corner, which was a comfort. Not many people understood my love for the rickety, old, classic car. By all rights, the car should probably be retired. But I had history with this car. After everything we'd been through together, I couldn't leave her now.

Blowing out a breath, I turned on the radio as I started the engine. Not long now. I lived a little way outside town. Not as far as the ranch, and not so far I felt completely isolated, but definitely far enough that I was outside the town's boundaries. I liked a little space since I was with people all day.

Now that I was off them, my feet were aching. I couldn't wait to boil water and make the biggest cup of tea known to man.

Underneath the pop song on the radio, the car shuddered.

"No," I said to Bessie. "Don't do this, girl. Please. We can make it home, right?"

The telltale shaking didn't subside, and dread seeped down into my stomach. I'd owned the car long enough and had felt this exact sensation enough times. I knew what was about to happen.

I guided the car to the side of the road before the

engine choked and died, letting me drift the last few feet before it stopped, the machinery ticking with heat when I turned off the radio.

The headlights pierced the darkness, illuminating a frozen and muddy patch of ground.

The panic crawling up my throat this time was different. The last time Bessie broke down at night was the night Evelyn and I were taken. I had to watch as he— I could barely think about that night without throwing up. He tortured her while I watched. I almost died.

I would never forget the sound of Evelyn screaming, or the feeling of all those needles in my arms. The number of nights I woke sweating and choking on air, remembering the sensation of fading into nothing with the knowledge I was never going to wake up…

It wasn't something I told anyone. At first, I hadn't been ready to talk about it. And then it felt like it had been too long to say I wasn't dealing with it well. This was the kind of thing Resting Warrior did—they helped people with trauma. I just couldn't bear to tell them about mine.

Evelyn had it so much worse, being the one who was actually tortured. I loved being the bubbly, shining, bright spot in people's lives. What would our little community be like if I were suddenly the dark cloud? I didn't want to bring people down. Besides, they all had their trauma. They didn't need to deal with mine.

What had actually happened to me?

I'd gone to sleep and woken up in the hospital, high as hell. There were worse things.

They told me Jude was the one who found me where Nathan had left me. Left…my body. Jude was the one who picked me up and carried me to the hospital, and he didn't leave until he made sure I was okay.

It was one of the many reasons I felt safe with him, no matter what.

Okay, Lena. Breathe. I tried to focus on the here and now. It was November. Not summertime. Nathan was dead. There was no way he could do anything to me anymore.

My windows were fogging from how fast I was breathing, obscuring the outside, which just made the panic worse. If I couldn't see outside, I couldn't see who was coming.

Movement outside the car startled me, and I screamed, heart pounding. The deer on the other side of the road looked over at me, uninterested in the terror and adrenaline racing through me.

I was shaking, and my mind was blank. I was on the side of the road, and it was late. Come on, Lena. You need to call someone to drive you home.

My finger was on the button to call Evelyn, and my vision blurred. It was too familiar, terror clawing up my throat like a living thing. No, I couldn't call her. I couldn't let her see me like this. She'd feel guilty, and she already carried too much on her shoulders.

My fingers were moving before I fully registered the contact I was finding. But the screen flipped over to the call, and I stared at it. Jude.

The feeling barreled into me like a train. I needed Jude like I needed to breathe. He was the only person who could make me feel safe right now. I didn't question the feeling as I lifted the phone and heard him answer.

"Jude?"

Chapter 3

Jude

My phone buzzed on the counter. I glanced down at the screen and did a double take at Lena's name. She was never far from my thoughts, but she rarely called me. Something was wrong.

I snatched the phone and swiped to answer.

"Jude?"

Every instinct I had roared to life. Lena's voice was imprinted on my mind. I knew it better than I knew my own, and right now, she was terrified.

"Are you all right?"

She hesitated too long. "Bessie died again."

I was already moving, grabbing my keys and my coat and heading to the door. "Where are you?"

"Just outside town."

"But you're all right? You're not hurt?"

Again, the pause, and her voice, which sounded far too small. "I'm fine."

"I'll be right there."

I ended the call, though I didn't want to. She was frightened, and the need to protect her at any cost was rising faster than I could control it. The feeling was familiar. Similar to when I'd found her on the verge of overdose and unconscious. I didn't remember much of that trip to the hospital, but Daniel told me I wouldn't let anyone touch her.

She had her reasons to be scared. She and Evelyn had been taken from the side of the road. I related. Obviously, I had my own shit that haunted me in the dark. But I was a soldier, and I'd chosen that life. All Lena did was try to be a good friend to anyone and everyone she encountered. She didn't deserve the fear I heard in her voice.

I saw the lights before anything else. Lena was still sitting inside, which was good. It was cold, and she could keep the doors locked in case anyone else came by. With this gang Noah was dealing with close to home, I didn't want anyone in our circle taking chances.

Lena was pale when she got out of the car. Pale and stiff. The opposite of the Lena we all knew. I stepped out of the truck and met her halfway. It was an effort not to pull her into my arms right then. That was the only thing that would solve the *itch* under my skin—the visceral need to make sure she was safe.

I nearly crushed my keys in my hand instead.

"Thank you for coming."

"Of course," I said, nodding to Bessie behind her. "All locked?"

"Yeah."

We walked back to my truck, and I opened the door for her to get in before starting it up. She didn't relax the entire rest of the ride, and she said nothing. For Lena, that was strange, and it spoke to how shaken she was.

Her house, a small two-story that used to be a farmhouse, wasn't far away, but too far to walk from the car. Out here, she could still see her two nearest neighbors. My house was far more isolated, but I was glad Lena had people close to her. If there was anything wrong and I couldn't be there, I wanted her to have help.

I stopped the thought from going further. *If I couldn't be there*, as if I could be there at all times. I couldn't. Wasn't it just this morning I said I needed to let her go?

I'd been to her house a few other times, but only as far as the driveway. Going inside was a recipe for disaster. My self-control was only so strong, and being in her house? Near her bed? It was asking for trouble.

But she looked over at me. "Do you want to come in?"

She was still scared. I saw it in her eyes, as plain as if she'd spoken out loud. There was no way to say no to that look. No matter if I had to let her go, I wanted more color in her cheeks before I left.

"I'd like that."

I made it around the truck before she stepped down, and her hand was nearly frozen when it touched mine to lean on. Lena had never shown any indication of this before. I knew the signs of trauma better than anyone, and as closely as I watched her, I'd never seen even a hint of this. It had been months.

Had she been hiding this the whole time? Or was there something specific tonight that triggered her?

As we walked toward her house, her shoulders dropped, and her body relaxed. Good. She felt better here.

Sudden nerves sprang up in my gut. I'd never been inside, and it felt…significant. I firmly ignored the small voice in my head telling me this was a bad idea, and I followed her up the porch stairs.

She had a little wind chime near the door that I had to

duck to avoid. Each chime had a different weather symbol attached. Clouds, lightning, rain, sun, and wind. It was exactly something I would expect to be in Deja Brew, and it made sense here.

Inside was warm, and Lena was moving fast. More the speed I was used to, taking off her coat and shoes, putting them in a cubby and hanging the coat on a hook. The entryway was a spring green.

If I were honest, I'd always wanted to know what Lena's house looked like. You could tell a lot about a person by their home, the way they chose to lay things out and to decorate.

"I'm going to change quickly," Lena said. "Then I'll make us some tea. Make yourself comfortable."

Taking my cue from her, I toed off my boots and hung up my coat, then I stepped into Lena's world. The living room in front of me was somehow completely different and exactly what I expected. A big, old-style fireplace dominated one wall, and there was a bookshelf far bigger than the TV in the corner.

The walls were white, but it didn't feel spare or barren. Prints of various things hung on the walls, and a green velvet couch sat in the middle of the space. The chairs and pillows all looked impossibly comfortable, and I couldn't help but imagine Lena here, relaxing. The image made perfect sense.

I scanned the spines of her books. I *knew* Lena, but this was different. This was her mind and heart. Who she was when she wasn't putting others in front of herself. Romances lined the shelves, and I smiled. A small crystal sat on the shelf, nearly the same green as the couch.

The whole space felt lush and peaceful. It was the home of someone who'd made it just for them, regardless of what anyone else thought. She loved beautiful things.

The kitchen was simpler, but still warm. I sat at the kitchen table to wait for her, not sure where this was going. A small creak let me know she was coming back, and I immediately regretted coming inside.

Lena wore black leggings and a camisole which, while modest, was still the most skin of hers I'd ever seen. Those leggings showed off the curves that were *begging* me to touch them, and I was glad I'd decided to sit down so I could hide how she was affecting me.

I could see myself breaking. Shoving my control aside and reaching for her. The vision tumbled into heat and shared breath and everywhere we couldn't go. Just because she was close to me and driving me crazy didn't change all the reasons I needed to hold back.

One stray touch could—and had—send me into a spiral of memory it wasn't easy for me to pull out of. Those memories were anything but sexy, and being in that state was dangerous for whoever was around me. I needed control, especially in the bedroom, where I was the most vulnerable.

Aside from it helping me stay grounded, I loved it, the strength it took to surrender to someone. I loved the trust that accompanied it. Being in charge of someone else's pleasure brought a satisfaction nothing else even came close to.

Back when I was still freshly rescued, I'd tried. The look on the woman's face when I'd shown her exactly what I needed was still with me. She'd claimed she was interested in an exchange of power. But as soon as I told her, she changed her mind. I was every woman's worst nightmare—always taking and never giving. I never tried it again.

I knew I could find someone who wanted what I did, but none of those people were Lena.

And every day since I'd met her, I'd wished I didn't need it. Didn't crave it. As if everything that happened had taken what I liked and turned it into a necessity. Because Lena wasn't a submissive. The fiery woman I knew wouldn't want to be held down.

So I kept my hands where they were.

Still, as Lena filled the kettle with water and put it on the stove, I couldn't help but stare at the curve of her ass and pray I could hold on to my own sanity.

Since she'd come down the stairs, neither of us had said anything. Now, she turned from the stove and came to me. Even seated, I was nearly as tall as she was. Her lower lip was caught between her teeth, fingers fidgeting together and apart. She was nervous. Her breathing was fast, and she was now flushed instead of pale. But I couldn't pinpoint the source of those nerves. There had to be something I was missing.

Of course, being stranded and having it dredge up memories might take her a while to settle from.

Lena was so close now, it felt like a magnet was pulling me toward her. She was staring at me, eyes wide, and I could see the shades of gray in her eyes as clearly as storm clouds in the sky. "Are—"

My words never made it past my lips. Lena leaned down and kissed me. For long moments, it didn't register that Lena Mitchell was kissing me, and holy *fuck*, her lips were perfect.

For a single, glorious moment, we were frozen together. And then I kissed her back. She tasted like strawberries and coffee, and the way she was fitting against me was the puzzle piece I'd always been looking for. I pulled her closer, guiding her lips deeper, already controlling where and how the kiss went. It was as natural as breathing.

Lena's hands skimmed my shoulders, wrapping around

my neck, and stillness slammed into me like a battering ram. I was still here, in this present moment, but the single touch on my back was enough to make my brain remember—and be afraid.

I wanted more of this. I wanted to take control and push her up against the wall of the kitchen, not stopping until she was moaning my name. I wanted to consume every inch of her until she was putty in my hands.

But Lena didn't want that. The passion in these lips spoke volumes, and with the way her hands slipped down my chest to my ribs and back, I felt the panic creeping upward from the place where I kept it locked.

Orders were on the tip of my tongue. To put her hands on my shoulders and not move them until I told her to. I was about to become every woman's worst nightmare, and I couldn't do it. I couldn't endanger her.

Leave. The thought surged through my mind. I needed to leave before I couldn't make myself do it.

When I pulled back, she looked at me, confusion and worry on her face. But I couldn't explain it; I couldn't handle the way her face would change from longing to disgust. Lena would be happier and safer if I was out of this house right fucking now.

I stood, and Lena's eyes followed me. I saw hurt in her gaze that I desperately wanted to soothe and couldn't. The same hurt was aching in my own chest, and there wasn't any cure for it except time.

"I'll come back in the morning to give you a ride to work."

Lena parted her lips, as if she wanted to say something, and then closed them. Her shoulders curved inward, and she wrapped her arms across her body in a movement so instinctual I wasn't even sure she was aware of what she was doing. She was shrinking in front of my eyes, and I couldn't bear to watch.

Only silence followed me as I grabbed my coat and shoes and closed the door behind me. Silence had never been so loud.

Even the house seemed to stare at me accusingly. But this was right. It had to be right. When I could talk to her without wanting to pick her up and lay her out on the dining room table like a fucking feast, I would explain why it was better this way.

I would always keep Lena safe. Even if that meant she was safe from me.

Chapter 4

Lena

I covered my face with my hands as I flipped off the bathroom light. It was probably three in the morning, but I couldn't sleep. I kept waking up and reliving the most mortifying moment of my entire existence, when I finally went for it with Jude and he just...walked away.

It was like those movies where the girl in high school has something really embarrassing happen and you can barely watch the screen because you're so uncomfortable for her. But it was me. I was the girl.

My stomach was in knots and went back and forth between feeling hollow and threatening to have me heave my guts up over the toilet bowl. My mind just kept replaying the feeling of him going still as if I'd electrocuted him, pulling away, and walking out of my house as if the earth hadn't just shifted under my feet. Because I would never be the same after the kiss, *that* was for damn sure.

The clock on my phone confirmed it. It was nearly four

in the morning. In a couple hours, Jude would be here again to give me a ride, and I was very seriously considering texting him to forget about it. At this point, I didn't think I was going to be able to look him in the eye. But then again, if he came back, maybe things would be different? Maybe I'd done something he didn't like and there would be an explanation.

It was the only thing keeping me from typing out a message saying I'd see if Evelyn would be willing to give me a ride instead.

The kiss itself? That part was amazing. He did kiss me back, and it wasn't a simple, casual kiss. Jude pulled me in and held me against him like he *had* to do it. He took control immediately, and that wasn't something I usually liked. But with him? Something about it made me curious. The forceful nature of his kiss made me wonder what it would be like to go further with him. I imagined it would be like standing in the eye of a storm made entirely from pleasure.

I wanted that. I wanted to explore him, and until last night, I would have said Jude wanted it too. I would have bet money on it. Hell, I would have bet Deja Brew on it.

The image of him walking away and the embarrassment that followed had me questioning everything. I couldn't explore him if Jude didn't actually want to kiss me. Of course, I wasn't going to force him if he didn't want to. I just…never imagined he'd walk away.

When I invited him inside, I imagined waking up with him, not tossing and turning, trying desperately to figure out what the hell happened. Because something changed in the middle of the kiss. Was he just being polite? Kissing me back at first? Was it just a natural male reaction to being kissed and then realizing he didn't have any interest in kissing *me*?

I placed my hands on my stomach as the anxious, embarrassed nausea rose again. Damn it, I hated feeling like this. Like the only tether I had to the earth had suddenly been cut, and I was floating with no way back to the ground. That was how certain I'd been. Sure, it had been years of us dancing around each other, but it wasn't exactly a secret.

My friends teased me, and I denied it, but we were both aware of the line of tension that always sang between us.

With it gone…

I pulled the blankets up over my head and buried my face in my pillow like it could hide me from the mortification currently binding itself to every cell in my body. No more Lena, just a creature of embarrassment.

At least for a couple more hours, hiding was okay.

The blaring of my phone jerked me back awake, and I groaned. I felt like a zombie, which made sense, given how much of the night I'd spent staring at the ceiling and letting my brain spin its wheels like a bicycle.

I needed to move. Jude would be here soon, and I needed to be ready. After last night, I wasn't about to make him wait. It would be perfect. *I* would be perfect.

The instinct to make sure I looked good was twofold. If the man had suddenly decided he didn't want me after this long, I wasn't going to give him the satisfaction of looking like I'd had a sleepless night. And if something had triggered him and he needed a little more encouragement, I was going to put on a show.

By all rights, November in Montana was far too late to be wearing dresses. I didn't care. The dress felt right, and one look in the mirror told me this was a good choice.

It was fifties-style, with a skirt that poofed right below my knees, and I did my makeup to match. Winged eyes and red lips. Part of me wanted the lipstick bright enough to smear everywhere if Jude decided to ruin it.

Please, please want to ruin it and tell me last night was some kind of misunderstanding.

I had comfortable baking shoes at Deja Brew, so I wasn't worried about the pain when I pulled out a pair of red high heels that made my legs like a supermodel's, if I did say so myself.

By the time I heard his truck pulling into my driveway, I was feeling a lot better. The embarrassment had faded to a manageable level, and I wasn't about to pretend it didn't have everything to do with the confidence a killer outfit could give you.

Jude went stock-still when I opened the door, not even making it up the stairs to knock on the door. From here, I saw his gaze travel down my body, taking in the dress—visible beneath my open coat—my legs, and the high heels. The fact that I stopped him in his tracks was good enough for me. "Morning." I put as much cheery energy into the word as I could.

"Morning." I must have been imagining that his voice was rougher than normal. It was just the morning and nothing to do with me.

I'd hoped the outfit would break the awkward ice between us, but as soon as Jude climbed into the truck and started the engine, the same atmosphere that had filled my kitchen last night seeped in like the cold morning air.

Jude was always quiet. I think I'd met him three times before he said more than a couple of words to me. But over the years, he'd gradually become less quiet with me. This felt like the way it used to be—Jude Williams, the giant, silent Navy SEAL. Devastatingly sexy and completely unattainable.

Okay, Lena. You can do this. You broke through his shell before. "Do you have any plans today?"

"Just ranch work."

I pressed my lips together and took a breath. "I have to deliver a bunch of cookies, and hopefully I have some people coming in to order cakes. Ever since Grace and Harlan's wedding, I've got a bunch of people asking about wedding cakes, and I love it. Granted, wedding cakes aren't my specialty, but just the idea someone would trust me with something so important is really cool."

Jude didn't say anything, and I had to stop myself from biting my lip and getting my bright red lipstick all over my teeth. If he wasn't going to talk about last night, then I had to be the one. We couldn't keep going like this, and we were almost at the bakery. If I wanted to say anything and break this horrible, miserable silence, it had to be now.

"Last night." My voice sounded strangled, and I cleared my throat. "I'm sorry. I took you by surprise. I know I should have asked first. I was just… After feeling like that with Bessie, I thought—" My palms were sweating. "I guess I don't know what I thought."

Jude said nothing, pulling up outside Deja Brew. He was out of the car and coming around to open my door before I could make him stay and say something. *Anything.*

The door opened, and he helped me down. *Take the risk, Lena. Someone has to.* "My whole point being, I'm sorry I startled you. But I would very much like to kiss you again, Jude."

I reached for him out of instinct, and he pulled back just out of reach of my fingers. My soul was crumbling inside my body, and I had to blink away the sudden rush of emotion. He didn't need to see me like this. Especially if he wasn't interested. But I—

I cut off the thoughts. "Okay."

Stepping around him, I headed for the door. I was going to be able to hold myself together for only so long. It was still early—I could take a few minutes to cry in my office before I needed to get anything done. I'd wipe off the stupid red lipstick, put on my comfortable shoes, and life would go back to how it always was.

Me, alone. And lonely.

I pressed my lips together as I got my keys out of my pocket. It was the only thing I could do to hold back the rising tide inside me. How in the hell had I managed to misread him so badly? Not just me—*everybody*. Maybe that was the problem. Everyone around us was so convinced Jude was in love with me that I'd believed it even as I'd denied it. But had anyone here seen what Jude was like when he was in love? Maybe this was just the way he was. Attentive and kind. Helpful. But completely not interested.

Lie.

The instinct was there. He'd kissed me back before he stopped, and I would never forget those few precious seconds when everything I'd ever wanted seemed within reach and everything felt *right.*

I fumbled with the keys but finally got them inside the cold lock and turned them, opening the door and stepping into the smell of pure comfort. Now that it wasn't dark, my shop really, truly was one of my happy places. It didn't make the feeling in my chest better. But it was a little more bearable, at least.

Shrugging off my coat, I went straight back to the office to change my shoes, trying and failing to avoid the thoughts popping into my head. We'd had moments. I was absolutely sure of it, and now they were piling into my brain without mercy, taunting me.

The first one that appeared was Grace and Harlan's wedding. She'd seated us together and had us walk down the aisle as a pair, but nothing had really mattered until Jude asked me to dance, and I'd nearly fainted on the spot. He was his usual quiet, strong self. But the feeling of him pulling me in and leading…cradling me even though he was so much bigger. I'd never felt anything like that restrained gentleness, and I convinced myself what I felt was him trying to hold himself back for reasons I still hadn't known.

Jude had driven me home on nights when I'd drunk too much with the Resting Warrior girls, but he never came inside. That should have been a clue, too.

Hell, even him coming to Deja Brew every week for the pickup, I'd twisted into him wanting me. When maybe he just liked the consistency of the routine. I felt my face flush, and a new wave of sharp, cutting embarrassment washed over me. How could I have been so stupid for so long?

If I didn't have so much work to do, I'd consider going and burying myself in a hole for a week so no one could see me and I could dig through all this emotion in peace. But as a business owner, I didn't have those kinds of luxuries.

Tears welled behind my eyes, and I quickly grabbed a tissue to save my mascara from running. I could cry later. Once I was home. While I was at it, I carefully blotted off the red lipstick. I still looked good, but the lipstick was going to be a reminder of him all day if I left it on.

"Okay, you can do this." I stepped back out of the office and into the front of the bakery and froze. Jude was standing on the other side of the counter. I hadn't realized he'd followed me inside. "Oh."

The single word sounded so insignificant in the gigantic silence which currently formed the bubble around us.

"Would you like me to get Bessie to the shop?"

My heart stuttered. Here he was, doing the things which made me want him and feel like his attention meant more than it did. I didn't want to give in to it, but I also needed my car, and I had enough to do today that taking time out to get back there and wait for the mechanic to tow it would be too much.

"If it's not too much trouble," I said. "I have a full day, and it would be helpful."

"Of course."

"Thank you." I'd forgotten to bring my spare keys I usually used when Bessie was in the shop, so I grabbed mine and handed them to him.

Silence spun out between us again. And all I could think was how much I wanted him to be going to get the car because he liked me and not some sort of…protective obligation from being a SEAL.

The chimes over the door rang as Evelyn came in. "Morning!" Her cheery tone was perfect for combating the clouds currently hanging over the two of us. "Hey, Jude. Little early for you to be here."

"I'm just going," he said, eyes still on me.

I smiled at Evelyn when she passed into the back to drop off her bag and get her apron, and she gave me the knowing smile I was afraid of. The worst part—well, maybe the second worst part—of all this was going to be everyone else's expectations. It felt like the whole town was going to grieve the fact that Jude didn't want me when they found out, and I wasn't sure I could bear it.

"I'll make sure Bessie gets there safely," Jude slipped his hands quietly into his pockets. "Promise."

There was something in the word at the end that made me want to hope. Instead, I smiled as best I could. "Thank you again. Call me if there are any problems."

"I will."

I turned, making a show of switching on the espresso machine. But I still felt Jude's eyes on me, and I felt the look he was giving me change. It was heavier, more significant. Everything in me wanted to turn back to him and look—like he was giving some sort of silent command. But I didn't. I didn't have any idea what it meant, and I didn't have any more strength this morning.

The chimes sounded again as Jude left, and I let out a breath in both pain...and relief.

Chapter 5

Jude

I called Daniel from the truck. He was free today and could help me with the car. I could do it myself, but Lena's classic car was both heavy and a pain in the ass to deal with alone. I respected the fact that she loved it, and the car even made me smile at this point *because* she loved it so much. But it was still a menace to have on the road.

"Hey, Jude."

"Feel like helping me tow a car?"

I heard his confusion. "Where?"

"Just outside town. Bessie broke down last night. Told Lena this morning I'd get it over to the shop."

"This morning, huh? Did you tell her this after spending the night?"

There was a smile in Daniel's voice, but not in mine. "No."

On top of the guilt I felt for walking away, for leading her on when I needed something she couldn't give, I was now going to have not one but *two* memories of pure hurt on her face.

When she'd come out of the kitchen, her eyes were red and the lipstick that had nearly put me on my knees when she'd opened her front door was gone. She'd cried, and I'd done that. Sickness had settled in my gut, and I already knew it was there to stay. For a long fucking time.

Daniel heard my tone and didn't question. He was good that way, by far the most intuitive of all of us. "Okay, I'll be there shortly."

He met me at the car; it wasn't exactly hard to spot. "How long has it been sitting here?"

"Since last night, and no, I don't want any more jokes about it."

He raised his eyebrows in surprise, but he didn't make any jokes. I already had my truck backed up to the front of Bessie, and it was far, far easier to get it hooked up to the truck with two. Modern cars were heavy, but old ones were monsters.

"You dropped Lena off at work?"

I nodded, silently begging him not to ask further. My mind was already a jumble of thoughts and emotions I hadn't had a chance to pick through. I'd barely slept, knowing Lena was probably not sleeping either, wondering about me. And when I'd pulled away again, instinctually avoiding her touch, I saw her break.

"I'll guide it." Daniel spoke into the awkward silence. "Let's get moving."

He sat in Bessie's front seat, "driving" the car in neutral while we took it across town. I'd drop him off back at his truck later.

As we pulled up, Ben Phipps, Garnet Bend's mechanic, came out, and he was already speaking when I shut off the car. "No. You can't bring this car to me again. It's just going to be in here next week, and I'm going to feel bad about charging that woman for the work because her cookies are so fucking good. Take it somewhere else."

"Hello to you too," Daniel said.

Ben just rolled his eyes. "Any idea what it is this time?"

I shook my head. "Unfortunately, no. Just got a call last night that it was dead again."

We unhitched Bessie and, in neutral, guided it into the garage. "The car should really be retired," Ben said. "It's being held together with my best shoestrings at this point."

I laughed. "Can't say I disagree with you. But if Lena has a working car, then she'll stop calling me for rides."

Ben stared at me, and Daniel turned his head slowly. I hadn't fully processed I'd said those words out loud. Fuck. It wasn't supposed to be said, and it certainly didn't sound the way I meant it.

"I'll, uh…start looking at what's wrong," Ben said, sensing the sudden shift in the room.

Daniel was watching me coolly. "Outside."

It wouldn't make much difference if he chose to rip me a new one. The garage doors were wide open. "Daniel—"

"No." He held out a hand. "I want you to listen first." A sigh came out of him as he looked at the ground. "I want to know what it's going to take."

"For what?"

"For you to make a fucking move, Jude." He shook his head, staring at me in disbelief. "Every single one of us knows you're in love with that woman, and you have been since the *first moment* you saw her. The whole town knows. You want her, and she wants you. It's been like watching the slowest romance movie in existence for the last three years. So, what is it?"

I stared at him. Daniel never spoke like this. He was steady, like me. But right now, he was pacing and agitated.

If I didn't know better, I would say he was jealous, but Daniel had never shown romantic interest in anyone as long as I'd known him. No, this had to do with me.

But the true answer wasn't one I wanted to give. It was my burden and no one else's. My brothers had enough to deal with without my moping ass.

"Is it the pressure?" Daniel asked. "Because everyone knows, and it will be harder because people will be watching both you and Lena?"

I shook my head. "No."

"Are you just being a masochist?"

"No."

Daniel huffed out a breath. "Tell me, Jude. Because I see the way you look at her. It's the same look and *more* than the way Lucas looks at Evelyn. Or Harlan with Grace. They are happy, and trust me when I say we all hate watching you decide not to be."

"I'm not choosing to be unhappy."

"Jude." His voice was low. "We all know the rules and what we decided. We don't butt into one another's trauma. We respect one another's boundaries. But you remember the other part of that? We get to call each other out when we see each other sabotaging ourselves or acting like assholes. Because the only way we can have each other's backs is by having the trust that we *will* do that for each other, no matter what. No matter how much it hurts.

"So, give me a straight fucking answer. Tell me why it looks like you're burying your head in the sand and ignoring the best thing to ever happen to you."

Anger and grief came roaring to the surface. The carefully crafted layers of protection I kept around everything meant nothing when Daniel punched a hole right through them. They thought I was keeping my head in the sand? Yes. Yes, I was, so I didn't break *everything else*.

I felt the snap before I started speaking, but I knew now I wasn't going to be able to stop. "Fine," I said. "You want to know the truth? I'll tell you. You're right. I do want her. I walked into that coffee shop when we moved here, and it was like the sun came out.

"Fuck, it was like the sun disappeared and was replaced by her. There's not a single day when I'm not thinking about her and wanting her. Hoping she's happy and wanting to make sure she is. Protecting her with my life if necessary. Is that what you want to hear? Congratulations, you all got it right."

"Then why the hell aren't you with her?" Daniel sounded shocked.

"Because I *can't.*" My voice was ragged. "I can't. Daniel, I can't make it through one fucking night without waking up and trying to strangle my bedsheets. I should invest in a bedding company, because I've gone through so many I'm practically keeping them in business. Sometimes they're torn to bits before I'm conscious. Other times, I have them wrung so tight I could use them to actually strangle someone.

"You know why I've never painted my bedroom? Because white is the easiest color to paint over spackle. My bedroom walls are made more of the fucking stuff than the original material. Sooner or later, I'm going to have to replace the walls entirely. I keep a can of it and a can of paint in my bedroom closet so it's always there. Can't sleep after the nightmares most of the time anyway. Might as well clean up the mess I made, right?"

My breath was coming in heaving gasps, like one of those nightmares was holding me hostage right now. "I always wake up right before the hit, Daniel. Not once has it been enough time to pull back the punch. And it's not only when I wake up from a nightmare. If someone touches me and I'm not ready, my mind snaps into defensive mode, and we both know I'm not talking about the defense they teach in college."

"When we spar—"

"When we spar, I'm ready," I cut him off. "I know the hits are coming, and I've already prepared myself. But if someone comes up behind me and touches me? It's all over."

Finally, my voice cracked. "I know how to kill, and my mind tells me to do it. It's the first fucking instinct. Kill first, ask questions later. And all I can think about every time I wake up ripping a pillow to shreds or my knuckles splitting apart on plaster is how fucking grateful I am that it's not Lena.

"It's not her. And I can't put her in danger. I won't. I could kill her, Daniel. Without a thought. Without even *knowing*, I could kill her. I couldn't live with that. You know I'd rather die than hurt her, so there's your answer. It doesn't matter what I want. It matters that she's safe, and she never would be with me. I'd always planned to get a handle on it and then 'make a move,' as you called it. But it's been *years*, and I'm not any better. It's not fair to her. I need to let her go."

The world had never felt quieter than it did in that moment. I hadn't even noticed how loud my voice had become. Every word needed to come out, but now all of it was in the forefront of my mind, and it *hurt*.

No doubt Ben heard all of it, but at this point, I didn't care. The whole town would eventually find out we weren't going to be together. It didn't matter.

None of it mattered.

I hated the way it felt like those words hung on my shoulders. Weights I would never be able to get rid of.

Daniel stood, still and quiet for a long time, just

observing me. This was the Daniel I knew—contemplative and calm. Not the man who'd pushed me nearly to breaking. Which, of course, he'd done on purpose. Not out of anger or malice, but because he'd seen I was in my own head and needed it. The most observant one of us and it was annoying.

"Feel better?" he asked.

"No, asshole."

His mouth quirked up into a smirk. "I know, but hopefully you will. There's a reason we tell people not to bottle this stuff up. There's a reason we're a team and have the resources we do. You don't have to do this alone. If you're struggling, why not ask for help?"

My stomach twisted. It was a cliché, not wanting to ask for help because I'd appear weak. I'd met enough men who'd done it to know it wasn't helpful. But the thought of baring that part of myself and admitting, even after doing what I should, I wasn't improving? It felt like a depressing defeat.

"I don't even know what to ask for." I shrugged. "It's not like I'm sitting at home alone, stewing in my own shit. I do my sessions with Rayne. I talk with all of you. I'm up and moving, and nothing helps. It's time for me to figure out how to live with it instead of fighting it."

He looked at me again. "Or, maybe, since the same things haven't worked in all these years, maybe you could try something different."

"Like?"

Daniel leaned against the side of my truck, crossing his arms. "It seems like being alone during the nightmares isn't helping you. Maybe having someone with you would keep your mind calm?" I opened my mouth to protest, and he shot me a look. "I'm not telling you to endanger Lena.

Don't give me that. But you have to know you're not the only one of us who has nightmares."

I did know that. Noah had been with me in those caves. He had his own trauma that he dealt with. We didn't talk about it much, each dealing with it in our own ways, but there was an understanding between us. Something deeper we understood because of the shared experience. "I'd wager to say most active vets have nightmares. Your point?"

"So far, you're the only one of us who's letting the nightmares hold him back from happiness."

The words hit me in the chest. I hadn't thought of it like that. Of course I hadn't. Because they were the strongest force in my life. Present every fucking day, dragging me from sleep and making me relive the worst moments of my captivity. How was I supposed to just ignore them and the danger they caused?

"So you'd have me take the risk?"

"I'm saying I think Lena might. You haven't told her, have you?"

"No."

He nodded. "Well, think about it. Because after all the shit you've been through, Jude? You're miserable, and we see it. Fucking hell, it's justified. But you also deserve to be happy." Daniel looked at the sky and then around us. "I think I'll walk back to my truck. It's nice, only a few miles, and I think you need to consider some things."

He walked away down the sidewalk and left me staring after him.

The last thing I expected coming to the mechanic was to have my world and thoughts flipped entirely upside down. But no matter how much I'd already turned it over in my head, the fantasy of being with Lena always collided with the reality that I could harm her—or worse.

But Daniel also had a point. I was bringing the nightmares to the forefront and letting them have more power than they deserved. Funny how hearing it from someone else could be the thing that made you see more clearly.

I wasn't sure which would be worse—continuing like this, pining after Lena, never letting her close because of the truth I lived night after night, and losing her, or taking the risk of being with her, hurting her without even being aware of doing so, and losing her anyway.

Fuck.

Daniel was right about one thing. I was miserable. Being caught between my past and resisting the glowing sunshine that was Lena, I was left inside my own shadows.

"I'll think about it," I said quietly, even though he was too far to hear me.

Chapter 6

Lena

"Seems like I showed up just in time." Evelyn peeked her head out of the kitchen, tying her apron back. "I didn't see Bessie out there, which means tall, dark, and handsome dropped you off. Does that mean anything? And I'm *loving* the dress, by the way. I'm sure he loved it too."

I swallowed. This was the part of the teasing game my friends played where I denied there was anything between Jude and me, and they just grinned and we all played along.

For the first time in forever, the denials weren't on the tip of my tongue. I couldn't exactly pretend it didn't mean something. It just didn't mean what Evie thought it did.

Clearing my throat, I continued with the espresso machine, though there was nothing left to do with it. "Bessie broke down last night on the way home. I didn't want to bother you and Lucas, so I called Jude. He offered to bring me to work this morning."

I practically heard her roll her eyes. "Lena, that car."

"I know." The words came out too quickly. "I know."

"Lena, are you—"

The door to the bakery opened, and one of our morning regulars came in. Tracy. Coffee and two scones. She always took an extra one to work for her boss. I served her with a smile and pretended nothing was wrong, because it was all I could do.

I wasn't going to be able to keep the truth from Evie forever, but the embarrassment still felt like it was going to crush me. I couldn't breathe when I thought about it. But she was going to ask. Everyone was going to ask. Might as well rip off the Band-Aid and get it over with so everyone could immediately know *not* to ask.

Tracy left, and I sighed, leaning on the counter. It was coming.

"Lena." Evie's voice came from behind me. "Are you okay?"

Taking a breath, I closed my eyes. "No. I am very much not okay."

She looked startled when I turned. And no wonder. I was always okay. The sunshine baker who made everyone's days better. It was my job to make people happy. So I was happy.

I didn't think I could be happy today.

"What happened?"

"I—" My throat closed, and I swallowed. The tears came faster than I could blink them back, and the mask I'd been trying to maintain broke.

"Oh, honey." Evie was pulling me back into the kitchen, and she guided me to one of the stools we sat on while we decorated cookies. "Shit. It's too cold for the patio. Just sit here for a second, okay? I'm going to close us for a minute. The town won't perish if we take a short break today."

I didn't argue.

My chest felt like it was cracking open, and tears just flowed. This was what I wanted to keep until I could get home. But I was lying to myself if I thought that was realistic. Ripping off the Band-Aid was going to hurt like hell. The pain in my chest wasn't small. This was *deep*, and it was going to take a long time to heal over.

How could things change so quickly?

Evelyn appeared again with one of our biggest mugs in hand, something steaming out of the top of it. As she set it down, I saw the paper tab of my favorite tea peeking over the side. "Hold that thought," Evie said, quickly grabbing the bottle of honey from the front counter and one of the small creamer cartons. "There." She pulled the other stool across from me, and I laughed once.

Her care in setting me up with what she knew I loved was comforting, and it only made me want to cry harder because I knew she cared and she was going to be disappointed too. I covered my face with my hands.

"What happened?" she asked again quietly.

"Nothing happened," I said. "And everything happened."

She made a face and smiled. "That doesn't tell me much."

"I know." Forcing my breath to be more even, I squeezed honey into the mug and mixed in the creamer until the tea was the exact shade I liked it to be. Then I started talking.

"Last night, it felt so similar to…you know… I called Jude to pick me up. Not only because I didn't want to bother you, but because I feel safe with him. When he dropped me off, I asked him to come inside, and he said yes. He's never done that before."

Evie gasped. "Lena, that's huge!"

I tried for a smile and took a sip of the tea. "Yeah. I wasn't planning on anything happening. I just wanted to talk and calm down. But when I saw him in my kitchen…I kissed him." Evelyn said nothing, waiting for me to continue, though I could tell she was on the edge of her seat. "He kissed me back for a second, and then he stopped. He froze, got up, and left."

"He *what?*"

I took another sip of tea. "The only thing he said was that he'd be back in the morning to bring me here, and that's what he did. I thought there was some kind of misunderstanding, so I tried to talk about it on the ride. Tried to kiss him again when we got here, but nothing. I don't—" My breath and voice shook. "I think I've been wrong. I don't think he likes me like that, Evie."

"That is *bullshit.*" She hopped off the stool and began to pace. "I would bet Lucas's life savings on the fact that Jude worships the ground you walk on."

"If he did, wouldn't he have done something by now?" Fresh tears followed the lines of the old ones down my face. "I didn't realize it until just now, but I didn't mind that it was taking this long because I thought we were a given. I know it's an assumption I shouldn't have made, but I did. I figured we were going to be together, no matter how long it took for us to get there, and now—"

I couldn't finish the sentence, but I now knew it wasn't going to happen. "If it's not a given, I don't think I can do this, Evie. I don't want to keep waiting anymore. And I try not to talk about it, but I am *lonely*. This hurts, and I can't do it."

Evelyn reached forward and placed her hand over mine on the table. "I'm sorry."

"Please don't think I'm jealous, Evie. I mean, I am, but I am so happy for you and Lucas, and Grace, and Cori. I'm over the moon for all of you. But…"

"But it hurts," she said. "I get it."

Standing, I grabbed a tissue and cleaned up my face. There would be more tears later, but the flood seemed to have stopped for the moment. "I'm a romantic. Never tried to hide the fact, and I always knew it was going to make things more difficult for me. I want someone to share my life with." I heaved in a breath. "And if it's not going to be Jude, then it's time for me to move on so I can recover from this before trying to find someone else."

"That's not going to be easy." Evie's voice was quiet.

"No fucking kidding." I crossed my arms and tilted my face back toward the ceiling. "And it's going to be so much worse because I feel like everyone expects it, you know? Everyone in town thinks of me as taken because of Jude, and it's the same for him. We're together without being together, and it's been that way forever. I know I tell you guys no and stuff, but we all knew better."

"Yeah." She leaned on the worktable, propping her head up with her hand. "I don't know, babe. I would have sworn he liked you. More than liked you. If someone had asked me, I would have told them Jude was in love with you. He watches you whenever you're in the same room. Not in a creepy way, but like he can't take his eyes off you. And you already know about the hospital."

I nodded. "I do. It was the whole reason I called him. Because he found me after Nathan, and it felt so similar. I don't know. I almost can't believe it, you know? I was *so sure.* Just like you, it was just a known thing. But I can't stop feeling him push me away, and I can't stop seeing him walk out the front door. Or him pulling away outside."

The now familiar sharpness of shame fell over me, and I pressed my hand to my stomach. I felt sick with it. And… "I feel so stupid, Evie."

"Hey, no, don't do that." She hopped off the stool and came to me, pulling me into a hug. "You're not stupid."

"Are you sure?" My voice cracked, and I hated how quickly tears came back. "Because it feels like only someone stupid could let this happen. I feel like I should have known, right? It's been three years. Anyone else would have left it alone by now."

I felt her shake her head. "If you're stupid, then so is everyone else. And before you say anything else about what this is, or start saying it has to do with you and who you are, I'm going to tell you, lovingly, to shut the hell up."

A laugh broke out of me, and she pulled back. "Listen, I was on Team Lena and Jude. And if there's any chance this is a mistake or he's just being an ass, then I'm *still* on Team Lena and Jude. But if this is going to hurt you? Of course I don't want that."

"Thanks." It didn't feel great, but at least I'd have someone in my corner when everyone else came and started saying what a shame it was Jude and I didn't work out.

"You work so hard, and you're half the reason anyone in this town has a good day. You *make* so many people's days and bring joy to everyone. You fully deserve all the happiness you bring everyone else. And you will get it. I'll make sure of it."

I laughed again, crossing back to the table to take another sip of tea. It was steadying. "Thank you."

Realistically, my plan of finding someone wasn't going

to start for a while. You didn't get rid of an imprint from someone like Jude Williams overnight.

"Want to take the day off? We could close up shop and play hooky."

"Part of me wishes we could," I sighed. "But we've got like three weekly orders to make, and I want to see if there are any specials we can offer for Thanksgiving. People have already been asking about putting in orders, and I've been avoiding it. But at least today, it will give me something to focus on."

Evie touched my shoulder as she passed. "Okay. I'll go open us back up."

She headed to the front of the shop, and I heard the chimes jingle, followed by her talking to a customer who must have been waiting. I didn't go out—every part of me was still shaky, and I needed to look in the mirror. I probably looked like a drowned rat. Not the way I wanted people to see me.

It was good I'd told Evie. I felt lighter, if not better.

Grabbing my planner and my notebook from the office, I went back to the worktable. Something about being closed away in the office was entirely unappealing at the moment.

I started on the plans for Thanksgiving, based on what ingredients I could get and how much. Pumpkin, obviously, would be a big one. Apple and cherry too. But then there were the pies that flew under the radar but were still popular. Lemon silk and chocolate cream. I wanted to offer a couple of pies that were less common and a little off-the-wall too, simply to see if I could get people to expand their horizons. Maybe something like a cinnamon pear, or something with caramel? A custard pie could be nice.

Work like this always calmed me down and centered

me. Figuring out new recipes, and even figuring out how much of things I needed to order, was a puzzle I enjoyed putting together. By the time Evelyn had taken care of the morning rush, I was feeling much better and ready to bake.

The day passed with me—mostly—able to keep my mind off Jude and out of the hole of embarrassment. Until evening, when I saw Bessie pull up outside. My traitorous heart leaped into the air and fell and crashed onto the sidewalk when I pushed open the door and saw Ben, the mechanic, getting out of the driver's seat. "Hi, Ben."

"Lena. She's good as new."

I smiled. "We both know that's not true."

"Sadly, we do."

"How much do I owe you?"

Ben backed away down the sidewalk, hands in the air. "This time? On the house."

"Ben—"

"No arguments, Lena," he called with a smile. "Just throw in some free coffee next time I'm in."

He turned and jogged around the corner before I could insist on paying him for his work. "Thank you!"

I reached out and patted Bessie's roof with my hand. She was a good car, no matter what anyone said. Especially now, it felt like she was the one constant in my life. I needed her.

The heaviness in my chest didn't leave, and I knew it was because Jude hadn't been the one to drop off the car. Every other time he'd helped me with Bessie, he'd been the one to pick her up and drop her off again. It was a sign, if ever I needed one.

How many little things I was used to and relied on were going to change now? Dread filled me at the thought. Because I was willing to bet there were far more than I realized.

I wrapped my arms around myself against the November chill. We were closing early today. I was going home to read the book and have the cup of tea I never ended up having last night, and I was going to do everything in my power *not* to think about Jude Williams.

Chapter 7

Jude

I dodged the punch aimed directly at my head and jumped away, throwing a missed punch of my own. Most of my sparring matches with Noah were missed hits. We knew each other too well and had for too long for either of us to land hits easily. But I was also sloppy. Days had passed since I'd last seen Lena, and I was slowly dying inside. At least, that's what it felt like.

Daniel's words about the nightmares were still ringing around in my head, as they had every time I'd woken since I'd heard them. With Noah, the questions were on the tip of my tongue, but I didn't want to overstep.

Holding up a hand, I stopped to catch my breath. "Can I ask you something?"

Noah nodded, heading to the edge of the mat for a sip of water. "Sure."

It wasn't a secret on the ranch that Kate was staying with Noah. While they were both tangled up in this messy gang situation, it was the safest place for her to be. I'd seen the way he looked at her, and it was exactly the kind of look Daniel described. Like she was life itself.

"I'm not trying to pry. I have a different question, but this comes first."

Noah raised an eyebrow. "Ominous, but okay."

"You and Kate are together now?"

He froze, glancing at me nervously before easing up. "I—yes."

"I'm not trying to bust your ass about it," I told him. "I like Kate, and what she's willing to do for her brother is great."

His face shifted into a smirk at my hedging. "All right, I get it. What's your real question?"

"Your nightmares."

"Ah." He looked at me. "Do I still have them?"

I shrugged. "More like, how are you dealing with them when you have someone in your bed? Are you afraid you're going to hurt her? Or scare her away?"

He stared at me, and in that stare, I felt him see through the pretense of my question. There was no point in trying to act like I was asking for any reason other than Lena. "Please."

"First, a caveat. My nightmares have never been as bad as yours. But I definitely had the thought, and I was concerned about it. However, recently, I was having more trouble falling asleep at all instead of waking up, so I think it was easier for me to let it happen."

"And?"

Noah smiled. The kind of smile you couldn't hold back because it was too real. "It's actually been great. Having her beside me…it's like my subconscious knows she's there now, and because I knew I wasn't alone, it didn't attack me.

I've been sleeping *far* better with her than I ever did without."

The mix of emotions in my chest was dragging me in multiple directions. It was exactly what I wanted to hear, and yet it wasn't, because it gave me hope that might mean nothing. Part of me had wanted Noah to kill off the hope I still held so I could let it die. But the other day, Daniel had planted a new seed in my mind.

Now, Noah told me he was doing well, and he was well aware of my trauma. More than most. All this time, had I been locking myself out of something for no reason?

"What's going on in there?" Noah asked. "You went quiet."

"Not exactly unusual for me."

He chuckled. "No. But you look like you need to talk. So, talk. Something is clearly bothering you. Even sparring, you usually have me on my ass by now."

I made a face. That wasn't strictly true, but I glanced at the clock, and we'd been going far longer than I realized. "Lena."

"Mm." He made the sound far too innocently.

"You know?"

"I don't know anything but whispers that something changed, and I didn't dig, because it's none of my business."

Briefly, I outlined what had happened and what I'd done. What Daniel said, and my own fear about hurting Lena.

"But there's more than just the nightmares. I'm not the same person I was when I went into the caves."

Noah snorted. "None of us are. If you can spring back from that like nothing happened, you're either dead inside or a psychopath."

"I don't like surprises or being startled. Why do you

think I bought a property out in the middle of nowhere and covered it with cameras? I mask it well, but I need control over my environment to make sure I'm okay. I need to be the dominant one."

Part of me had always liked it. Even before everything happened—the captivity—I liked control in the bedroom. It was everything else that turned it into a need, more than just enjoyment. And I did enjoy it. Taking charge and allowing my partner to let go? Heaven. And the control gave my own pleasure an edge that couldn't be matched.

I didn't know if I could let it go. For Lena, I would be willing to try. But I still didn't think she wanted anything to do with that kind of dynamic.

Noah raised an eyebrow, and I sighed. "Yes, it's exactly what you're thinking."

"I don't give a shit what you like in the bedroom," he laughed.

"You've never felt that?"

He shrugged. "Here and there, but not in the way you're talking about. But like I said, I don't have a problem with it."

Grant had similar inclinations to my own, but it wasn't quite the same. Even without Noah having those desires, I was more comfortable talking about this with him. And that said a lot. "I don't think Lena is submissive, is the problem."

Sitting on the mat and stretching one leg, Noah gave me a look. "You think? Or you know?"

"You know her too," I said. "She's passionate and loves her freedom. I don't see that changing in private."

Noah laughed again, but this time, it didn't seem funny. "You've dug yourself deeper than I realized."

I started stretching too since we'd both silently agreed we were finished sparring. "What do you mean?"

My friend stared at me for so long I wondered if he'd fallen asleep.

"Noah?"

"I'm sorry," he said. "I should have been paying more attention, and I should have pushed you for answers more. Checked in and made you respond."

"What the hell are you talking about?"

"Jude, you can't see what's in front of you."

Anger flared at the accusation, but I checked it. Noah didn't say things without a reason, so I waited.

"You're not the only one who has trauma."

I rolled my eyes. "Of course not. We all do."

"And so does Lena."

My entire body went still. I knew that. It was the whole reason she'd called me—the similarity to the night she was taken. So why didn't I equate it to the same things I held?

"It's not the same," Noah said. "But if you don't think she can understand what you're going through with the nightmares and everything else, you're not giving her nearly enough credit."

"She's seemed entirely okay." My voice rasped around the weak excuse.

Noah snorted, sarcasm dripping from his tone. "Right. Because looks on the surface are a totally accurate picture of how someone is dealing with trauma privately."

There was nothing I could say to that.

"As for the other thing, I don't see a problem."

"You don't?"

Noah shrugged. "No. If it's something you need, and you and she are meant to be together, then talk to her about it. *Ask* her, and don't assume she's not interested. What you shouldn't do is look straight ahead and decide everything yourself. Which is what I think you've been doing, and for longer than we should have let you. You can't carry everything alone, Jude. Even if you feel you need to."

The air in the gym went taut. He was talking about Isaac. I'd shouldered a lot of the blame for his death, because I felt like I had to. I still did, even if I was rational enough to recognize I'd been in no state to help him when I was rescued.

But when he came back—

"Have you heard from Ellen?" Noah asked, interrupting my thoughts.

"No. I doubt I'm a person she really wants to see right now."

Noah shrugged. "Five years. It's a big thing. Maybe we should reach out and see how she's doing?"

I managed to keep the instinctual cringe off my face. Even if Isaac's death wasn't my fault—and it still felt like it was—surely I was just a reminder of everything she'd lost. I didn't know if she would want to see me and be reminded of it. The last thing I wanted was to cause her more pain.

Noah took another swig of water and clapped me on the shoulder. "Do me a favor? Think about everything we've talked about. Not because you think it's going to make me or Dr. Rayne happy. But because it feels like you've traced a path through your own guilt and grief, and it's the only place you're allowing yourself to walk."

I raised my eyes at the metaphor, and he chuckled.

"Seriously. Just try. Take off for a few days if you need to, go to the lake property and camp for a bit. Get the silence you crave and think about it. Because you're carrying more than your fair share of too many things. And finally, I think the cracks are showing."

"Finally?"

"At risk of another metaphor," he said with a grin. "If

you don't build a foundation properly, a house collapses in on itself. Take a look at yours. I think there are some holes you may have put there yourself."

I huffed a laugh, and he raised his water bottle in a mock toast.

I had to ask. "She's changed you that much so quickly?"

Noah considered. "I don't think Kate has changed me at all. But she brought out parts of me I've been ignoring. And showed me there's more than letting it own you. She's now seen me at my worst."

He was referring to himself being unintentionally triggered at our recent family dinner. And the fact that he'd had to resort to violence to protect Kate, though he hadn't wanted to.

"Not only at my worst, but at my most vulnerable and darkest. She didn't push me away—she pulled me closer. And…" He sighed. "It's helped more than I know how to describe."

"So, you're in love with her?"

He smiled. "It's probably too fast to say that. Anyway, I have to go. Got an appointment with Dr. Rayne, and I need to shower. And then Kate's at the house."

The door to the gym closed behind him, and I decided I wasn't quite finished.

I had an invisible hole in my chest, filled with the emptiness of longing. Jealousy of Noah, who was going home to a woman he loved—no matter if he didn't want to admit it yet. Fear that I'd royally fucked everything up by not seeing what was actually happening in front of me.

I didn't want to go home yet and face an entirely different kind of emptiness there. Instead, I pulled a pair of boxing gloves off a hook and tightened them, lining up with one of the bags. I imbued the bag in front of me with every unseen enemy, every flinch at an unexpected touch, every impulse that made me push Lena away out of fear and the need for her to be safe.

She didn't push me away—she pulled me closer.

It all coalesced in my head at once, and I might have to take Noah's advice and get out for a couple of days to think it all through.

The guilt of Isaac's death still clung to me like a shirt I could never take off. It seemed as if I was never able to let it go. And deep down, I blamed myself for his suicide in spite of all the evidence that it *wasn't* my fault. Because no matter rational thought, I couldn't control how I felt.

Yet, at the same time, maybe I hadn't tried as hard as I needed to in order to work through all of it.

Maybe I'd been lying to myself and everyone else about my progress, and I'd made a show of being better than I was because I felt like I deserved the punishment.

Fuck.

I deserved the punishment of keeping myself away from Lena, because I hadn't been able to keep Isaac alive. And if I allowed myself to be with her, it would be the same. Only this time, I would be the one to hurt her. Kill her.

That was what my brain was telling me.

And because I was so wrapped up in my own version of the world, I'd ignored what was in front of me, just like Noah said. I was choosing for Lena, when I should have just fucking talked to her.

I stopped, heaving in breath and resting against the punching bag, allowing the horror of realization to overcome everything else. After all this time, I was still surprised at how things could come to light. I'd seen it more than once in the people who came to Resting Warrior to heal.

Things they already knew, phrased just right from a different person, and puzzle pieces clicked into place. I never imagined it would be me, and it was humbling. Fucking hell. I needed to go over all of it in my head again. And again. Because if I was this blind—this wrong—then I was on the edge of losing everything I wanted, if I hadn't lost it already.

I tossed the gloves back onto their hook and pushed out of the gym, ready to figure out my life all over again.

Chapter 8

Lena

I groaned, letting my head flop back on the arm of the sofa. I was lying sprawled under a blanket with a fire crackling merrily, though I didn't feel merry. What I wanted right now was to throw the book in my hands into those flames and watch it blacken to a crisp.

A bit dramatic, maybe, but I couldn't get the discomfort out of my chest. The discomfort of knowing my world was *wrong*. Unsettled since that night with Jude.

Normally, romance books brought me joy. In the stead of my own happiness, I lost myself in the love stories of others, knowing and expecting that mine was on the way. Right now? With all my thoughts about Jude? It was more frustrating than anything else.

Where once I savored the little moments and gestures the heroes made, now all I saw were things that weren't real and would never be real for me. I wasn't like most of the women in these books. Ones who were wilting flowers.

Lovely and thin and ready to let their hero sweep them off their feet and to the bedroom, where they had nothing to think about but their next orgasm.

Must be nice.

Every man in a romance stepped up and made himself better. And Jude *was* that man. I knew he was. I just didn't know where we'd gone wrong.

I stared into the flickering fire, allowing myself to remember those too-brief moments when he kissed me back. I definitely wasn't a wilting flower. If anything, I liked to have fun and have more control during sex than most of the women in the books I read. But there was something about the way he kissed me I couldn't get out of my head.

He'd pulled me in and angled my face so he could kiss me deeper, like it was the most natural thing in the world—like he'd thought about it a hundred times before. But it wasn't just that; it was the strength and sureness of his touch. He simply…knew what he wanted and made it happen.

My face flushed, and I covered it with my open book. Why did the thought make my body temperature rise and make me squirm with embarrassment at the same time? I could see the way it might have gone—as if Jude were just like one of those romance heroes, ready to sweep me off my feet and have his wicked way with me. With a touch like that, it was tempting to believe he'd know what I needed even before I did. It was tempting to give in to a fantasy I'd never indulged—letting go entirely.

Was that what I wanted? I'd never thought so. But even those brief seconds when he swiftly and easily took control had me desperately curious for more.

But there's not going to be more, is there?

I sighed. It had been a full week since I'd seen Jude. For the first time in years, he hadn't come to the bakery for the ranch's weekly pickup. No one came. Evelyn just took it home with her at the end of the day and dropped it off. And it hit me harder than I expected it to.

Had he realized I'd decided to move on? Or try to? Had someone told him? I knew Evie hadn't, but it still made me wonder. Jude was always able to read me better than anyone else. But he had to see me to read me.

There was a big, Jude-shaped hole in my life now, and I didn't know how to handle it. What I really needed was to get my head on straight about him and what I needed. Moving on was good. Healthy. It was a solid plan, if my stupid brain would get on board and help me execute it.

But my brain was a traitor. She—and I was referencing her as a separate entity at the moment—kept thinking about Jude nonstop. Possibly even more than when everything had been moving along swimmingly. It felt like everywhere I turned, I saw him and a new memory hit me.

I could barely cook meals because I would look at the chair and remember the surge of joy I felt when he pulled me closer—and then the feeling of being thrown off a cliff onto jagged rocks as he walked away.

Even when I wasn't looking at the chair, I felt it staring at me like a ghost.

Now things were popping up at the bakery. Noticing when another customer ordered his favorite drink or wondering if he liked anything from the pickup he hadn't made.

Turning, I shoved my face into the pillow I was lying on as if I could escape from my own embarrassment. I just needed to stay the course. That was all. It would get easier, especially if I kept not seeing him. It would get easier.

Those were the words I kept repeating in my head, hoping eventually, if I said them enough, I would believe them.

It would get easier.

It would get easier.

It would get easier.

My phone rang, breaking me out of my reverie. The device was buried in the cushions beneath me, and I flailed under the blanket trying to get it. Evie's name was on the screen, and I sighed, swiping to answer the call. "Good timing. I was just getting lost in my own self-pity."

"Lena?" Evie's voice was raw with panic.

I sat straight up. "Evie? What's going on?"

"The ranch is on fire. It's *on fire.* The fire department is on the way, but everyone else is gone helping Kate and Noah. Please."

She didn't have to specify that she was asking me to come help. "I'll be right there."

I didn't bother to change out of my sweats and T-shirt, throwing my coat and shoes on and grabbing my keys. I sent up a silent prayer Bessie wouldn't let me down tonight. If someone got hurt or anything else bad happened because my car broke down, I couldn't bear it.

She roared to life without any trouble, and it was almost as if she knew I needed her to be solid. Even the sound of the engine seemed stronger as I raced down the road.

Against the darkening sky, I saw the light of fire over the high walls of the ranch and blanched. Seeing fire and hearing about fire were two incredibly different things. One was almost mythical. Pictures you encountered from news stories and the internet. Seeing a place you knew with flames licking out of the windows was a horror all its own.

The gate was broken. It looked like it had been torn apart by a dinosaur or something, dented and ripped off its hinges. Smoke hung thick in the air from all different directions. Multiple buildings were on fire—at least two guest cabins, the gym, even the lodge had some smoke coming from it.

I slammed to a stop, barely shutting off the car before I was out and running toward Evie and Mara, who were carrying both buckets and fire extinguishers toward the lodge.

"What can I do?" I shouted.

Mara held out a fire extinguisher without saying anything, and I took it.

"Should I try to save the guest cabins?"

Evie shook her head while running. "No, they're too far gone. We'll have to wait for the fire department for them. We're trying to save the lodge since the fire is confined to one corner. Cori and Grace are on their way. They'll work on the gym."

"What the hell happened?"

"It was a truck." Mara sounded out of breath. "Big, like a construction one. They rammed through the gate then drove through and started throwing lit bottles everywhere out their windows. I was near the gate doing some last-minute work on one of the garden beds. I was lucky they didn't see me."

It was more words than I'd ever heard the shy woman say. But there was no time to be shocked. The cabins in front of us were going up—there was probably no possible way they could be saved.

The heat… Holy hell, I would never take firefighters for granted again. Flames licked the side of the closest building, spreading into the dead, dry grass.

I looked over and saw Evie stock-still beside us, staring at the flames in horror.

Shit.

She wasn't even here right now. I knew the look. It was the look that came over her when she flashed back to

Nathan and him burning her. This had to be a nightmare for her.

"Evie, go!" I shouted over the roar of the flames. "Help Grace and Cori get what they need. You don't have to get near the fire."

Her eyes locked on mine. "The hell I don't." Determination was written in every line of her frame. "This is my home. My asshole of an ex doesn't get to make it impossible for me to protect it."

Later, it would be hard. I knew it, but I wasn't going to stop her. We needed her. "Okay. These buildings are gone. Let's save the lodge."

We'd be able to do more good there since the fire seemed much more contained—stop it before there was true damage.

Together, the three of us ran for the lodge. I pointed the fire extinguisher at the tendrils of fire crawling across the low beams at the back corner of the building. The flame-retardant foam sprayed out, defeating the blaze right in front of me, and suddenly Mara was on the other side, helping me cage it in.

"Inside." I ran up the back porch stairs.

"Lena, wait!" Evie yelled.

I didn't. I almost felt outside of myself. Total calm ruled me, but it wasn't what I really felt. There was panic and dread. Fear too. But none of it rose to the surface, as if there was a barrier keeping it at bay so I could function.

I touched the back door handle, letting out a small sigh of thanks when it was cool. I opened the door.

Nothing was on fire inside the lodge. It had been contained to the outside. Thank God. The damage would probably only be cosmetic.

Behind us, sirens sounded as the Garnet Bend fire

trucks sped down the road toward the burning cabins. The blaze was even bigger.

"Do you think Grace and Cori are here?" I asked, breathless as we all backed away from the lodge.

"I hope so." Evie's fire extinguisher hung from her hands. "We need everyone we can get."

"Lena." Mara froze. I wasn't sure why. She was looking deeper into the ranch.

And then I heard the sound no one who lived near a ranch ever wanted to hear. The sound of terrified animals.

I dropped the extinguisher and sprinted toward the fire trucks over by the cabins. There was a crowd there. Grace and Cori were there too, looking on as the flames were sprayed down.

"Help!" The women looked at me first. "The stable is on fire. The animals."

That was all I managed to get out before Cori cursed and was shouting. Firefighters broke off, and the sound of an engine roared.

"Are you okay?" Grace's hand came down on my shoulder.

I nodded. "I'll be fine. But the animals…"

"Let's go help as much as we can."

We all jumped in vehicles and drove to the stable. Staying out of the firefighters' way, we used our canisters to put out any flames in the grass and feed. The professionals quickly got the stable fire under control as we helped lead the terrified animals out and to safety.

Then one by one, the firefighters got the rest of the flames out. By the time it was all over, my friends and I stood there, taking in the damage.

The cabins were a total loss. The stable would need to be replaced too, although fortunately no animals were harmed. The lodge would be fine except for the back porch.

"We got lucky," I said. "Really lucky."

Grace nodded. We were all still breathing hard even though we weren't running around anymore. The adrenaline was still coursing through our systems.

A phone rang. Mara pulled it out of her pocket and held it to her ear.

"No, it's under control," she said, perfectly clear. "Everything is out, no people or animals hurt. If someone was trying to divert your attention, don't let them succeed. There's nothing that can be done right now."

So much for that woman being mostly mute.

I was staring when she hung up, and she shrugged. "That was the guys. They heard about what happened and were coming back to help. But they're needed elsewhere. Evidently whatever they're doing to help Noah and Kate, someone didn't like, and this was an attack to divide their efforts."

What I'd been told of the Noah and Kate situation sounded serious. They needed the help more than we did. My calm fading, I felt a spike of panic drive through my stomach. Jude would be with them. Was he in danger?

Please, let him come back.

Just because I planned to move on didn't mean I didn't still care about Jude. More than care. I needed him to be okay in the same way I needed Resting Warrior to be okay.

"I've never heard you say so many words," I said to Mara with a laugh. "It's nice."

She gave me another little shrug. "When I have to."

Evie talked to the firefighters as they packed up their equipment. Like Mara had said on the phone, there was nothing more that could be done here tonight.

Mara started back toward the lodge, and I followed

slowly. The fire trucks were pulling out when I started climbing the front porch stairs and went inside. Thank God this building, the heart of the ranch and the team, hadn't been harmed.

"Want one?" Cori asked.

"Yes. Please." I sank onto the end of the couch, feeling like I'd just run a marathon. I smelled like smoke—we all did—but we'd just have to pay to get the furniture professionally cleaned. "I'm exhausted."

"Same." Evie was slouched in one of the armchairs, staring at the ceiling. "I never want to do that again."

"Are you okay? Because of the fire."

She shook her head. "Not really, but I'll deal."

Cori handed me my drink. I honestly didn't care what was in it. It wasn't going to help the exhaustion, but at this point, I needed it. Both to relax and to take the edge off. I didn't even take off my coat. Now that I was sitting down, I was shaking. I would just have one so I could still drive home.

"Do we know who did this?" Cori asked. "Because I'd like to have words with yet *another* person willing to burn animals alive. And *words* is a loose term."

"No idea," Grace said. "But it seems like a pretty big coincidence someone crashed the gate when none of the guys were here."

So it probably had to do with whatever they were doing right now. "I'm just glad the damage wasn't worse."

"Thank you." Evelyn lifted her glass. "For coming so quickly."

"Of course."

All of us sat in silence, shell-shocked, nursing our drinks. Even Mara sat with us near the fire. Eventually, we talked about stuff, but no one was really paying attention to the conversation. We'd just saved Resting Warrior from burning down, and most of the women in this room were waiting for their partners to come back from a situation that could be even more dangerous.

It was like a knife in the chest that I wasn't one of them.

The waiting was excruciating. My drink was long since finished when we heard the sound of tires on dirt and gravel. "Oh, thank goodness," Evie said, jumping up.

She waited in the doorway, watching, and it was Lucas who came barreling through first, lifting her off the floor and wrapping her in his arms. I heard a single sob from Evie before he carried her directly out of the lodge again, headed toward their personal cabin.

My heart ached. Evelyn was one of the strongest people I'd ever met. But when she was faced with one of her worst fears and memories, I hoped she would find the safety and comfort she needed at home with Lucas.

Mara stood and slipped out the door without saying anything. Grace and Cori stood as their men came inside. "Are you okay, Lena?" Cori asked. "We can get you home."

"I'm okay," I promised. "I just need a couple minutes, and then I'll head home."

I could have gone earlier, but I wouldn't have been able to sleep without knowing if they were all back safe.

Grace leaned down and hugged me before Harlan tugged her to him, embracing her and kissing her forehead before they left.

Cori and Grant left too, so I was alone in front of the fireplace.

All the men looked exhausted, too. Whatever happened, it hadn't been easy. I would hear about it later from Evelyn and Grace. We would need another girls' date soon. The one we'd had for Kate to welcome her to the group hadn't been nearly long enough.

I should leave. There was no one here, and no one needed me. I could go back home and finish reading my book, though, at this point, sleep was more appealing. The only thing the book would do was make me think about Jude.

Heavy footsteps sounded on the stairs outside, and a large frame filled the still-open door. I hadn't noticed it was ajar, letting in cold air. It was Jude. I would know his frame anywhere, even in silhouette. I didn't know if I'd ever forget the shape of him. Ever.

He stepped into the glow of the firelight, and my heart jumped in my chest. It thundered. The expression on his face was the one I'd always seen when he thought I wasn't looking. It was wild, filled with barely contained hunger. And even now, no way could I be convinced it meant nothing.

He moved, crossing the space to where I sat and pulled me to standing. I always forgot how fast he could move. My hands landed on his chest to keep my balance, and he didn't pull away.

He didn't pull away.

Jude's hands were on me, running down my arms, and he was still looking at me like that. Like he could consume me alive, and I would be happy to let him.

"Are you all right?"

His voice was rough. "I am now."

"Jude—" His hand came up, slipping behind my neck, and my traitorous stomach flipped with hope. "What are you doing?"

Jude was so, so much taller than I was, and he was leaning down. "You can tell me to stop," he said quietly.

"Stop what?"

He said the words again, bringing our faces even closer. "You can tell me to stop."

No part of me wanted him to stop. I didn't want to move on from him, no matter the face I was putting on. I wanted him to look at me exactly like this, and I wanted everything else. "I don't want you to stop."

Jude lowered his head and kissed me.

Chapter 9

Jude

This was a dream come true. That was the only thing I could think as I pulled her more firmly against me and kissed her. Lena melted—*melted*—in my arms, and I felt an overwhelming sense of relief from her. And from me.

After what I saw tonight, there was no going back. No way for me to reconcile the fact that I'd waited so long to do this. So much wasted time.

Before we'd gone into the house, we'd had eyes and ears on it. I saw Noah with a gun to his head, and I heard him tell Kate to close her eyes so she wouldn't have to watch him die. But I also saw the love on his face and the knowledge that, if things had gone differently, at least they'd had even their short time together.

I put myself in his position.

If something happened to me and I never had a chance to hold the woman in my arms right now—never had the chance to love her and to give her that time—it would be worse than anything else. My stubbornness had hurt us both. I already knew that.

I slipped my hand from the back of her neck up into her hair, angling her head so I could kiss her more deeply. She tasted like the sweetness of tea and the bitterness of whiskey. Sugar and something more.

Feeling her against my body was everything I'd dreamed of, and it felt like a miracle. I dropped my free hand down her spine to cradle her waist, and she gasped into my mouth, twining her arms up and around my neck.

Right now, I didn't care about the need to command her pleasure and the instinct to tell her to lie down and open for me. I just needed to feel her.

Breaking away for breath, I looked down at her. Lena's eyes were wide, pupils dilated, chest heaving for the air we both needed now. It was an effort not to kiss her again or, better yet, take her on this very couch.

"I owe you both an apology and an explanation," I said. "But more than that, I need to take you home. I don't plan on leaving this time."

Her tiny gasp sent chills down my spine. The flicker of doubt I saw stabbed me in the heart because I was the one who put it there. If there was one thing I would do in this life, it would be to make sure Lena Mitchell never doubted her own worth again.

"Will you let me take you home?"

"Yes," she breathed. "Yes, please."

I didn't bother letting her go, instead lifting her off the floor and letting her wrap her legs around my waist.

"Are you sure—"

"I'm not letting you go." The words were a growl. Lena tightened her arms around me, and I managed to shut the door behind us. She was worried about me being tired or her being too heavy? I wasn't.

She didn't understand that if I had to carry her all the way to her house on foot, I would do it. I dug my fingers into the softness of her hips, itching to slip them down onto her ass. The frenzy building in my chest was ready to be unleashed, but I wanted to be in her bed when it happened. A place where she felt safe, and where the first time we did this didn't have to be rushed.

Still, I pushed her back against the door of my truck and kissed her again. The moan that fell out of her was enough to make me harder than I already was. The second her lips touched mine, I'd been harder than the rocks of the mountains all around us.

Lena shuddered, and I pulled back. Her lips were red, cheeks flushed, and the rest of her was pale. It was cold. That wouldn't do.

Stepping back, I opened the door and lifted her. "Get in."

"Bessie?"

"We'll come back for her," I said. "I don't think I can be separated from you right now."

"No complaints here." She barely left enough room for me to slide onto the bench seat.

Leaning forward, she kissed me this time, nearly sprawling over my lap in her attempt to get closer. Her words rang true. I wasn't complaining. But I also didn't want her to die on our way there. "You need your seat belt," I murmured against her lips.

"You'll be my seat belt."

"Lena." I put more command behind her name.

"Jude."

The kiss was desperate, both of us breaking, pulling toward each other without thought for anything else. I couldn't get enough of her lips on mine or the brush of her body. Every place she touched was a live wire, sending shocks through my entire being.

Finally, I pulled her back. If I didn't, we weren't making it to her house. "Put it on."

She rolled her eyes, but she was smiling as she slid across the seat and buckled. The fact that she wasn't touching me anymore was pure torture. I started the truck and backed up. The faster we got to her house, the faster I could taste those lips again, along with everything else.

I held out my hand across the seat, and she took it, weaving our fingers together. One glance over told me she was biting her lip, the tiny glow from the truck's headlights showing me only the barest details.

The silence in the truck was a living thing, surrounding us and spinning back and forth. I had so much I needed to say, and I imagined Lena had plenty to say as well. But there was nothing in this moment we *could* say to break the tension and the cloud of lust fogging the air.

Condensation was creeping up the edges of the windows, the haze made visible because of our need.

There. Her house came into view, and I nearly took the turn into her drive too fast. We were here. This moment was here. As soon as I heard the click of her belt, I tugged her across the seat to me. No more distance.

I swept her into my arms and kicked the door of the truck shut. "Keys?" I asked.

She squirmed, getting them from her pocket, and we tumbled into her house together. I didn't want to let her go. The image of me carrying her into the house like a bride struck me so deep and so true, I lost my breath. There was a rightness in this I couldn't deny.

But I had denied it. For far too long.

I bumped the door closed behind us.

"I have to shower," she whispered. "I smell like a chimney. And...I need a moment. Is that okay?"

I nodded, setting her down. "I need one too. Can I use your guest bath?"

I wanted to shower with her, but I would give her a chance to compose herself. And I needed the chance to make sure I had myself completely under control.

She pointed down the hall. "There's soap and towels in there."

Before I could say anything else, she darted away. Was she nervous? That would be my fault. Again.

A cold shower got me clean but didn't do much to calm me down. I re-dressed and was waiting back in the hallway when she came out of her own shower, wearing sweats and T-shirt, hair damp.

I'd never wanted anybody as much as I wanted this woman, right now.

She motioned for me to come to her bedroom. As I stepped inside, my instincts roared to take charge. I wanted to order her to strip so I could watch every inch of her appear. To turn around and place her hands on the bed. So many other things I wanted and fantasized about all this time.

But that was a conversation we still needed to have. Tonight, I was going to enjoy the woman in front of me. Later, we would deal with the rest of it. I was done making Lena wait.

I stared at her, and she stared at me, everything building between us until we moved at the same time. We came together with a clash of lips and teeth and tongues. Roaming hands and groans of relief.

"Do you need me to take this slow?" I whispered the words into her neck.

"Please don't."

I laughed softly. "Thank goodness."

Pulling her shirt up and over her head, I tossed it aside before freezing. This was as much of her skin as I'd ever seen. In the warm light of the lamp, I drank her in. Lena's hair was wild, mussed and damp. And her skin…I wanted to touch every inch of it.

Taste it—and her.

I shrugged out of my shirt, watching Lena's breath speed up in the process. Stepping closer, I wrapped my arms around her, taking the moment to draw my fingers across her skin and feel the softness. I found the clasp of her bra and let it fall away.

Lena looked up at me, cheeks blushing. "Is this real? We're sure I didn't fall and hit my head and this is all a dream."

Lifting her off her feet, I stretched her out on the bed before joining her. "Very real, Lena. And I'm sorry for making you wait so long."

I didn't give her a chance to respond, rolling over her and dropping my mouth to her skin. Nothing could hold me back except her words, and the only word I heard on her lips was *yes*.

My mouth had a mind of its own. My body too. Everything was simply too overwhelming. This was *Lena*. Her skin pebbled, and she arched to meet my mouth, where I kissed across her chest and down between her breasts. She sank her hands into my hair and pulled me closer.

I was caught between everything. My need to take control and my desire to savor every inch of Lena's body. The softness of her skin and the tiny, panting breaths she made every time I kissed her body. The need to talk to her and tell her every filthy thought speeding through my head and the urge to keep silent so we didn't break the atmosphere of reverence surrounding us.

"Oh my god." Lena both whispered and moaned the words as I sealed my mouth over one nipple, thoroughly enjoying the feeling of it hardening under my tongue. It drew into a tight peak that made it look so much pinker.

She dug her fingers into my scalp, following me as I continued my journey, tasting her skin and teasing her with brushes of my tongue until I reached the waistband of her pants. "May I take these off?"

"Burn them for all I care," she said, breathless.

I made sure she felt my smile.

Moving so I knelt, I hooked my fingers under the band of her sweatpants and pulled them off. She hadn't bothered with underwear after her shower, so she was completely naked in front of me. Lena looked up at me, total vulnerability shining in her eyes. This was the moment when we crossed a line neither of us could come back from.

It felt perfect and inevitable, but also fragile.

She was so small underneath me. My height dwarfed hers when she stood. Now I felt like I dwarfed her everywhere, and the caveman in me liked that. I loved having the ability to wrap myself around her and keep her safe and protected.

Deeper, there was an instinct I couldn't let myself consider right now. This woman was *mine*, and I was never going to let her go. Now that I'd seen the truth of my mistake, I never wanted to be away from her.

And I never wanted to see this unsure look in her eyes again.

Stretching myself over her, I kissed her. Softly and deeply. "Lena, you are perfect."

She choked on a laugh. "I don't know about that."

"Perfect," I whispered again. "Please don't doubt it."

Her cheeks tinged pink, and I watched her eyes flutter

closed under my kiss. Already, the way she was, hair spread over the pillow, face flushed…I regretted every second I'd spent not loving her. Watching her from afar and doing nothing about it.

I was going to make up for lost time.

Again, I followed the path, kissing different places on her body and listening to the way her breathing changed. I glanced up and found her watching me, gaze now filled with wonder instead of nerves.

Her eyes locked with mine, and I brushed my lips over one thigh and then the other, getting closer to what I really wanted.

"Jude."

I slid my hands up her legs until my fingers were on those same thighs, ready to spread them apart and reveal the promised land. "Do you want me to stop?"

Lena shook her head. "No, I don't want you to stop."

"Good." I smiled and gently lifted her legs open. The frenzy I'd been fighting caught up with me. I couldn't even pause to admire how gorgeous she was because I needed to taste her like I needed my next breath.

Holy. Hell.

Lena sank her hands into my hair again, and she cursed, hips lifting to my mouth. Life-changing, earth-shattering, and more. I drank in Lena and tried to hold on to myself in the process. I'd thought she was the center of my world already.

I was wrong.

Now she was the center of my world. The center of everything. And if I spent my life only bringing her pleasure, it would be enough.

"Jude," she moaned. "I need you."

Tracing circles around her swollen clit with my tongue,

I savored her gasp. "You'll have me," I said. "More than enough of me."

But first, she would come on my tongue. I wanted the burst of deep sweetness from her orgasm to brand me with a flavor I would never forget as long as I lived.

I gave in, taking more control, gripping her thighs and pushing them wider. She was completely exposed to me, just the way I wanted. The image of her bound for me like this entered my head, and I groaned. I could happily spend hours between her legs.

"Oh—" Lena stiffened. I dragged my tongue under her clit, finding the spot which had made her speak. I repeated the motion and felt her shake. There it was. The key to her undoing.

She dug her fingers into my scalp, and I scooped my hands under her legs, pulling her to my mouth like the feast she was. I didn't stop. That same swift, gentle movement had her hips jerking and stifled moans escaping.

"Don't stop," she whispered. "Please don't stop."

I didn't.

Sealing my mouth over her, I sucked her deep, keeping my tongue exactly where she liked it. Fuck, I was going to enjoy learning every inch of her. She was shaking now, hips moving on their own, begging me without words for more.

Her wish was my command.

I dragged my tongue over her once more, and she came. Lena arched, shuddering. She called my name, and I wasn't even sure she realized. I closed my eyes to enjoy her orgasm on my tongue, never letting go until her body sagged down onto the bed, newly spent with pleasure.

There was more where that came from. We weren't nearly finished.

Chapter 10

Lena

Stars danced behind my eyes.

I hauled in a breath, trying to catch it and recover from the orgasm. Which was…indescribable.

This. This was what I wanted. The chemistry that had always spun between us played out on our bodies.

Jude lifted himself from between my legs, and I drank him in. Every line of muscle that came from a lifetime of training and hard work. The dusting of hair on his chest that drove me mad. Lines that dipped below his belt to where his jeans were so tight it looked painful.

He came back to me, kissing me again, and I wrapped myself around him. Arms, legs, anything I could move. I twisted around him and pulled him down to me. He was so much bigger, I didn't get much purchase. I just wanted him closer.

Holy shit, we'd just done that.

I wasn't totally convinced I wasn't sleeping and was

about to be woken up from the best dream of my life. "This is real," I said quietly. Earlier, I had asked him, but I needed to say it again. "You're real."

"I'm real."

There was a rawness to his voice I didn't understand, but it was sexy as hell.

"Lena."

I looked up at him.

"I know you said we didn't need to take it slow, but I wanted it to be. So I can learn every inch of you. But—"

"I don't need slow," I interrupted, repeating the sentiment. "This isn't going to be the last time, and there's a place for slow. Right now, I need *you*. Fast or slow, I don't care."

A smile bloomed on his face before he kissed me again. He'd smiled more in the last half hour than I could remember. Jude's smiles were rare, and when you earned one, you believed it. That he was smiling so much—

It was me.

The realization stole my breath.

I made him smile. Us being together.

Jude lifted himself out of my arms and stood. He quickly removed a condom from his wallet before reaching for his belt, and I found myself transfixed, watching. I'd seen him like this, in summer moments when they worked the ranch. But everything else?

He pushed his jeans and underwear off his hips, and I stared.

My mouth went dry.

Another smile, this one tipping to one side. "Did I kill you?"

Jude was proportional. Meaning, he was huge, and I wasn't totally sure how we were going to fit. Other than that, he was long and straight, and I never thought I'd encounter a cock I thought was beautiful.

Clearly, I was wrong.

"No."

"Good." He rolled the condom on and joined me on the bed, settling over me and tilting my face to his for a kiss so deep it made me ache. "Killing you is the last thing I want."

I grinned. "I don't know. You might still kill me with that thing."

"If I do, I'll make sure it's from pleasure."

The word *pleasure* returned my focus solely to him. He was holding something back—I could feel it. Maybe he was worried about hurting me. Right now, I didn't think anything in the world could hurt.

He was right there. I felt him brushing against my entrance, and twin flames of nerves and excitement sprang to life. Taking his face in my hands, I guided his gaze to mine. "If you have any doubt—"

Jude silenced me with a kiss. It was all the answer I needed. There was no doubt in this kiss, only pure lust and longing. He didn't stop kissing me, moving his lips across my jaw and down to my neck as he pressed in.

The moan that left me was completely unintentional. He was so big, it was hard to breathe. But he didn't stop. Pressing in and in and in until every delicious inch was somehow inside.

We were connected, and it didn't feel real. Every time I'd imagined it was nothing compared to the real feeling of him. Emotion rose in me, and I fought it back as best I could.

It didn't work.

When I looked up at him, my eyes were wet, and I tried to speak, unable to do so.

But Jude didn't look at me with horror or concern; he just pressed his forehead against mine and breathed with me.

"I know," he said. "I know."

Then he began to move.

It wasn't slow.

I thought it was stars behind my eyes, but it wasn't. Whole galaxies were spinning in my mind as Jude drove home, taking us to a place I never wanted to come back from.

Pleasure swirled around me like the ocean, hitching itself to the first orgasm he gave me and leaving me breathless all over again. This wasn't polished or perfect; it was raw. Both of us letting out years of pent-up desire, taking what we needed without apology.

Jude kissed me, hard enough to bruise, and I wrapped my arms around his neck to make sure he stayed there. I was only aware of his lips on mine and the movement of his hips, friction dragging me back into bliss every time he thrust deep.

Locking his hands on my hips, Jude rolled us, never pulling back. Now I was looking down at him. Miles of man laid out all for me, pure hunger in his gaze.

He *was* holding something back. I felt the restrained power in his fingers gripping my skin, lifting me and bringing me back down onto him without having to do a thing.

I wanted to tell him I wasn't breakable. That I could take all the heat lurking behind his eyes and the power he was containing. But my voice was nowhere to be found. Every stroke hit me exactly where I needed it to, and I was shaking.

The orgasm crashed over me like a wave, collapsing over my body in a silvery, shining flood. I matched Jude thrust for thrust, riding out my orgasm like the cowgirl the position was named for.

My voice came back, and I heard myself saying yes, the words shaking along with my body before I collapsed on Jude's chest. I kissed him, desperate for more of this—of anything.

He was there with me, still driving up into me and causing aftershocks. Lightning bolts of pleasure that kept me moaning as he came. Thrusting once. Twice. And again before he groaned, holding himself so deep I never wanted us to come apart.

Breaking away from his lips, I laid my head on his chest, letting myself enjoy the feel of his breathing. The rise and fall of it was calming, bringing me back from oblivion with pleasure.

I just had sex with Jude. With *Jude*. A part of me still didn't quite believe it after all this time.

He stroked his hands down my spine, spreading warmth. "Are you all right?"

I laughed once. "A little better than all right."

Slowly, he rolled us again, cradling me so we didn't come apart. He was so big in every way, it made me smile. He could lie on top of me and I would disappear completely.

"Now for the rest of it," he said softly.

"There's more?"

He was braced on his elbows so he could look down at me, and he lifted one hand, tucking a strand of my wild hair off my forehead. "I owe you an apology. More than one. And I plan on making it up to you. I'm sorry, Lena."

I blinked away the sudden emotion fast enough to see a glimpse of the pain on his face before he kissed me. This was a gentle kiss. Soothing and apologetic. When he pulled back, I reached for him, slipping my hands around his shoulders, big as they were. "You're not going anywhere?"

"No." The promise in the single word was clear. It rang through me like a bell. So much that I squeezed him where he was still inside me, and he smirked down at me. "No, I'm not going anywhere."

He pulled back only long enough to separate our bodies and dispose of the condom before he settled again, this time beside me where he could tuck me into his chest and still look down at me.

"I—" Swallowing, I pressed my forehead to his chest. "I don't know what I'd like to know first. What made you decide to walk away, or what made you change your mind?"

Jude dragged a hand up my side, weaving a hand into my hair before he tugged me back far enough to see him. "I wanted to protect you."

I raised an eyebrow. "From incredible sex?"

"No, from…" He sighed and closed his eyes. "From me."

"What? How?"

He reached down and took one of my hands, moving it to his skin. A scar ran under my fingers. Of course he had scars—all the Resting Warrior men did. The ones across his back and chest, I'd already seen. This one was lower on his hip and thick. "I don't understand."

"I have nightmares," he said gently. "More often than not, I wake up fighting my memories. I rip the sheets in half and punch the wall before I wake up. And I never want it to be you."

My heart fluttered in my chest. Of all the reasons I'd considered and made myself sick thinking about, that wasn't one of them. "I'd decided I was crazy," I admitted. "That I'd been imagining us the whole time and making something up. Or that you'd simply changed your mind and just didn't want me anymore."

"*Never.*" The word was low and fervent. "Not for one second."

We rested in silence for a moment, and I let the knowledge settle and wrap my soul up in comfort.

"I was a prisoner of war for six months." His voice was soft.

"Just like Noah." I knew a little about the other man's history after we'd witnessed him deal with his PTSD at the family dinner.

"The same place. He was rescued. I, along with another member of our team, wasn't. When they finally came back for me, I was broken. Physically and mentally. I couldn't get Isaac out. Eventually, they let him go. By that time, they'd extracted everything he knew, which wasn't much, and were trying to make nice with our military." He slid his hand down my side again, pulling me closer, like he was making sure I was real.

I felt the same way.

Finally, he spoke again. "Isaac killed himself a few months after he came home."

"I'm sorry."

He smiled briefly, but I could see shadows in his eyes. "I did the work. I dealt with it. Fixed my body and my brain, and all this time, I thought the nightmares were something that would always be there and they would always stop me from being with you. Because I wouldn't survive waking up and finding out I—" One deep breath. "That I hurt you. Broke a bone or, worse, killed you without even knowing."

I swallowed. "I have nightmares too."

They were something I didn't like to think about, the

times I woke up sweating, remembering Evie's screams or the feeling of knowing I was going to die.

"It's one of the things that made me change my mind."

I blinked. "But I've never told anyone."

He hesitated and pulled me closer to kiss my forehead. "We'll come back to that." My stomach swooped with nerves. Not at talking about it, but the gentle firmness in the way he said it. We would talk about it, and that was the end of it. "I talked to Noah to see how he was handling it with Kate, and he told me the nightmares are better with her. He also, lovingly, verbally kicked my ass and pointed out you've gone through something too. He's not the only one who kicked my ass, by the way."

"You said it was one of the things."

Jude's face darkened. "Where we were… You'll all find out soon enough. Kate was taken. Noah went after her, and with the fire, we were split. He and Liam had to go in before we got there because they were out of time."

"Oh god."

"They're okay," he said. "Everyone's okay. But when we got there and set up eyes and ears, we could hear them. I could barely see them through a crack in a door. Noah was on his knees, and they were going to kill him."

My gut twisted, listening. But at least they were okay.

"He told Kate to close her eyes."

Jude went quiet, and I looked up at him. His eyes were closed, jaw tight. "Nothing more than that, but I understood it. He didn't want her to live with the memory of seeing him die. Only the memories they had. And I put myself in his place. If it had been me, I would have had no memories with you."

My heart kicked into high gear, breath going short.

"I was afraid to hurt you, and I still am. But after seeing them, I couldn't stay away from you anymore."

"You never had to stay away from me."

"I know that now." The words were murmured against my lips. "I'm sorry."

The way he kissed me could have set the house on fire and melted all the snow for miles. All-consuming. An apology entirely on its own, apart from everything else. If I knew anything about Jude, it was once he made a decision, it was made. End of story. The waiting really was over.

I still felt an edge of carefulness in the way he touched me. There was something more he was holding back, but I wasn't afraid of whatever it was. Now that we were doing this, we had time to tell each other things. He'd already said we'd talk about my nightmares, and I had no intention of doing it tonight.

But I couldn't keep the smile off my face. "So, we're doing this?"

"Yes," he said mildly. "If you want to."

I rolled my eyes. "Yes. Though I'm not sure if I'm looking forward to everyone knowing it's finally happened."

Jude chuckled. "True. But I'll take the brunt of it. It was me who kept you waiting."

"When you—" I took a breath before I said the next thing. "When you pushed me away, and then I didn't see you, I questioned everything. And I decided I was going to try to move on. I told Evelyn."

He winced. "Is she planning my murder?"

"No." I hit him lightly on the arm. "She was sad but wanted what was best for me. She'll be over the moon now."

"Lena." Jude tilted my face to his, keeping his hand where he could just brush my lips with his thumb. And there was something so *hot* about it, I was nearly distracted.

"I know I hurt you. And I made you wait. If moving on is what's best for you—"

"I said I was going to try. It didn't fucking work. If anything, I only thought about you more."

A pure, genuine smile cracked across his face. "That shouldn't make me happy."

"No, it shouldn't."

He moved, rolling over me so fast I blinked and he was above me, weight settling between my hips. He was hard all over again, and now conversation was the last thing on my mind.

"We'll take it slow." I gave him a look, and he smirked before kissing me. "Slow-ish."

"What does that mean for tonight?"

"Mmm." The sound flew straight south, lighting up my body as it went. "It means I'm going to start my exploration."

"Start?"

"Trust me, Lena," Jude locked eyes with me. "I've been fantasizing about you for years. It's going to take more than one night for me to explore your body." He placed a kiss between my breasts. "I plan on learning every inch of you."

He raked his fingers down my ribs, and I arched into his hold. Being memorized? I couldn't say I minded that.

Heavy warmth was what I woke to. My back was pressed against Jude's chest, and I had no confusion about what was different or wondering why there was another body next to mine. It was clear and right—like we'd been waking up together for years.

My alarm was chirping somewhere in my clothes on the floor.

"Good morning." Jude's already deep voice was rough with sleep.

"Good morning." I smiled over my shoulder at him. "No nightmares for you."

Behind me, he brushed my hair over my shoulder and kissed the back of my neck. "Having you close must have chased them away."

"I would like to sleep in all day and stay here with you, but I can't." I sighed, stretching.

"It's a good thing we have more than one day, then, isn't it?"

My stomach tumbled into butterflies.

I was with Jude. *Together.*

That he was here was hard to wrap my head around, but I couldn't wipe the smile off my face. I went with cute but comfortable for the day. I wasn't trying to seduce Jude the way I had the other day. But I still appreciated the look when he saw me in leggings and a shirt that slipped off my shoulder.

"You sure you have to work?"

"I do," I said with a pout.

Watching Jude get dressed was both a wonder and a crime. All those lean muscles were even more delicious in the clear morning light, but their disappearing was a damn shame.

"I'll drive you to the bakery and get one of the guys to help bring Bessie over later."

"Thank you."

Before we left the house, he pulled me against his body and kissed me. "I can't believe I can do that."

"Finally," I said with a grin before he lifted me into the cab of the truck.

Just like the night before, it was impossible not to touch him. This drive couldn't have been further from the one we'd shared after the kiss in my kitchen. Instead of awkward silence, it was perfect, Jude's arm around me to ward off the morning chill. He didn't even make me wear the seat belt, though I saw him consider it.

Deja Brew appeared too soon.

"Come here." He pulled me with him out of the driver's side and walked with me to the door.

Before I could reach for my keys, he spun me and backed me against the door until our bodies were touching. Not just touching, he was pressing me into the glass hard enough that *all* I could feel was him. "I owe you a kiss here," he said.

Just like last night, he wove his hand into my hair, holding my head still as he leaned in to kiss me. Pressed against the door and frozen by his hand, I could do nothing but accept his kiss. My head spun, dizzy, heady pleasure sizzling through me and making me desperately wish I didn't have a million things to do today.

I reached for him, and he caught my wrist with his free hand, not ever breaking the rhythm of his kiss. He was in control of it, and the heat that followed the thought startled me.

When he stepped back, all I could do was stare.

Jude let one corner of his mouth tip up, and he winked —*winked*—at me. "Have a good day."

"Yeah." My voice sounded like I'd run a marathon.

Finally able to tear my eyes away, I saw a couple of my regulars far down the street and coming in this direction. I had to get inside. Jude waited until I'd unlocked the door before getting back into his truck, and I started the morning routine feeling like I was floating on a cloud.

Chapter 11

Lena

The sensation of floating lasted for days. It was as if I drifted from task to task in a mist of happiness nothing could touch.

Everyone at Resting Warrior knew—once I told Evelyn, it was inevitable—but they were being good sports about keeping it low-key. As I predicted, Evie was so happy she started jumping up and down before she hugged me. And now that a few days had passed, I was starting to believe I wasn't in a fever dream.

The phone rang in the office, and I stepped away from the batch of cupcakes I was mixing to answer it. "Deja Brew, Lena speaking."

"Hello, Lena dear. It's Mrs. Rosenthal."

"Oh, hi." The older woman was one of my best customers, having a standing weekly order for Garnet Bend's retirement community. "I hope everything's all right with the cookies?"

"That's the thing… It's not."

My heart skipped a beat. Mrs. Rosenthal often called to compliment us on the cookies or to ask for something particular the next week. I'd never had her call to tell me something was wrong. "I'm so sorry. What happened?"

"Well…" She paused. "I'm not exactly sure."

"Did they taste bad?" I'd tasted them yesterday when we made them, and they'd seemed fine. Had I missed something?

She made a noncommittal sound. "I couldn't tell you. We weren't able to eat any of them. As soon as we picked them up, they crumbled into bits."

I froze. "What? All of them?"

"Yes. All of them."

Dread hollowed out the pit of my stomach. "I'm so sorry. I don't know what happened. I'll happily replace—"

"That's all right, dear," she said with a sigh. "With Thanksgiving so soon, the last thing I want here is for anyone to have a disappointment for the holiday. So I'll cancel the order for tomorrow and also cancel my weekly order until after the holiday. Or rather, until you figure out what's wrong and make sure it doesn't happen again."

My mouth dropped open, and anyone stepping into the office would have said I looked like a gaping fish. "Of course, Mrs. Rosenthal. I'll let you know when I find the cause."

She didn't even say goodbye before hanging up.

I sat down heavily, bewildered about what could have happened in such a short time. Evie and I made the cookies yesterday—we always did, so they had time to settle—and boxed them. They sat on the counter overnight, and then Evie dropped them off this morning. They'd looked perfect when they left.

Of course, I hadn't touched them, but I never did that.

"Lena?" Evie called, knocking on the wall before stepping into the doorway. "You okay?"

"Not really. Mrs. Rosenthal canceled her order indefinitely." I filled her in, and she was just as bewildered as I was. There was no sign we'd done anything different to the cookies.

"I swear they looked fine when I dropped them off."

I waved a hand. "This isn't your fault. It's probably a fluke. Maybe we need to calibrate the oven."

But I couldn't shake the niggling worry in the back of my mind. It felt silly, but people talked about my baking a lot. I was known as a good baker around town, and I liked that reputation. If Mrs. Rosenthal decided to speak to anyone else about what happened, it could be a cascading effect, and quickly. That was the way it worked in small towns. Opinions and experiences mattered, and now there was a bad one connected to Deja Brew.

"Well," Evie called, glancing over her shoulder. "Your day is about to get a little better, at least."

Jude appeared behind her, stepping into the kitchen. The clouds at the edge of my mind receded, and I smiled. Since we'd gotten together, he no longer stayed in the front of the store, instead coming back—at my insistence—to see me. It let me do things like this. "Take care of the front for a couple of minutes."

Evelyn looked like she was barely containing her laughter. "Yes, ma'am."

I pulled Jude into the office and shut the door. He didn't even wait for me to say a thing, pushing me up against it the second it closed. I was getting to like his habit of doing it.

"I'm glad you're here," I breathed.

"So you can use me for my body?" he asked, lips against my neck.

The line of heat drawn by his tongue on my skin nearly made me lose all power of speech. "Not only. I got some bad news, and seeing you makes the day better. That's all."

"What happened?"

My laugh was breathless. "At the moment? I don't really care."

"Tell me."

"I'd rather you kissed me until I forgot about it."

"Lena." He looked at me. "If you're avoiding it this much, it's really bothering you. Please tell me."

He was right, and I hated that he was. But the way he had me up against the door, I wasn't going anywhere. So I told him, my body wilting in shame and the same nervous worry trickling down my spine. "I just don't know what could have happened. Besides the cookies themselves, it's a big order. That's a lot of money to lose every week if she decides not to come back."

"She'll come back. People react before they consider. When everyone is missing your cookies—which *are* delicious—she'll place the order again. Everything is going to be fine."

"I just don't like that it happened at all. I don't want anyone to believe I'm a bad baker."

He smiled. "One bad batch of cookies isn't enough to make people think you're a bad baker after years of them being addicted to the things you make."

I hoped that was true. I couldn't fully explain the slow, oozing dread spreading through me at the thought. Or the embarrassment.

Those were thoughts I'd had before. I was the one who made people's lives better and not worse. By messing up the cookies, I'd failed. What would happen if I wasn't the person Garnet Bend came to for coffee and a pick-me-up?

A future that was both bleak and horrible.

"What's going on in your head?"

"A lot of things."

Jude pressed his forehead to mine. "Do I need to find a penny to give you for your thoughts?"

"There are too many. It would take longer than I have, and you wouldn't want to hear them anyway."

"Not true." He didn't move, keeping our faces close and me locked against the door so I was completely enveloped by him. "There's not a single thought of yours I don't want to hear and nothing about you I don't want to know." Then more quietly, he said, "I've already lived through hell, Lena. Whatever it is, I can bear it."

"It's nothing compared to that."

"That's not what I meant." One finger lifted my chin, so I was looking into his eyes. "My point being, there's nothing you can say that will shock me or make me think less of you. No matter how small or big the burden, I want to share it with you."

All of it was on the tip of my tongue. But as soon as I started, I wondered if it would all come pouring out of me and I wouldn't be able to stop. I had a list of orders as long as my arm to make for Thanksgiving, and getting caught in a loop of worry and shame wouldn't help if I added it all on top.

"Later?" I asked. "I need to get back to work."

"Later, then." He would ask me later. But at home, with just him and a little distance, I might be able to voice some of the things pushing against the wall I was barely keeping up.

"But," he added, "we still have why I came here in the first place."

"Oh?" I allowed myself to smile. "What's that?"

Jude's only answer was to kiss me. It had the magical ability to wash away everything I was worried about.

Nothing existed but the two of us in the moments Jude kissed me, and I hoped that would never change.

A knock vibrated through the door. Evie's voice was muffled. "I hate to break up the lovebirds, but the lunch rush is starting."

"I'll be right there," I called.

Jude kissed me one more time. "I'll be at your house when you get there. Try not to let it take over your mind, and you can tell me about it later."

"Right."

He gave me a look that told me he knew I was going to have it swirling around in my thoughts for the rest of the day, but I hoped not.

"See you at home."

The phone rang, and he let me go so I could answer, squeezing my hand before he slipped out of the office. My stomach was in knots when I answered, hoping it wasn't another person canceling on me. But it was just a delayed delivery, and I had to take several deep breaths to push back the anxiety.

This was an overreaction. Jude was right. One bad batch of cookies wasn't enough to undo everything I'd built. And I was smart enough to know, deep down, it had nothing to do with the cookies, and that everything I'd been pushing away since Evelyn's and my abduction was starting to come back to me.

At some point, I needed to face it.

Today was not that day, with a million and one things to do, along with the added pressure of making sure absolutely *nothing* went wrong.

Evie's grin was about as wide as the state of Montana itself when I finally came out of the office. "So. How'd it go?"

I looked at her. "What is it you think we did in there?"

She just waggled her eyebrows, and I rolled my eyes. "Do you honestly think we could have had sex in that amount of time? Or that you wouldn't have heard it?"

She shrugged. "I think Mr. Jude Williams can pretty much do whatever he wants."

"Well, we didn't."

"I'm not judging." She held up her hands. "If you'd done it in the kitchen, I might have judged a little, cause… sanitary. But it's your office."

"Oh my god, we *didn't.*"

She smirked. "Whatever you say, boss."

"Let's take care of the rush so we can get on with the pies. We're barely going to have enough time as it is."

We did. The influx of customers dissipated in less than an hour, and we went to work. I tasted *everything*. The filling, the pastry, the raw ingredients. The only thing I couldn't do was try the pies once they were baked. But they looked fine. I stacked them on the cooling racks and covered them lightly so they could cool. Most people would be picking up their pies tomorrow, and I'd finish up any last-minute ones, plus those I said I'd bake for the Resting Warrior meal.

The nice thing was, so close to the holiday, other than the cookies we'd made, all the other things we normally baked were put on hold. The town was used to it, and it would help limit the damage I imagined if word got around.

It was later than usual by the time I pulled Bessie into my driveway, but the lights were on, and knowing Jude was waiting for me warmed me up from the inside. It seemed almost too domestic for being together less than a week, but then again, nothing about the two of us was going to be normal.

When you circled a person for three years, wanting

them and never actually having them, things had a right to move faster than the average couple.

He was sitting in the chair when I walked in. *The* chair. The one where I'd kissed him and he'd pushed me away. I saw as he smiled he knew it, and he'd done it on purpose.

We'd spent every night since the first in my bed—though we hadn't had sex again—and that first morning he kissed me outside Deja Brew effectively erased my memory of his rejection there.

"Trying to get rid of all the bad things?" I asked.

"Maybe. Maybe I just needed to sit." As soon as I was within reach, he pulled me to him. "How are you?"

"Tired," I admitted. "I'll probably be tired until Thursday."

"Not worrying?"

I shook my head. "No, I think it will be okay. I hope it will be okay. The rest of it—" I sighed. "I'm not sure if I'm ready to talk about it tonight. I'm not hiding it. I just don't have the energy."

The way Jude was gently trailing his hands up and down my spine was distracting, as was the fact that it felt so *natural.* It shouldn't shock me we fit together so well after so long, but it still did.

He looked as tired as I felt. "Long day?"

"Not too bad. Why?"

I stroked a hand through his hair and winced. "You look tired."

"I am a little." Then he tightened his hands on my body. "Not so tired I don't want to take you upstairs. But first," he said. "I want to ask you one thing. Then I promise I won't let you think about anything else the rest of the night."

"I like that promise. Does it mean…?" I looked at him meaningfully.

Jude smiled. We hadn't had sex, but that wasn't to say nothing had happened. Jude had continued his thorough exploration of my body and maddeningly declared he still wasn't finished. Not that I didn't enjoy the way he reduced me to nothing but breathless sighs and shaking pleasure. But one of these days, I was going to get him to let me explore *him* and lick all those muscles from head to toe.

There was a sparkle in his eye. "We'll see. But this is what I want to ask—on Thursday, are you ready? Do you want me to pull back physically at all?"

It wasn't the question I expected, but I understood why he was asking. Thanksgiving would be our first time with the "family" as a couple. There were sure to be teasing and jokes, all in good fun, but he wanted to know how much of a couple we should be in public. "Well…" I tried to hold in my smile and failed. "Anything besides you staying all the way across the room from me will practically be like we're married."

He laughed, sudden and loud. "I was doing my best to stay away from you."

"What would have happened if you didn't?"

I watched as his eyes darkened and briefly dropped to my lips. "Nothing that would have been appropriate for family dinner."

"Yeah?"

"It might have been wrong," he said. "But the things I imagined doing…pulling you away and making us both filthy. There was a reason I needed to shove myself into a corner to be contained."

I slid my hands over his shoulders, leaning into him. "What about the wedding? When we danced?"

"Until the other night? The best moment of my life."

Wrapping myself the rest of the way around him, I let him hold me. This was what it felt like to not be lonely, and every piece of me loved it. "Do you ever feel like it's too good to be true?"

"You've always been too good to be true, Lena."

My heart skipped a beat. I thought I'd eat something before we went upstairs, but I wasn't interested in food anymore. "I don't want you to pull back," I said. "Not for Thanksgiving. Not for anything. They'll make their jokes and I'll be embarrassed, and then they'll get used to us together. But I don't want to pretend we're less than we are."

"Good," he whispered. "Because I'm not quite sure I'll be able to keep my hands off you. Even if it's just holding yours."

"I like that more than you know."

In one movement, Jude captured my lips with his and lifted me as he stood. He carried me upstairs and kept his promise not to let me think the rest of the night.

Chapter 12

Jude

Lena was a whirlwind Thanksgiving morning. A veritable tornado of sunshine and glitter. It was almost enough to make us late for dinner; the craving to carry her back upstairs to her bedroom and ravish her was so strong. But not yet.

We needed to have the conversation about control, and with everything she had on her shoulders to prepare for this day, I didn't want to bother her or distress her. Or worse…

I cringed when I thought of the worst. I truly didn't believe it would happen now, but there was always the possibility. Tonight, after we'd spent time with friends and were both in the happy glow of companionship and excellent food, I planned to talk to her about it and then thoroughly sweep her off her feet.

She came down the stairs, fixing one of the shimmering, dangly earrings she was wearing. Her dress made my mouth water. Though, there wasn't anything she could wear that would make me want her less. The fifties-style dress was sneakily sexy and was driving me wild. It showed just enough to tease me, and all I could think about was lifting her *and* her skirt, bracing her against the wall and making her scream. Exactly like the morning after I'd pushed her away and she'd tried to distract me on purpose.

"I know I'm forgetting something. I swear I'm all over the place today."

I picked up the bag she'd put together last night. "You've got it all here. And if you do forget something, I'll come back for it."

The little drop in her shoulders in relief, the gratefulness in her eyes—those were the things I lived for. It was the part of dominance I enjoyed most outside the bedroom, the ability to lift the burden off someone's shoulders and ease their worry. The fact that it was Lena made it so much sweeter.

"Okay," she said. "Thank you. Pie time?"

"Pie time," I confirmed.

We were picking up everything she'd baked for dinner. All the desserts came from Deja Brew. Hell, a lot of the desserts in the town came from Lena. They all looked beautiful too. As we loaded them into boxes and I carried them in stacks to the truck, I was struck by the little details she'd put on some of them. Woven patterns or decorative leaves. Vents that swirled and made lovely designs, exposing the filling. "These are going to be the star of the show," I told her when she hopped up into the cab, her skirt showing more of her legs than she realized.

She went pink at the compliment.

I looked forward to turning her an even deeper shade of pink later tonight.

"I hope so."

The ride to the ranch was quick with everyone home for the holiday, and soon I was arranging the truck between all of ours. Even at family dinners, there were rarely so many cars and trucks outside the lodge.

This year, we had even more to be thankful for—that we had a lodge still standing for us to have Thanksgiving dinner. That the fire had only damaged the outside back porch.

We each grabbed a pie, but I caught her before we went up the stairs. "Are you ready?"

"You mean am I going to be able to survive all the jokes about to happen? I will. As long as you're with me."

I smiled. "You'll be lucky if I leave your side."

Together, we walked inside, and there was nothing but cheering. For a couple of seconds, it was a little like being a rock star. They were already going to tease us. Might as well go all the way. I scooped an arm around Lena's waist and, careful of the pie she held, pulled her to me for a kiss.

It was so fucking tempting to ruin the delicious berry-colored lipstick she'd chosen, but I kept it chaste. As chaste as was possible for me. Everything was still so new and so real, I couldn't stop myself from coaxing her lips open and trying to make her dizzy.

I heard more cheers as we kissed, and it didn't matter. All that existed was the two of us. It showed in her eyes when I pulled away, and she was looking at me like I held the moon.

I wanted to see that look in her eyes forever.

"Finally," Lucas called, and everyone laughed.

Lena looked at all of them, holding back her smile just enough. "Help us with the pies, please. If you want to eat them?"

The men, myself included, retreated to the truck to

grab the pies. Daniel clapped me on the shoulder. "I see you thought about it."

"I did."

"And?"

"And I owe you for forcing me out of my own fucking head."

He laughed. "No, you don't. Just be happy. All of us can see you are. And we're relieved."

"We better get back in there," I said. "Before the girls make her tell them *everything*."

Grant laughed. "If you don't think they'll do that, regardless, you don't know them very well."

"Oh, I know they will. I just hope it'll be when I'm out of earshot."

Sure enough, when I walked back in, the girls were all clustered around Lena, and the questions were flying a million miles a second. I put down the pies on the counter and reached through the throng. Her eyes found mine instantly. She wasn't overwhelmed; she was happy. But the way she looked to me right away brushed up against the part of me I loved. The trust she still gave me, even though I'd broken it. "Would you like something to drink?"

"Yes, please."

I went over to the bar—familiar territory since I'd spent most of my time over here, trying to keep myself away from Lena. I poured her a glass of white wine and didn't pour myself anything. I wanted to be clearheaded tonight, no matter what.

"I assume you plan on joining us again now, Jude?" Harlan called. "You don't have to stay over there."

"Something I appreciate," I said.

Harlan leaned against the counter, Grace tucked up under his arm. They looked so natural together, it was a wonder we ever thought they were enemies.

"How long before dinner?" Cori asked. "I have a patient I really need to go check on. I'll be back as soon as I can."

"On Thanksgiving?" Evie asked. "Someone called you today?"

Cori shrugged. "No, this is at the clinic. I'm sure they're fine, but I want to check."

"I'll drive you." Grant wrapped his arms around her from behind. "I'm faster."

I noted the way he held her, his hand on her wrists, subtly pulling her arms across her body so she couldn't move them. You would only notice if you were looking for it, but the way he had her restrained was enough to make color appear in her cheeks. I noticed her smile and the way she swallowed before speaking, and I wondered if checking on Cori's patient was the only thing they'd be doing.

"Okay," Evie said. "But we're eating in an hour. Don't be late."

"We won't!"

They escaped too quickly for me to be wrong.

I handed Lena her glass of wine and slipped an arm around her. It felt strange being able to show affection in public, but we'd more than earned it. This felt right, being next to her and not in the corner imagining the way she'd look spread out underneath me.

Of course, I was still imagining that, but having her next to me was intoxicating.

"Did we miss something?" Noah was pushing through the door, Kate in tow. "Why are they leaving?"

"Cori has to check on a patient," Grace said.

Kate laughed and clapped a hand over her mouth. "I'm sorry."

"Why?" Lucas raised an eyebrow.

Noah laced his fingers with Kate's. "Because Grant

had her up against the truck, and they don't seem very concerned about checking anything but each other's mouths."

"Seems about right," Liam laughed.

He was in the corner I usually occupied, a drink in his hand. "Taking my place, Liam?"

"Maybe." His voice was mild. "But I don't plan on staying there nearly as long as you did."

I choked on the sip I was taking. "Fair."

The front door opened once more, and Kate's brother came inside, followed by Mara. Liam's neck nearly broke with how quickly he looked at her, and in between her and the brother. A second later, he saw me looking and shook his head.

That was new. I'd ask him about it later.

"Looks like the gang's…mostly here," Daniel said.

Evie shrugged out of Lucas's arms and practically danced over to us. "The *ladies* are going to…" She thought for a second. "Make sure all the side dishes are ready. Jude, why don't you go rebuild the fire?"

"You know they're ready, Evie." Lena laughed into her wineglass. "Everything is ready—or will be once the turkey comes out."

"Play along," Evie murmured through closed lips.

I leaned down and kissed Lena on her hair. "I'll rebuild the fire."

She rolled her eyes, but she was smiling as she let Evie guide her to the other side of the room where the women were gathering.

I played my part, examining the fire. It could stand to be built up a bit, and the men drifted in my direction, not wanting to disturb the sacrament of girl time.

"Take the piss out of me now," I said. "Spare Lena. We all know I'm the one who let it go on for so long."

"Oh," Liam said. "We will. But don't think it will end now."

Daniel sat down heavily. "Someday, Liam, you're going to be in the same position. I hope you're ready to take everything you've dished out over the years."

The younger man grinned. "Bet your ass. Don't give what you can't take."

I took my time working on the fire so it would last all night, glancing over at Lena more than once. Even from here, the joy on her face was clear. She was luminescent.

"You've got it bad," Lucas said.

"Was there any doubt?"

He raised his glass in answer. No, there wasn't any doubt.

Noah sat down on the coffee table next to me, glancing back at the girls. Kate was on the edges of the group, but she was still there. "She okay?"

"She likes them." He held out his hands to warm them with the flames. "Still a little gun-shy. They can be overwhelming."

At that moment, Evie threw an arm around Kate's shoulder and yanked her into the group. Both of us laughed. "I think she'll be okay."

"I'd like to know how you're doing," he asked in a low voice. "If it's not too invasive."

Given the conversations we'd already had, invasive had long passed. "I'm happy. So fucking happy, it doesn't feel real."

"I'm glad," he said. "But that's not what I asked."

I tossed the last log onto the top of the pyramid I'd built. Noah was a little like Daniel in that way. He knew how to get to the heart of things. "I'm tired," I admitted. "I took her home the night of the raid, and it was…incredible. But I didn't sleep. I've barely slept since. Stolen naps here and there. I know I can't do it forever."

"No," he said. "You can't. She knows?"

"She does. But her *knowing* I might hurt her doesn't make the possibility easier."

Noah nodded. "Have you talked to her about the other thing?"

"Not yet. Planning to later tonight. The night of the raid, I didn't care. And since then..." I didn't want to get into the details of what we'd done together and my journey to learn what Lena liked and *loved* before I took her to bed properly again. It wasn't time wasted. Any amount of time listening to her moan and learning the taste of her skin was time fucking well spent.

"After this long, I thought you both would want to move faster." He looked surprised.

I smiled at that. "After I make sure we're both on the same page, I'll speed up. We're getting there."

"No matter what they say or how much they tease, we're all happy for you. I hope you know that."

"I do." I stood, stretching after so long crouched in front of the fire. "And I can take it. But Liam's going to take it in the teeth." My voice reached him—I made sure of it.

Kate wandered closer to us and hovered at the edges. She looked expectant, and Noah went to her. They fit together in a way that looked familiar to me. The subconscious ease of two bodies that had found their match. Something so instinctual, it couldn't be denied. Every couple in this room had that.

"Daniel." Kate addressed the man, and he turned. "I was wondering if they ever found her?"

I was opening my mouth to ask who, but Daniel didn't

need to. His face went dark. "No," he sighed. "It's like she vanished completely."

Noah looked troubled as well. "Well, we definitely got her out of the cages. Hopefully she's all right."

Oh. The woman who had been imprisoned alongside Kate. I hadn't realized she had disappeared.

"If she ever turns up, please let me know." Kate hugged Noah a little tighter. "I think about her a lot."

"Will do."

From across the room, there was a chime of a glass. "All right, everyone," Grace called. "Time to eat all this food."

Little name cards had been placed at the extended table, Lena's and mine next to each other. I caught her before she sat and pulled out her chair. A faint blush rose to her cheeks. It made me want to kiss the hell out of her all over again. But the kind of kiss I wanted to give her wasn't one for in front of people.

That would come later, when I took her home.

"Thank you," she murmured.

I grabbed her hand under the table. "You're all right?"

"Better than all right. I'm perfect."

"Good." I couldn't help myself. Leaning over, I kissed her cheek quickly. She smelled like sugar.

"Get a room," Liam said, and I glared at him before raising a single eyebrow and looking down at the other end of the table where Mara sat.

His eyes went wide, and I fought the laugh building in my chest. He would behave now. I wouldn't embarrass him, but right now, he didn't need to know that.

Grace set the turkey down on the table, and we descended into cheery madness.

Chapter 13

Lena

"I don't think I can eat another bite," I said, leaning my head on Jude's shoulder. "Pie is canceled."

A chorus of protests rose from around the table, and I laughed. "I'm kidding. Of course pie isn't canceled, though I'm seriously not sure if I'll be able to eat any."

"That won't be a problem for most of us, I think." Jude turned his head and kissed my hair. "You know, the things you send us in the week barely make it through three days."

I gasped, turning to him. "Why didn't you say something? I could send more."

Daniel laughed. "Don't worry, Lena. We need a few days without the sugar."

Rolling my eyes, I took a small sip of my wine. I'd been making this glass last. I wasn't sure what Jude had planned for later, but like hell was I getting so drunk I couldn't take part. "Like you guys have any problem burning a few calories between the ranch and the gym back there."

"True," Lucas said. "I think all of us will need it after this."

I stood, pushing back my chair and going to where the pies sat on the counter. I'd probably made too many, but then, the leftovers could stay here. I knew the guys would eat them, no matter what they said now.

"Ladies first," I called. "Who wants what?"

"I would kill for some apple." Evie got up to help me. "I've been dreaming about this pie. Plus, it's cute."

She'd helped decorate this one, cutting out shapes from the dough to create the tree and leaves, which wound around the cooling vents in the crust. "It's almost too pretty to cut."

"*Almost* being the key word there." She grinned.

With her help, we got everyone settled with pie. Evie was the last to sit before me, while I served myself a piece of the lemon. "Go ahead," I said. "You don't have to wait for me."

The clatter of silverware followed, and where there would normally be a chorus of sounds of enjoyment, there was nothing. I turned with my plate and froze. No one at the table was moving. Evelyn was entirely motionless with the fork still in her mouth.

I recognized the pose. I'd used it myself more than once when I was in the beginning of my career, overconfident, and had created something that was truly awful.

Dread poured down on me. "No."

Setting my plate on the counter, I cut a bite of the pie and ate it. Rancid, sour flavor exploded in my mouth, and I nearly gagged. It was as if I'd made the pie with all expired dairy products, on top of baking it, which made it all worse. It was rotten, and judging from everyone's faces, it was not the only one.

I turned, stepping to the trash can and spitting out the bite of pie, trying to keep myself calm. But panic was spinning up my spine, and it was only a matter of time. I couldn't be here. Not this second. I needed to breathe.

Not one person looked at me as I ran for the door, but I heard the scrape of chairs on wood behind me. "Lena." Jude's voice followed me, but I didn't stop.

How could this happen?

The door slammed behind me, and I went down the length of the porch and around the corner, where they wouldn't immediately see me. The door closed a second time. I didn't mind that he'd followed me, but I couldn't even speak. Couldn't respond when he called my name until he came around the corner.

"Lena, it's all right."

"It's not." I shook my head. "It's not all right."

Evie came skidding around the corner. "Lena, it *is* okay."

I gave her a look. "Of course it's not. The pies are ruined. Thanksgiving is ruined."

She rolled her eyes. "Okay, no. Thanksgiving can't be ruined by not having some pie."

"I don't understand. We tasted everything. *I* tasted everything. I should have made an extra pie to try after they baked, clearly. Has something happened to the oven? Maybe something I used was heat sensitive. Old flour..." I was grasping at straws. "I don't understand."

"You're right. They were fine when we made them, and I don't know what happened. But no one is mad at you for something that was clearly an accident."

"Yeah."

Rationally, I knew that was true. But it didn't make anything feel better.

"Come back in when you're ready," she said. "I'll take care of the pies, and we've got ice cream and loads of whipped cream to eat."

Evie glanced at Jude on her way back to the door with a forced smile. I needed to go back inside. Staying out here would only make it worse and make everyone think they needed to be careful around me. Or walk on eggshells. I didn't want that.

"Come here." Jude opened his arms, and I didn't remember making the conscious decision to walk into them. But I was wrapped up in them all the same, his hands rubbing comforting circles down my spine.

My mind was entirely blank, trying to figure out how this had happened. It was just...beyond me.

"You tasted it?" I'd served him a piece of the chocolate pie.

"I did."

"I'm sorry."

"Lena, this isn't you. Something happened. You know no one in there is going to blame you for this. Or even be upset. Mistakes happen. Accidents happen."

"They tasted fine, I swear..." My thoughts tumbled to a stop. We'd made most of the pies two days ago and left them overnight for the customers to come pick up yesterday. Some of ours, we made that day, and a couple of them we made last minute yesterday. That meant... "Was it all the pies?"

I looked up, and I saw confusion on his face. "What?"

"Was it *all* the pies?" I slipped out of his arms and ran back to the door. "Evie, was it all of them? Every one I brought?"

She wrinkled her nose but nodded. "Yeah. Looks like

there was a piece taken from each one, and they're all like that."

I went to my coat hanging by the door and grabbed my phone out of the pocket. If it was all of our pies, and they were made on two different days…

My phone screen was buried in notifications. I wasn't very careful about giving out my number. Not when I had to make so many deliveries. It was just easier. Now there were text messages and missed calls. Voice mails. I barely had to scan them to see they were all the same. Some anger, some horror, some wondering if I was okay or the victim of a practical joke.

I felt the blood drain from my face, and Jude caught me under the arms before my knees had a chance to buckle, guiding me on wobbly legs back to my chair at the table.

"Lena." He crouched in front of me. "What is it?"

Somewhere I found the strength to swallow and look him in the eye—I doubted I could do the same to anyone else right now. "It's not just our pies," I whispered. "It's all of them."

You could hear a pin drop in the room. Everyone was shocked by the declaration.

First the cookies, and now this? Obviously, there was no way to contain this. Everything was already out and wrecked. How many Thanksgivings had I ruined? It didn't matter if Jude and Evie were right. Sure, the idea of Thanksgiving wouldn't be ruined without pie or dessert, but people's expectations would be.

What they thought of me, too, would be changed.

If this kept happening, I needed to check my suppliers. Maybe shut down the bakery and tear the kitchen apart. The ventilation. Anything and everything something could touch or be put inside of that might have an impact on the outcome.

Jude still crouched in front of me, his big hands over my knees. There was nothing harsh in his gaze. Only sadness for me and comfort. I blinked back the emotion threatening to overwhelm me. "What am I going to do?"

"Here." Evie put a big bowl of ice cream down in front of me. A mixture of vanilla, chocolate, and doused in chocolate sauce and a maraschino cherry. "Eat that. No one was ever hurt by a bowl of ice cream. The rest of you, the ice cream bar is open. Get your asses up and make some sundaes."

It was a spell that unlocked everyone, and they moved. Soon, there was conversation and laughter as Liam and Noah shoved each other to get to the sprinkles, and Grant put some chocolate sauce on his finger, dabbed it on Cori's nose, and kissed it away.

But every time one of them looked in my direction, I made sure not to meet their eyes. If I did, I was afraid I would fall apart. This was everything I hadn't wanted. I was the one who made things better and not worse. And I'd ruined everything.

I could see the way it would all crumble. First, my reputation, which I was sure was already hanging by a thread. Then the business. I couldn't keep it open if they thought they were going to get a rancid baked good every time they purchased something from me. Or something that would crumble to bits before they even had a chance to eat it.

Then I would have to do something else. Move to a different state and become a nun. That might be a little dramatic, but I wasn't crossing it off the list of options yet.

"Do you want to go?" Jude asked.

I shook my head. The mood was already tenuous, and

I didn't want to make the cloud of failure worse by abandoning my friends. "No, not yet. I can't do that to them."

Jude's mouth tightened. We'd never gone back and talked about my nightmares, but I was sure this was on the list of things we would eventually get to. I just hoped it wouldn't be tonight. I wasn't sure I could handle it now.

"Will you share your ice cream?" he asked, allowing a small smile.

The bowl Evelyn had put in front of me had enough for about three people. "Yeah."

"Come on." He tugged me up out of the chair and grabbed the bowl, settling us together in front of the fire. I was mostly in his lap, and if nothing had happened, maybe I would have thought it was too much, too soon for everyone to see us tangled up like this. But right now, Jude's touch was the only thing keeping me from freaking out entirely.

My phone kept buzzing in my hand.

"Evie?" Jude called her over.

"Yeah?"

He took the phone from my hand, and I didn't fight him. I wasn't reading the messages anyway.

"Can you put this with Lena's things, please?"

She caught a look at the screen and the literal phone book of notifications. "Yeah."

We ate the ice cream together, sharing a spoon. The sugar helped, but then again, sugar always helped. That was the point of the fucking pies.

Everyone else was at the table, in their seats. Was this worse? Was I making everyone feel bad by sitting over here with Jude and depriving him of the Thanksgiving with his family?

Anxiety was hot under my skin. I couldn't seem to get it under control. Part of me wanted to run outside and scream until my voice was raw. Another part wanted to hide under a blanket until the entire world disappeared. Being caught in between those two opposites made me itch.

"I'm probably being silly, overreacting," I said. "Making everyone feel bad."

Jude glanced over his shoulder, where Liam finished telling a joke and everyone collapsed into laughter. "I don't know." He shrugged. "They seem okay to me."

"Yeah."

He pressed his lips against my temple. I leaned into the kiss—I needed it more than I realized. "Sweetheart, you're not overreacting. It's okay to be hurt by something that hurts you."

This was going downhill, and fast. Crying wasn't high on my list of things to do today—or any day. But if he kept saying things like that…

I took a bite of ice cream and tried to breathe. "I just wanted everyone to have a nice day. And I don't want them to feel bad or pity me."

He was looking at me, and I could almost feel his thoughts churning, but I didn't look up. "What do you say we go back to your house?" he asked.

"But—"

"No one is going to mind. I promise."

My cheeks burned. All I could think about was how they were going to talk about me after I left. Poor Lena. She really fucked up. It'll be a Thanksgiving to remember.

Those thoughts weren't fair to my friends. I knew it, and yet I couldn't seem to stop them from happening. "Okay."

"Stay here for a second."

He picked up the bowl of half-finished ice cream and took it to the kitchen. I heard him say something, and I looked over long enough to see him speaking to Daniel. It was too much. They were all being careful not to look at me, and I couldn't bear it.

I stood and made a beeline for my coat. "Happy Thanksgiving, everyone. I'll see you later, okay?" It was a miracle I got it all out without my voice cracking.

"Happy Thanksgiving," came a chorus of all the voices, but Evie wasn't about to let it stand. She jumped up and nearly tackled me in a hug.

"It's going to be okay. Promise."

"You don't know that."

"No." She pulled back and grinned. "But you and I and everyone in this room have survived worse things than bad pie. And I need you to hear me when I say this, Lena. No one thinks less of you."

I didn't believe her, but it was a nice thing to say.

"I'll see you tomorrow at work."

Nodding, I shrugged on my coat and let Jude pull open the door for me. He bundled me down the stairs and into his truck. At the very least, I was out of sight of everyone else. As it was, I would be lucky to make it home before I fell apart entirely.

Chapter 14

Jude

I wasn't sure what to say.

Lena was completely inside her own head, and I knew the feeling. She was worrying and spiraling and flaying herself to bits about what went wrong with the pies.

But I knew it wasn't just the baked goods. It was deeper. A few things she'd said let me know she was struggling with more than just her experience with Evelyn and the abduction. It sounded like she held herself responsible for others' happiness—at least in our direct circle. And those thoughts led to her struggling to accept that she was *allowed* to struggle.

Her first thoughts about the pie weren't for herself and her business; they were for us and if she'd "ruined" the holiday. Sure, the business was on her mind too. But now, I saw. What people thought of her—especially those of us who knew her—mattered even more than Deja Brew.

The dominant need to show her she was wrong and

that we loved her rose up. It wasn't an ideal time to have the conversation, but I wasn't left with much choice. She needed what I could give right now just as much as I needed to give it.

She sat on the other side of the cab, not even close to the way we'd been driving lately, all cuddled up together. Hell, I missed her, and she was feet away. We needed to talk, and I desperately wanted to get her out of her own thoughts.

Her phone was in her hand, and she was scrolling through the mountain of notifications from angry customers, wondering what had happened. I got a glimpse of some of them. They weren't pretty. People could be cruel in the heat of the moment.

"Why don't you leave that for now?" I asked gently.

"What good will it do? Not like the messages are going to go away."

"No. But I've always found messages like those are more easily dealt with after a good night's sleep."

She let out a shaky sigh but put the phone back into the pocket of her coat. Her house was a welcome sight. Here, I knew she felt the most safe, and I hoped she would let down her guard with me. I didn't like to see her so shaken.

To someone else, they might look at her and say she was overreacting, like she'd said. But I looked at her and saw a woman who'd watched her identity crack in two and wonder what she'd done to make it happen. It didn't matter if it was an accident; the edict was the same.

I followed her into the house and watched her hang up her coat, absently putting water on for tea like it was second nature. "Thank you for driving me home."

"That's it?"

She forced a smile. "You don't have to be here for this. It's okay. I'll be fine."

Letting out a breath, I took off my coat. "Lena."

"I don't—" Her voice cracked. "I don't want you to see me like this."

"Like what? As human? As someone who's hurting?"

She shook her head.

I walked over to her and reached past her to turn off the kettle. This was going to take longer than it took to boil water, and I wasn't going to be interrupted by a whistle. "You and I are new together, but we've still known each other for a long time. If you think me seeing you like this will change how I look at you, or make me not want to be with you, you're wrong."

"Jude."

"You're *wrong*," I said firmly, pulling her into my arms. Her entire body was shaking like a leaf, and it was only seconds before she burst.

The tears were silent at first because she was still trying to hide. But when I picked her up, she let go. I hated that she was crying, and I hated that she was in pain. But I loved how I could envelop her and make sure she knew I wasn't going anywhere and I would do what I could to shield her while she took the time she needed.

"I feel so stupid."

"Why?"

I sat with her on the couch, and she looked at me, trying to steady herself and failing. She swiped angrily at the tears. "Because I care so much. I know I shouldn't put so much stock in what people think of me, but I do. I'm the person who makes people feel *better*. They come to Deja Brew and they get a kick of happiness, and it makes their day.

"Now what? Now I'm the woman who ruined everyone's Thanksgiving and baked bad cookies for innocent senior citizens. Everyone knows I'm good at this. And if I'm not, then I have no idea what to do, Jude. I don't even know who I am if I'm not this."

I pulled her close so she was lying across my chest, and I ran my fingers through her hair. She had her face pressed into my shirt, but she was already breathing easier. All of that needed to come out, and badly.

"We're going to figure it out."

"How?" She sounded miserable.

"Starting tomorrow, we close the bakery. I'll help you tear it apart and look through everything. We'll call whoever we need to call to get your machines checked and all of your ingredients. And when everything's okay again, you'll reopen. I guarantee Evie will help, and I'll be the guinea pig for anything you make.

"I'd help with the baking itself, but I don't think you want to see me bake."

At least the thought drew out a smile. "You'd look handsome covered in flour."

"Noted."

Lena's eyes were closed. "You really think it's going to be okay?"

"I do."

"Okay." It didn't sound like she believed me, but she didn't have to. I would believe for both of us, and eventually, she would believe it too.

"I had a plan for tonight," I said mildly. "But I'm not sure it's a good idea now."

"What kind of plan?"

"Well…" I shifted her so she was more upright, straddling my lap, the skirt of her dress poofing over both of us. "I'd planned to sweep you off your feet after our first public experience as a couple. But if you're not up for it now, that's all right."

"No." She moved, reaching up and curling her arms around my neck. "I'm up for that. I'm very up for that."

Her lips met mine, and I pulled her back gently. "There's a little more."

"Oh?" She looked more mischievous than sad, and I would take it. I just hoped the rest of the conversation would go as well.

"I'd already planned on talking about this with you before everything happened. I know it's not ideal now, but I can't put it off anymore."

Lena's face fell. "Please don't tell me this is bad news."

I kissed her lightly. "I don't think so."

"Okay… Still sounds a little ominous."

"Not ominous. Just a part of myself I don't want to hide from you."

There was still tension in her body—I felt it under my hands, and I tried to soothe it, running my palms up her ribs. I found it was harder than it should be to speak it out loud. The old fear that she'd look at me with disgust and run popped up, but I knew better. At the very least, she'd listen.

"In the bedroom, I like to be in control."

Lena searched my face and waited. "Is that it?"

I laughed once. "It's the main part of it, yes. But I want to explain it."

"I'm listening." Nothing about her seemed angry or disgusted. Yet.

"Even before I went into those caves, I felt the need to dominate. Taking control in that way—it might sound strange, but it gives me more satisfaction than I can describe. And now, after everything, I *always* crave control. But especially in the bedroom.

"Unexpected touches can send me into flashbacks. It makes it easier when I control who touches me and when. It's why my house is out in the middle of nowhere. I control who's there and in what capacity."

"I touch you all the time." She frowned. "Have I ever…caused that to happen?"

I winced. "Once. When you kissed me in the kitchen."

Her lips fell open in shock, and all I could think about was how adorable the expression was. "I'm so sorry."

"How could you have known, when I didn't tell you? And I'm the one who could have handled it better. But this…my need for control is another one of the reasons I stayed away from you for so long. I didn't think you'd want any part of it."

She bit her lip and dropped her eyes, and down low, hope sprang to life inside me. "Maybe I shouldn't say anything, but a while ago, Cori said some things that made me…curious. And there've been a couple times when *you* made me curious. Like when you pushed me up against the door when you dropped me off." She blushed furiously. "You really thought this would make me not want you?"

"It's happened before."

Anger flared in her eyes. "When?"

I smiled at her reaction. Not because it was funny, but because her immediate instinct to protect me was endearing. "A long time ago. Before I met you." I brushed her hair back. "It's only been you since we met."

"Good."

"So, what do you say?"

Her smile was shy, and instead of looking at me, she examined my fingers as she toyed with the fabric of my shirt. "I'm intrigued. I want to see what it's like. And after everything that's happened today, I don't want to control anything. I just want you to love me. So, let's do it and see how it goes."

I blew out a breath in relief.

"This is what you've been holding back?"

"What?"

"The first time we had sex, I could feel it. You weren't giving me everything, and I wanted to say you didn't have to treat me as breakable. But I figured it was just the first time. Now I really know."

"Thank you," I said, pulling her more tightly against me. The way she was perched on my lap was only making the hardness in my pants more uncomfortable, but I savored it, simply because it was *Lena*. "For not looking at me like I'm crazy."

"Are you kidding? After some of the things Cori's—" She froze, and I laughed.

"Grant and I are on the same page. Different execution, maybe. But I know."

"Okay, phew." She curled her fingers into my shirt and suddenly became shy again. "How would it work?"

A good question. "It's both easier and harder than it sounds. You don't have to make any decisions. But you also don't *get* to make any decisions."

"That sounds nice right now."

"I'll show you." Moving one hand, I slid it up into her hair and tightened my grip. Not enough to be painful, but enough to be in control. I sat up straighter, pressing her hips into mine. Her breath shook, but she wasn't afraid. I'd seen her afraid. "For the next few minutes, you don't have permission to speak, and you don't have permission to move. Keep your hands on my shoulders."

Lena opened her mouth, realized what I'd said, and closed it again. We were close enough for me to watch her pupils dilate with arousal. So maybe this wasn't as foreign as I'd thought.

I brushed my mouth over her jaw. "See?" She shuddered when my kiss reached her ear in slow motion. "Two very simple commands, and yet you're dying to move now that I've told you not to."

A sharp intake of breath. I smiled into her skin, reveling in being right.

With my free hand, I tugged the strap of her dress off her shoulder. There was something about seeing a strap fall off a shoulder that brought every instinct I had roaring to life. So simple, and yet the image it created—arched neck, eyes closed, and the bared skin there like an offering.

"This is what it's about." I continued my trail, kissing along her collarbone until I reached her shoulder. "An exchange. You surrender your power, and I borrow it. In return, you don't have to think about anything, and I take care of you."

"Whoever the bitch was who told you this was wrong, she missed out." Lena gasped, realizing she wasn't supposed to talk.

I grinned as I pulled back to look at her. "Harder than it sounds sometimes, isn't it?"

Lena nodded. "What happens if I mess up?"

"It depends. Some people like to give punishments. I only like to do that if both people enjoy it."

She took a deep breath, and I was distracted by the way her fallen strap revealed more of her as she breathed. I was going to have fun with her tonight.

"Cori mentioned rope. Is that something you use?"

"I can, but it's not really my thing." I knew enough about rope bondage to tie someone safely, but that was the extent of my knowledge. "I prefer using my hands to restrain you. Or handcuffs. But I don't have those with me."

She burst out with a laugh. "Is it weird that I'm both excited and nervous at the same time? Because I am. Every time you've done something like this, I've just…liked it. But it's all new, and I—" She cut herself off. "I know it was already your plan, but thank you for distracting me with it."

"My pleasure." I smirked. "And hopefully your pleasure, too."

The comment turned her pink enough that I was about to lose control.

"We're going to figure everything out, and it's all going to be fine. But I don't want you to think about the pies, the cookies, or Deja Brew anymore. Put it out of your mind as best you can, and I'll take care of the rest. Tonight, if it's too much, tell me to stop. But otherwise, you do what I say. If we need to figure out some other boundaries once you try, we'll do it."

"Okay."

"One last thing." I dropped both of my hands to her hips. "I need to hear you say yes. And I need you to know when you say it, unless you change your mind about that yes, it's the last decision you'll be making for the rest of the night."

She let out one long, slow breath as she looked into my eyes. No fear there, no disgust. Only anticipation. "Yes, Jude."

I stood, lifting her with me. My need to get her upstairs had already been teetering on the edge. Now I had a yes? There was no more time to lose.

Chapter 15

Lena

Butterflies were whirling in my stomach as Jude carried me up the stairs like every main character in every romance I'd ever read. I hadn't lied to him. I *was* curious, and I *was* nervous. But excitement tingled under my skin too. Above anything else, the idea of letting go and not having to think or make decisions—especially today, of all days—was incredibly appealing.

We reached my bedroom, and he set me gently on my feet. I wasn't sure what happened now. He told me it was the last decision I was going to make—how deep did that go? I guessed I was about to find out.

He sat on the end of my bed, and all I could do was look at him. Dress shirt rolled up to his elbows. Darker jeans that looked dressy for the occasion we had today. And the look in his eyes that pinned me to the spot. The look had *weight*, and I startled, realizing this was the real Jude.

Every inch of him exuded power, and he was comfortable owning it.

It was unbearably sexy. How could anyone look at him like this and tell him they didn't want it? I wasn't sure I was going to like all of this, but I was willing to try because it was him.

And there was a smaller, whispering part of me that was laughing, already suspecting I was going to fucking love it and I was just being stubborn.

"Take off your dress."

My stomach dropped in a way that made my whole world swoop. Like the ground under my feet just dropped a foot. No room for argument, careless power behind the words. He would be obeyed because he expected it, and there was something so *hot* about that.

I slipped the other strap of my dress off my shoulder and shimmied it down so it dropped to the floor in a pile of fabric.

"The rest too."

It wasn't like he hadn't seen me entirely naked at this point, but I still blushed. The intensity of his gaze would have made me self-conscious if it weren't for the fact that he looked like a man starving and I was about to be his next meal.

My bra joined the dress on the floor and then my underwear. Already, I saw what he meant about it being both easy and hard. The things he ordered weren't hard to do. But standing there waiting for him to choose the next thing was far from easy.

He smiled. "Come here."

I moved to stand in front of him, and he pulled me between his knees. "You are so fucking beautiful. You know that?"

Jude kissed the place where my neck met my shoulder,

and I melted. I loved that spot. He seemed to find it without even trying, and every time, it turned me into a mess. "Am I allowed to talk?"

He laughed low. "Until I tell you not to."

"Then I could stand to hear it a little more."

"Noted." Another chuckle.

I swallowed. "What now?"

"Now…" He moved his mouth again, sliding down my chest until he could reach my breasts. He covered my nipple with his mouth, swirling his tongue and making me gasp. "I'm going to enjoy you."

The words barely interrupted him, and by the time he switched to my other breast, I was wet. I reached for him, wanting to sink my hands into his hair, and he caught my wrists. "No."

"But—" Surely that wasn't a bad thing? I blinked.

Jude took my hands and wrapped them behind my back before encasing them in one of his big ones. The way he had my wrists, I couldn't move them. I tried.

Heat curled under my skin, sinking lower down to my core. And again, I had the sensation of dropping.

"I didn't say you could do anything but stand here. I'm not finished."

"I just like your hair," I said by way of explanation.

He smirked. "I'll let you play with it again. But not tonight. Tonight, I want you to feel all of it. Without any lenience, so you understand. When I say control, this is what it means." The hand holding my wrists squeezed them for emphasis.

I swallowed. "Okay."

Holy hell, it was more than okay. I was on fire. My skin felt like it was burning, and arousal was building in my core as if every word he said was throwing more kindling on the blaze.

Jude went back to lazily exploring my body. His free hand and his mouth drawing patterns and teasing me until I was barely able to keep still. He was doing this because it was what he wanted, not what I wanted. Jude wasn't a selfish lover—he wasn't going to take without giving. But knowing he was only pleasing himself sent another wave of heat rushing through me, along with embarrassment.

Should I find that hot? Wasn't it wrong? My mind faltered, and I tried to banish the thought, but it wouldn't go.

"What was that?"

I shook my head. "I didn't say anything."

"No, but your whole body language changed. I did something, or you thought something. What was it?"

"I—" Hesitation blocked the words. I didn't want him to think I didn't want this when I did. I *really* did.

My hands, still caught in his, made it easy for him to yank me against his body. "The only way this truly works is to be honest, Lena. I don't want you to hide anything from me. Whatever it is, we'll handle it."

"The way you were touching me." I swallowed. "I knew it was only to please yourself, and I liked it. And I was embarrassed that I did."

"Why?"

"Because I don't know if it's okay to enjoy it when it isn't about me. Like…" I struggled to find the words, and he released my hands, pulling them forward and massaging my wrists. "What does it say that I find you using my body…I don't know how to say it right."

"Is it okay to enjoy the fact that someone else is enjoying your body, even though the pleasure isn't centered on you?"

Discomfort swam in my gut. "Yeah. I'm not sure what tripped me up."

"First—" he smiled, though it was the kind of smile that made my toes curl "—I want you to know there will be pleasure. I've been thinking about being able to control your pleasure for a long time, and I want you screaming my name before the end."

The wicked heat of arousal was back, fueled by his words and his hands, which now circled each of my wrists like handcuffs, locking me to him.

"And second, this isn't an easy thing. Giving up control is hard and brave. But no, there's nothing wrong with it. It can be difficult to let go, but think of it this way. You're allowing yourself to be an object of pleasure for me. And it wouldn't be the same if it wasn't you."

Using my captured hands, he pulled me so we were flush against each other and kissed me. This kiss was Jude unleashed. He held absolutely nothing back. All the control he craved and all the dominance that came as naturally as breathing.

It stole all the breath I had in my body, and I didn't care. He moved swiftly, lifting me and laying me out on the bed like I was his own personal feast. Just as fast, Jude had my hands over my head, pinned to the mattress. His lips brushed the shell of my ear. "No more questions. No more worries. No more talking. If you need to stop, tell me. Otherwise, the only sounds I want to hear from you are sounds of pleasure."

All the heat returned. I resisted the urge to respond to him after he'd just revoked my speaking privileges. It wasn't easy. Questions bubbled at my lips, but I held them back.

Jude straddled my hips, leaning into the way he held my hands. "Later, you can ask all the questions you want. I swear it."

I nodded, and he smiled. The approval in the smile

warmed me like stepping into the sun. I wanted to bask in it like a cat.

"Hmm." He let his gaze trace my body and the way it was spread underneath him. "What am I going to do with you?"

The words were light, but they hit hard. They had me squirming unintentionally, trying to get closer. My reactions to this shocked me. I always thought I wanted more control. When I read about the heroines of romance novels turning into puddles for the men who did exactly this, I thought it wasn't me.

Oh, it was me.

It was *very* much me.

I hadn't been with too many men, but it hit me now that I'd never been with anyone I trusted like Jude. He saved my life. He would stop if I asked him. So, the thought of voluntarily placing myself at his mercy was freeing in a way it never could have been with anyone else.

The realization unlocked my brain, and I relaxed. Everything was warm and soft and I wanted Jude to move, and I also never wanted anything but the way he was pinning me down—anchoring me.

"There you go."

I asked the question with my eyes instead of my words.

"It takes a little time to realize you trust me."

The words "I do trust you" were on the tip of my tongue, and I held them back. Again, that smile made me want to arch and stretch into sunshine.

Jude leaned close. "I saw you pull that back. Good girl."

My whole body froze, and my heart started to pound. Need spiraled down my spine, and my head was light. What the fuck?

I wasn't a girl. I was a grown-ass woman. And yet, I

was going to need to ask Jude to record himself saying those two words so I could listen to it over again.

His low chuckle made everything tighten. I was a mess of wetness between my thighs, and I decided in that moment to let everything go. Throw caution to the wind and let this happen.

"I'll remember you like that. Right now, I need you to keep being good, and when I release your hands, you're not going to move them. No matter what I do. Understood?"

I nodded once.

"Good girl."

Holy shit, I was going to pass out if he kept saying those words.

He lifted himself off me, releasing my wrists, and I kept them there. I wished my bed frame had bars so I could hold on to something. In the middle of whatever he had planned, I didn't know if I could focus enough to keep myself still.

I watched as he stripped off his shirt with quick efficiency, eyes never leaving mine, before he approached the end of the bed again. "Open your legs."

I did, closing my eyes and letting the new feelings of submission wash over me.

"Wider."

Oh. My. God. I slid my legs farther apart and tried not to move anything else. Jude stroked his hands up my thighs, easing my legs the few extra inches apart they would go. I was entirely exposed to him, and I knew without having to look it was exactly what he wanted.

"I can't get enough of you," he said quietly, and then his mouth was on me.

I already knew his tongue was magic. Now, it was heaven. Tiny, barely there strokes which made me focus so intensely to predict where he was going next. Every touch was a jolt of lightning unfurling into a new bolt of surprise and pleasure.

Bolder touches now, Jude using his tongue to circle my clit and find the place he already knew drove me crazy. But his movements were still lazy and easy. He wasn't pushing me to the edge.

Yet.

Again, I had the sense he was taking his time for his own pleasure. Tasting me at his own pace like I was his dessert. After all, he'd planned this already. No matter the pie, he'd always planned to have me. I was his pie.

He pressed a hand low on my stomach and sealed his mouth over me, pulling hard. My hips tried to arch off the bed, and he held them down. Without the ability to move, I felt the pleasure shake me. It had nowhere to go except twisting back on itself and rushing up and out and sweeping me closer to the edge.

There. The moans coming from me were entirely involuntary. The one spot and rhythm that made me ache and sigh. I bunched my hands into fists, arms shaking with the need to reach for him.

Pleasure rose, and I leaned into it. So close, so close, *so close.*

Jude pulled his mouth away. "You don't have permission to come."

"What?"

I didn't remember I wasn't supposed to speak. The quirk of an eyebrow was all I needed as a reminder, along with his smirk, which told me he knew exactly what he was doing.

"Trust me, Lena." He sealed his mouth over me again, driving me higher.

Somehow, my arms were still above my head. A miracle. But I was focusing on anything but my orgasm that was coming toward me like a freight train, and I had no idea how I was supposed to stop it.

I was so close; I was moaning and writhing when he backed off, letting me catch my breath. But not for long. He used his tongue like I was an ice cream cone and I was his favorite flavor.

All the way up to the edge again, before he backed off. I couldn't keep silent. I couldn't. "*Please,* Jude."

He swatted the inside of my thigh lightly. "Just for that, you get one more before I let you come."

An inferno of arousal scorched my veins. I was light-headed and falling through space back into the mattress, and yet I wasn't moving at all. It didn't take long for him to have me back at the edge, biting my lip and barely holding myself on this side of ecstasy.

Jude lifted his mouth and looked at me, locking eyes while he licked his lips, and I groaned. The denial of another orgasm almost hurt.

Almost.

He stroked his hands up and down my thighs as I caught my breath, letting the pleasure fade into absolutely nothing. But I was like tinder—one strike of a match and I would go up in flames.

Finally, Jude brushed a kiss low on my stomach. "This time, you have permission."

He didn't hold back.

I was barely aware of his mouth and the steady stroking of his tongue, of the way he sealed his mouth over me to suck me deeper. It was secondary to the pleasure crashing into me like a tidal wave, crushing me underneath it.

Everything ignited, and I was lost in a flash of light and a flare of bliss that was sharp as a knife and soft as velvet.

A contradiction all wrapped up into one, lifting my hips off the bed into his mouth and leaving me with even less control than Jude.

And then there was the other piece of it. I'd held on even when it felt impossible and did what he asked, only to be rewarded with one of the best orgasms I'd ever had in my life...

Okay, yeah, I understood why all the heroines loved this. Changed woman and all that. My mind felt numb in the aftermath, the rest of me melting into a puddle. Jude's mouth was still between my legs, tongue sending flickers and aftershocks through my body.

He moved, straddling my hips once more and towering over me. The scratch of his jeans on my bare legs emphasized the difference in power, just a little reminder of this game we were playing. Jude pinned my hands to the bed again, and the way he leaned, I gasped.

Jude was entirely hard through his jeans, pressing against me where I hadn't bothered to close my legs. After all the pleasure he'd dragged out of me, I was so sensitive, the rough fabric of his jeans was enough to make me want more.

Smirking, he flexed his hips. The man knew exactly what he was doing to me, and he loved every second of it.

"You did so good," he said. "And I want you to talk to me for a second."

"I messed up when I talked before. I'm sorry."

He flexed his hips again, driving another gasp from me before he lowered his mouth all the way to my skin. "This isn't about perfection always. We're human, and I was teasing you on purpose. You were incredible, especially being new to this."

It was impossible to explain the sunshine feeling that came with his praise and approval. My heart was fluttery, and I felt like I was being pulled away from what I knew and realigned with something entirely different. "Can I move my hands? I really need to touch you."

The small, pleased smile brought crinkles to the corners of his eyes and made my stomach do backflips. "Yes, you may."

I reached for him, and he met me halfway, running his hands over my shoulders and massaging them. They ached a little from the tension of holding them above my head while he wrung pleasure from me like a sponge. But the way he dug his fingers in and made them loosen felt amazing and let me know he absolutely knew what he was doing.

My own hands, I spread over his shoulders and wrapped behind his neck. How long would it take before this would feel normal? Not just him being dominant, but him being here at all. It still didn't feel real.

"What are you thinking?" he asked.

The words didn't come at first, and I opened my mouth and closed it, causing him to smile. "I think..." I swallowed. "I think I like this a lot more than I thought I would."

Jude froze for a second, and then he was kissing me. Hard. His whole body pushed me into the bed, and the way we were intimately connected caused me to moan into his mouth. "Really?" The whisper brushed against my lips.

I shivered. "Yes. I don't know what it means or how far it goes or anything like that. But *fuck*, Jude."

He chuckled. "I'll take it. And I'm sorry."

"Why?"

"Because if I hadn't had my head up my ass about whether you would like this, and hadn't chosen to make the decision for you, this could have come a hell of a lot sooner."

My stomach flipped again. "I see where you're coming from, and I accept your apology. But also, some things happen the way they're meant to. Both of us wishing we'd done this sooner is only going to take away from the now."

"Excellent point," he conceded. "And I think that's enough talking for now."

My eyes went wide, and my mouth dropped open. He grinned and raised an eyebrow. "You didn't think I was finished, did you?"

I closed my eyes, a shudder of need racking my body. Was this something I always would have liked? Or was it him? Did it really matter?

"And I promise," he said softly. "I won't take away your voice every time. But it's a very fast and effective way to emphasize surrendering."

Surrendering.

God, that's what it felt like. Yielding. Falling into someone's arms, knowing without a doubt they would catch you.

"Up on your knees," Jude said. "Put your hands on the headboard, and then you don't have permission to move. But," he added, "you have permission to come as much as you like."

Oh fuck. He lifted himself off me, allowing me to move, and I heard the sounds of his buckle as I did and then the sound of a condom wrapper. My knuckles turned white, holding on to my headboard.

Now that he'd told me not to move, all I wanted to do was turn and watch him. See the way he stroked the condom onto his cock and look at all the gorgeous lines of his body. But I didn't. I held on harder, willing myself to stay still like it was the only thing keeping me alive.

I felt the warmth of him behind me before he even

touched me. One hand slipping around my waist and down between my legs, the rest of him pressed against me. Would it feel like this every time? Because if it did, then I would never get enough. It felt like I was high, in a good way, and I could easily become addicted to him and the feeling of his control.

"You didn't look back even once," Jude murmured, teasing me with his fingers. "You know what that makes you?"

Everything in me waited with breathless anticipation.

"A very good girl."

The sound that came out of me was strangled and needy, and I was no longer questioning my reactions. Everything now was about enjoyment, and I would figure out the rest later.

"Don't move," Jude reminded me. "If I move you, you stay where I put you." He used one knee to push mine wider, fitting himself against me and thrusting in with one smooth, even stroke.

I almost broke the rules to speak—I definitely broke the rules for moving. This was only the second time he'd been inside me, and it was just as overwhelming as the first. Now I was warm and aroused; everything was glitter and shine. The barest movement, and I saw stars.

My forehead was now resting on the headboard between my hands, and I hadn't even realized.

Jude made a sound of disapproval. "What did I tell you?"

He pulled me back up and against his chest. One hand still teased me between my legs, almost idly, while I got used to his size all over again, and the other circled my throat. There was no pressure behind it; the feeling of it was more than enough. "Don't move, Lena."

Jude moved then, and I was grateful I had permission

to come, because there was nothing in the world that could have held me back.

Holding me exactly where he wanted me, my hands gripping the headboard, Jude took me. Every stroke was brutal and beautiful, and I drifted into an entirely new space that was only him. His pleasure, his command, his hands on me.

An orgasm washed over me in a wave of golden stars. There wasn't any need to tell me not to speak or not to move—I couldn't do either. I was entirely at his mercy, and it felt like I was blossoming under that same mercy and care.

I never imagined it would be like this. How could the contradiction possibly be true? Letting someone take control made me feel safer and more cared for than I could remember in my life, and the freedom it brought allowed me to accept a whole new level of pleasure.

Everything faded into a haze of breath and moans, of Jude's whispers in my ear, and the delicious friction of every driving thrust.

He drove me over the edge twice more, my body now so attuned to his guidance he played it like an instrument. When he came, his hands landed on top of mine, holding us together, connected and shaking as we both caught our breath.

"Here." He lifted my hands off the headboard, massaging them just as he had my shoulders, completely ignoring the fact that he was still buried to the hilt inside me.

I didn't think I could have moved if he hadn't moved me, gently separating our bodies and laying me out on the bed before taking care of the condom and even cleaning me with a warm washcloth I hadn't told him where to find.

A blanket slid up my body, and he joined me beneath

it, pulling me against him. My brain felt deliciously scrambled. Like I was a little drunk and at the same time floating on a cloud. "Is this normal?"

"Is what normal?"

"Feeling like this?" I gestured vaguely. How the hell did I describe this? "I think you made me high."

Jude chuckled softly. "Yes, it's normal. You've got endorphins flooding your brain. But it will pass."

"I'm sleepy."

His lips warmed my forehead. "I've got you, sweetheart. Sleep."

"But I have questions." My words were a little fuzzy and I did have questions, but I couldn't seem to remember them.

"You can ask them in the morning."

I snuggled closer, enjoying the sensation of his arms wrapped around me. "Okay."

Jude stroking his hands down my spine was the last thing I felt.

Chapter 16

Lena

I woke with a start, my brain wondering why it was so light without my alarm going off. "Fuck." Rolling, I went to leap out of bed, convinced I was late, only to find a large arm around my waist hauling me backward.

"Good morning," Jude said, kissing just below my ear.

"Morning. I have to go. I don't even know what time it is, but I'm late."

He didn't let me go. "Lena, look at me."

I did, finding the steadiness in his stare. It shouldn't have calmed me down the way it did, but I found my heart easing and my breathing evening out.

"I turned off your alarm. You're not late. You're not opening Deja Brew today, remember?"

All of yesterday crashed down into my memory all at once. Jude had managed to fuck all of it right out of my head. "Oh."

That's right. We were going to pull the place apart

today and see if we could find the problem, though that was the most unappealing thing I'd ever heard of at the moment.

"So you can take your time." He tugged, turning me back toward him so we lay face-to-face. "Morning."

"Morning," I mumbled. Sleep still fogged my brain, and the morning-after shock of what we'd done together on top of all the bakery stuff made me want to put the pillow over my head and sleep until noon.

He ran his hand down my arm. "How are you feeling?"

"About Deja Brew? Or about…you know." I didn't know how to put voice to it.

"About me taking control last night, and you letting go."

I let everything play over in my head, and every single moment was just as hot as it had been at the time. My face flushed, and that alone was enough to tell him what I thought. "I liked it. A lot. And I honestly wasn't sure I would. I know I told you already."

"I don't mind hearing it again."

Biting my lip, I tried to conjure the questions that had seemed so urgent last night. "I'm just not sure where we go from here? Like…" I shook my head. "You just start ordering me around?"

Jude laughed, slipping a hand behind my neck so he could pull me close enough to kiss my forehead. "No. Of course not."

"Okay." My stomach did a little flip-flop of nerves and excitement. "So, paint me a picture? What does this look like for you?"

"Hmm." He brushed a teal strand of hair back off my forehead. "Well, first, I want to talk about what it's not."

I nodded once.

"It's not both of us turning into robots, me giving orders and you taking them. It's also not a set thing that has to stay the same forever. We're both human, and we need different things at different times. That's why talking about it is always the best policy—if there's ever a problem, or even if there's not."

"Makes sense."

"But," he said, shifting us both so his body was over mine, weight pressing me into the mattress, "I'll tell you what it looks like for me."

"Is this coercion?" I smirked up at him, thoroughly enjoying the feel of his naked and hardening body on mine. "Because if it is, it's working."

Jude smiled. "Maybe."

I laughed, relaxing into his hold. "Tell me."

"I have no interest in controlling your entire life, Lena." His voice was serious. "You were doing perfectly well before me, and if I weren't here, you'd still be doing amazing."

"I'm not so sure about that," I admitted. But it wasn't the conversation we were having right now. I saw him bookmark the comment for later, along with my nightmares.

"Furthermore," he said, "if there's ever a time in your life, permanent or not, when you *want* me to take control, I'm happy to. I will gladly take what you give. But the only place I won't compromise on is here."

I fought to keep my face serious. "My house? How presumptuous."

Jude kissed my neck, and any jokes disappeared. If he was going to do that…

"In bed." The words slipped across my skin. "Anything sexual, for that matter, regardless of where we are. You're *mine*."

The word made me shudder, shades of last night echoing through my mind. The image played out in my head. Me, doing everything I normally did at the bakery and day-to-day, even coming back and doing the same things at home. Dinner with Jude. Reading and tea. And then as soon as we crossed the threshold, he was in charge and I wasn't, and…

There was something so relieving about it. As a single person before Jude, and as a business owner, my entire life was making decisions. Things as small as what to make for dinner or as large as whether to purchase a new piece of equipment for the kitchen, and it was exhausting. Having one place where I didn't have to make *any* decisions sounded like heaven. Especially if it was going to end in the kind of explosive, see-fireworks-behind-my-eyes, holy-fuck orgasms I'd had last night.

I swallowed and nodded. "I think it sounds nice."

"Nice?"

A blush tinged my cheeks. "Sorry. Not the right word." I blurted out all the thoughts that had just crossed my mind and the reasons it sounded beyond nice.

"I won't lie, though," I said. "There might be the occasional time when I want to explore you or be on top or something. Will that be okay?"

Jude's knowing smile sent tingles all the way down to my toes. "What makes you think I won't order you to do those things?"

My mind went immediately and blissfully blank, arousal flooding me in a single rush. "Right."

He chuckled and kissed under my jaw. "Like I said, we're two human people. As much as I *need* this, there's always push and pull."

"I wonder if it's something I needed and didn't know." I didn't meet his eyes on purpose.

Jude frowned; I saw the corner of his mouth turn down. "Are you embarrassed by that?"

"I mean…yes and no. No, because it makes sense not to know if you like something until you try it. And yes, because I've always read books like this and thought it wasn't for me. If I responded so deeply to something, shouldn't I have had some kind of clue?"

"Not necessarily. Not a perfect comparison, but think about it as trying a new recipe. Something you'd seen from a distance, and the ingredients maybe weren't your favorite, so you assumed you wouldn't love it and didn't try it. But then you decided to make it, and it turned out the way those ingredients mixed was something you never knew you'd love. Would you be embarrassed by not knowing you would like it?"

He had a point there. "Fair."

"Now." Jude's grin made my whole body tighten. "Since you're opening late, call Evie and tell her you'll be in by noon."

"Noon?" I blinked. The clock on my bedside table said it was only nine. "Why?"

"Because we're still in the bedroom, and if you don't have to be at the bakery, then I intend to keep showing you more of this."

The way his voice darkened with promise had me growing wet, and I reached for the phone.

The kitchen was an absolute nightmare. On any other day, if the space was like this, I would be losing my shit. As it was, I felt like I was floating on a magic carpet, gently drifting from place to place.

Everything in my professional life was falling apart, but

I was choosing not to focus on that and instead focusing on Jude and me. If I clung to the idea of us and what we agreed to, I could keep it together.

If I had to explain to one more person knocking on our locked doors—in spite of the sign explaining our temporary closure—I was absolutely going to lose it.

Evelyn was working in our pantry, counting and labeling everything, checking expiration dates, and making little sample bags of literally every supply we had so we could do some experimenting and find out if one of the ingredients was the cause. If it was, maybe it was the fault of the supplier and not on our end.

As much as I didn't want to shift the blame to someone else, I also couldn't deny it would be a relief.

Grace and Kate were here too, helping me scour every inch of the kitchen for holes, cracks, leaks, or anything else which could possibly cause a contamination. Later, when all of us were finished, we would pull out the ovens and clean inside them and behind them and make sure they were perfect as far as I could.

I knew my way around an oven by this point, and I was confident I would be able to tell if something was fishy. But if there were any question, I would call a repair person.

The ventilation system was a different beast altogether. That, I would need to outsource.

"Okay," Grace said, head popping up above the worktable from where she was checking the back baseboard. "We're all clear over here, and I think I need a coffee break."

"I second that." Kate pulled off the rubber gloves she was wearing. "Just a couple minutes."

"I'll put some on," Evie called. "It sounds perfect."

I rolled my eyes. "Gang up on me, why don't you?"

"Don't think I don't have an ulterior motive." Grace

pulled up one of our tall stools to the worktable. "I do. I want to hear about the man, the myth, the legend, Jude Williams."

Just hearing his name made me flush to my hairline, and I turned away from my friend. "I think Evelyn needs help with the coffee."

"I most certainly do *not*." Evie pointed back into the kitchen. "Don't use me to hide. I want to know too."

"Me three," Kate added. "Though I don't know him as well as you guys do."

They were all staring at me, and it took me a second to realize my mouth was open. I cleared my throat. "What do you want to know?"

Grace gave me a look that told me she wasn't going to buy any of my bullshit. "Everything, Lena. We want to know everything. After *pining* for the man for three years, you're together, and all you can say is, 'What do you want to know?' Details, woman."

"I—" My throat was dry, and I had to clear it again. "It just seems strange now that we are together, you know? Everything about the two of us has been so public, I'm not sure I want everyone knowing all of it."

"Not all of it!" Evie called from the doorway, balancing too many cups. "Just enough to make us be happy for you. We've barely had a chance to talk about it, and yesterday when he took you over by the fire, I almost died from the cuteness."

When I was losing my shit. "Yeah, it didn't feel cute."

"It was, though," Kate said. "He revolves around you. You move, and he turns toward you like he always wants to have you in his sight."

"That's not new, though." Grace took her cup and a big swig of it before Evie had even brought the cream and sugar. "He's always done it, but now they're together, he does it closer."

I snorted. "You're not wrong." The three of them stared at me intentionally, and I relented. "Okay, fine."

They cheered, and I took my sweet time making my coffee the way I liked it. "It's...honestly amazing. Because we've known each other for so long, some of it feels effortless. It just makes sense."

"You know what we're really asking, girl. Don't be coy." Evie smirked. "God knows you know enough about my sex life."

"And mine," Grace said. "And Cori's. I'm sure we'll get there with Kate."

The platinum blonde blushed but smiled. "We have a good time."

"See?" I pointed. "Exactly. We have a good time."

Grace leaned her elbows on the table. "Okay. I will promise on whatever you want me to that what you say here will not get back to Harlan." She looked over at the others meaningfully. "Or Lucas or Noah. Just give us something."

I blew out a breath. They weren't going to let me off the hook, and honestly, I needed someone else to talk about it with besides Jude. "If any of you says anything—" I tried to think about an appropriate threat. "Just please don't."

Evie's face grew serious. "Of course, girl. We're not trying to mess this up for you, and if you're really uncomfortable, then we won't bug you."

Grace looked at her as if to say "*Speak for yourself,*" but she nodded too.

"Last night." It was an effort to even speak without flushing like an idiot. "Let me start over. Kate, you weren't here for this, but you guys remember when Cori told us why Joel broke up with her and what she was curious about?"

"Bet your ass I do," Evie said. "Is that what happened?"

"Not in the same way, but last night, he took complete control, and I let him."

They stared at me. Finally, Kate said, "And?"

"And it was fucking incredible." I blew out a breath. "It's nothing like I thought it would be or what I thought I wanted, but it's what he loves, and I have literally no arguments. Seriously, it brought out something I never imagined."

"Damn," Grace said. "Honestly, I can see it. Dark, brooding, stoic. Totally makes sense."

"Dark and brooding?" I laughed. "Hardly."

They all shared a look.

"What?"

Evie smiled into her coffee. "You know the only person Jude smiles at is you, right?"

"That's not true. He smiles at other people. At jokes and stuff."

"Yeah," Grace said. "At jokes. But you're the only person he spontaneously smiles at. So maybe you see a different side of him, but to us, he's a bit dark and broody. Hot, but dark and broody." She pinned me with a stare. "Don't tell Harlan I said Jude was hot."

Kate snorted. "If any of these guys has an issue with that, they all need to line up at a mirror. Noah is everything I want, but I can appreciate Resting Warrior is a beacon for seriously hot men."

We all collapsed into laughter. She wasn't wrong.

"Am I interrupting?" The man of the hour stood in the doorway to the kitchen. I'd given him a spare key this morning after he finally let me out of bed, though I was a boneless mess and it had taken me time to be able to stand.

"Not at all." I crossed to him, and when he pulled me in to kiss me, I had no thoughts in my head about being watched or worried about what anyone might think. That was gone, and I didn't want it to ever come back. "Thanks for coming."

"Find anything?"

Jude had had a couple of things to do at the ranch, but he had promised to come and be a second eye in case anything was wrong. So far, though, nothing. "No. Unfortunately."

"Let's poke around some more, then."

We put our coffee away, and the girls kept their word, not saying anything about what I'd revealed, and Jude gave no indication he'd overheard anything. He wouldn't care. If there was one thing I knew about Jude, especially now, it was that he was confident.

Wanting what he did in bed wasn't an embarrassment for him. If anything, his hesitation about sharing it was more about my reaction than his.

The oven looked fine. None of the connections was damaged. There were no contaminants in the vents—nothing which could have made fifty pies go rancid. Jude got on a ladder and checked all the vents as best he could, but we would still have to wait for the all clear from the specialist.

Tasting the ingredients went just fine, too, but I was still nervous. "I think I'm just going to ditch everything that's open. It's not worth the anxiety I'll have using it."

"Are you sure?" Evelyn looked worried. "That's a lot of inventory."

It was. "If we don't have customers, we won't have any inventory anyway. Better safe than sorry. If you can work on it and make me a list of everything to reorder, I need to start calling people to let them know what we're doing and how we're starting from scratch. Hopefully it will rekindle some confidence."

"I'm sure it will." Jude wrapped himself around me from behind. "If you're okay, I'll head out, but I'll be back to pick you up."

All eyes were on my face as I turned pink. But they didn't know the flush went all the way down to my toes. "Sounds good."

His lips brushed my ear, and his words were low enough no one else could hear. "I have time to go get my handcuffs, sweetheart. Keep that in mind for later."

One searing kiss later, and I was staring after him in a daze. He looked over his shoulder and winked. God, I liked this side of him.

The door shut, and Grace slammed her hands down on the worktable. "Okay, what the hell did he just say to you because you're red as a tomato, and your face went all *gooey*." She was cracking up.

"That," I said, "I'm keeping to myself."

Because if I didn't, it was all I was going to think about, and the last thing I needed in my mind while talking to customers was how badly I wanted my boyfriend to handcuff me to my bed and fuck me.

I slipped into my office before they could notice I was blushing all over again.

Chapter 17

Jude

There was a spring in my step as I came down the stairs of my house and got back into the truck. I'd packed a bag with a couple fresh pairs of clothes, my handcuffs—as I'd promised—and more essentials. Lena's house was far more inviting than mine, and I was content to spend all our time there, though I would have to bring her here eventually. She'd already asked.

Now that I was looking at everything through the lens of Lena, my house was kind of sad. I preferred the quirky, colorful space she'd created for herself.

But the spring in my step wasn't because of the amazing sex or that she bloomed like a fucking rose under my control. Those things were perfect, and I couldn't quite believe they were real.

No, the extra energy I had today was because I'd *slept* with her. Last night after we'd done all of it, I was too tired to keep myself in the shallow, half-asleep state I'd been staying in so far whenever I slept over.

And I didn't hurt her.

I didn't even wake up once. It felt like a miracle, and once again, I had to confront the possibility that a lot of the assumptions I had about myself might be wrong. Maybe Noah was right and the loneliness which had been my constant companion had been making the nightmares worse.

I certainly felt more at ease when I had Lena close. Not just because she helped me sleep or because we were together, but because deep down on the instinctual level, where my purest reactions came from, Lena was mine. I already knew it, but every day we were together proved it more.

Those instincts told me to protect her at all costs. Keep her in my orbit so I could be there if she needed me. To extend both my control and my support in any way possible.

It was only one night, so I wasn't going to dismiss my concerns out of hand. There was still a very good chance my demons would pop up to haunt me again, but the hope I felt now was like one of those clear Montana sunrises—completely beautiful and incomparable.

I couldn't wait to pick up Lena and take her home. Spend hours listening to her moan while I instructed her in every filthy thing my brain had been concocting for the last three years, and finally holding her as I slept. If I could let myself.

But first, I wanted to get her flowers. Something to make her smile.

Since it was past Thanksgiving, the selection of flowers in the local shop was different than it'd been in the summertime. The blooms were darker and richer than

I would have chosen for Lena, but I still wanted something.

I smiled at the shop owner. "Hi, how are you?"

"Hi, good to see you. Can I help you find something?"

The last time I'd been here had been during Lucas and Evelyn's ordeal to ask whether the shop carried the black roses Evelyn's stalker had tormented her with.

Would Lena be shy of roses because of it? We still needed to talk about her nightmares, and that might be a good opening. But I also didn't want a gift I was buying out of kindness to be attached to something so dark. "I'm looking for flowers for my girlfriend," I admitted. "I'm just not sure what she'll like, and I'm not sold on roses."

She looked at me for a second. "I have a couple things I can show you. I have a few flowers which look similar enough to roses but aren't quite the same. Lisianthus, for one thing." She gestured to a bunch of white flowers, but white wasn't exactly what I had in mind. Not when I was planning on taking her home and ravishing her until she had no voice left.

"Anemones too. These are great for the time of year."

The gathering of blooms she stood in front of was a wild mix of colors, everything from white to pink and red. But it was the purple ones that caught my eye—a deep royal color that would look beautiful in Lena's home surrounded by all that green. The flowers themselves were oddly lovely, somehow a cross between a daisy, a rose, and a black-eyed Susan. "Can you make me a bouquet of those, but only purple?"

"Of course," she said with a smile. "Give me a few minutes."

I wandered the store, looking at the various flowers and plants and enjoying the scents. For working on a ranch, I knew almost nothing about this area of horticulture.

Movement across the street drew my eye. Someone going into a store. I watched and did a double take. That wasn't a store; it was a *coffee shop*. There was another coffee shop in Garnet Bend? A sign sat on the sidewalk, but I was at the wrong angle to read it. When the flowers were finished, I needed to check it out. The shop looked decently busy.

"Here you go," the owner called. The bouquet was gorgeous, with some greens and baby's breath, which was dyed a light purple to complement the rest of the flowers.

"It's perfect, thank you."

"I hope she likes it."

"She will, I'm sure." I swiped my credit card. "Question. Out of curiosity, how long has the coffee shop across the street been there?"

She made a face, thinking. "Couple weeks, maybe? There honestly haven't been many people until the last couple days. I've tried it since it's a lot closer than Deja Brew. Coffee's good. Cookies could use some work."

I chuckled and kept the knowledge these flowers were for the owner of Deja Brew to myself. At least this was proof Lena's worst fears hadn't come true. Her disaster hadn't spread to everyone in town. If the florist had known about it, I was sure she would have made a comment. "Thank you."

"No problem!"

I jogged across the street to the small store. The green awning was cheery in the cold weather, and the little chalkboard sign told me this was "Mountain Jewels Coffee."

Not a bad name for a place like Garnet Bend.

There were several people in line, but I stepped inside anyway. That alone felt like a betrayal, but I needed to know. The scent inside was good. Coffee, with an undercurrent of sweetness, but it wasn't the same as when you walked into Deja Brew, where the smell had been seeping into every corner of the shop for years.

"Hey, Jude." I focused on the man in front of me, who'd turned around in line. Ben, the mechanic. I hadn't recognized him from behind.

"Oh hey, Ben." I extended the hand that wasn't holding flowers. "Good to see you." The garage was on this side of town, so it made sense he could walk over here.

He nodded to the flowers and grinned. "Those for Lena?" I stared at him for a second before I remembered he'd heard my whole outburst with Daniel while dropping off Bessie.

"Yeah. Finally got my head out of my ass."

Ben stuck his hands in his pockets with a chuckle. "A bit ago, I saw you kiss her outside the Deja early in the morning, so I figured something had changed."

I nodded. "By the way, who do you trust to look at a ventilation system?" Lena hadn't decided yet who she was going to call.

"Why?" He frowned.

"We want to just make sure everything's on the up-and-up at the bakery," I said easily. If he didn't know about what happened either, I wasn't going to volunteer it.

He stepped forward as the line moved. "I could come over and take a look if you want. I'm a car guy now and they're definitely more fun, but I came up on HVAC."

"If you're willing, that would be great. I'll have Lena talk to you and set up a time in the next couple of days."

"Sounds good." It was his turn. He smiled and nodded before turning away and starting his order.

A blond woman was behind the counter. Bubbly and smiling, waiting on people as quickly as she could. It didn't seem like she had a lot of experience dealing with a rush.

But slowly, the line moved forward until I was at the counter.

She looked at me and then behind me. "Oh, thank goodness, you're the last one. I can take a breath."

"I didn't realize there was another coffee shop in town."

"Ah." She winced and covered with a smile. "I've been getting that a lot."

"How long have you been open? And I'll take a coffee to go."

She poured my coffee. "Two weeks tomorrow. I'm Allison, by the way, but everyone calls me Alli."

"Nice to meet you." I wasn't sure it was the truth, but I didn't need to be rude. Yet. Something about this place had my instincts tingling—and not in a good way.

Alli placed the coffee on the counter while I handed her the couple of bills I owed. "Have a nice day," she said. "And whoever's getting those is a lucky girl."

She was, but I didn't know if she was going to feel lucky once she found out about this place. "Have a nice day." I shot her a wave and left, taking a sip of the coffee. It wasn't bad at all, but I'd had better at Deja Brew. In this area, I was completely biased and didn't care that I was.

I looked at the storefront from down the block as I got back into my truck. It was strange we hadn't heard about this shop opening in the last two weeks. The timeline placed the opening before the first incident with the nursing home and Lena's cookies.

With the way gossip spread in this town, I would have thought the news of a rival coffee shop would have had people racing to tell Lena. Maybe at the time not enough people knew and were still loyal to Deja Brew?

All I knew at the moment was that the timing for a new

coffee shop and two disasters in a row for Lena, which clearly benefited this place, was awfully convenient.

There was nothing to do about it now, and the woman seemed nice enough, but I made a mental note to do some digging. It wouldn't be hard to verify if she had the proper permits and everything was in order. If I happened to find any information that told me she'd intentionally come after Lena in the process, then so be it.

At the very least, I was going to keep an eye on Mountain Jewels Coffee until I figured out why the hell it was driving my instincts crazy.

Chapter 18

Lena

I flopped back on Jude's leather couch, looking at the ceiling. Every piece of me was tired. The last few days had been nothing but a craze of getting Deja ready to reopen. Accepting deliveries on new supplies, cleaning *everything* in the kitchen until it shone. Having Ben look at the ventilation system and him giving the all clear.

Every night, I had to kick out Evie, and then Jude came and found me, head buried in scrubbing something or organizing the pantry. Tonight, he'd simply picked me up, turned off the lights, and walked out the door.

I could have protested harder, but it was going to be fine. Most everything was done by this point. We could start baking in the morning and hopefully be open again in the early afternoon.

The good news was the customers were sympathetic. There were only a couple who didn't seem okay with my explanation of what I was doing to prevent another mishap of the same kind. But my offering a boatload of free coupons definitely smoothed a lot of feathers.

My entire body felt so boneless, I didn't want to move. Which was saying a lot, because I desperately wanted to snoop around Jude's house when I could muster the energy to stand.

This was the first time I'd ever been here. I'd only ever known approximately where he lived, but I never knew he had a gorgeous house in the middle of a property that was downright *lush* for Montana, even in winter. Beautiful woods around an older-style, two-story house.

He was adorably nervous about letting me come here, but I begged and begged until he said yes. Now, he was in the kitchen, cooking dinner.

From here, I saw a small room with a security setup that rivaled the one at the ranch. Cameras covered every inch of his property. But given everything he'd gone through, it made sense. I would want that kind of reassurance too.

Jude appeared in the doorway to the kitchen, a glass of wine in his hand. He laughed when he saw me, and I thought about what the girls said—that he really only smiled with me. It was a pity, because Jude's smile was the best thing in the entire world. "You okay? You look like you melted."

"I kind of feel like I melted," I sighed, reaching up to take the glass when he handed it to me. "But I'm trying to rally so I can snoop around your bachelor pad."

He rolled his eyes. "It's hardly a pad. It's hardly anything at all."

"Don't say that." I knew where he was coming from, but I didn't agree. The house was plain and not decorated, but the bones of it were *gorgeous*. If this were my house, I would have a fucking field day.

Slow your roll, Lena. Don't think about it yet.

Jude's eyes narrowed. "What was that thought?"

The man was too fucking observant. "Nothing." I sipped my wine. "Nothing to worry about."

He slid onto the couch beside me. "Are you going to tell me? Or am I going to have to pin you down and deny you until I get it out of you?"

My eyes went wide. "It wasn't a big thought, and you wouldn't."

"Wouldn't I?" His gaze was full of mischief, and I knew he absolutely would, and he would enjoy every second of it.

"Fine," I sighed. "I just thought if this were my house, I would have a great time decorating it because the bones are beautiful. That was all. I didn't want you to say it's nothing because it's not. It's just plain."

"It is plain." He didn't sound offended in the least. "Let's go back to the first part of the sentence."

"We don't have to."

Jude took the wineglass from my hand and set it on the coffee table before he pounced. Pounced was the wrong word, because Jude was an absolute predator, stalking me with grace and ease until I was fully pinned beneath him on the couch. "I think we do."

As I looked up at him, it was easy to see he was tired. It was written in the lines of his face, and I felt it in his body, even if the same body was making what he wanted very clear. "You've been running yourself ragged between the ranch and me. I'm sorry."

"I'm fine," he said.

"You're tired." He opened his mouth to protest, and I put a finger on his lips. His gaze flared with dominant hunger, the urge to take my hand and pin it to the couch for trying to shush him, but he didn't. "We can go to bed early."

"I'd rather not sleep."

"There're only so many times you can say it before you get so loopy you start seeing things."

Jude leaned down, pressing his lips softly to my cheek. "I'm okay, Lena. Promise."

"I know. But you've been taking care of me. It's allowed to go both ways." I wiggled, and he let me up. "How's dinner?"

"Finished and ready. But I'm warning you, I'm no Grant. It's not gourmet."

I retrieved my wineglass and took another sip. "Jude, I make cookies and coffee. Home cooking is just fine with me."

And it was fine. The pasta he made was actually delicious, though he wouldn't accept the praise. Simple things could be amazing. I already knew that.

But Jude was still dragging after dinner as I helped him put the dishes into the dishwasher. I took his hand when we were finished. "I think it's time for bed."

He looked worried, and I suspected he hadn't told me the full extent of his nightmares and it was why he didn't want to go to sleep. But we hadn't had any problems so far at my house, and he'd been sleeping there more often than not.

"I promise I'm not going to bite," I said with a wink.

That finally drew a smile from him. "Okay."

I'd brought a little bag with me so I'd have a change of clothes, and I was glad I'd included comfy pajamas. I'd tucked something else in there too, in case Jude was feeling frisky. But I wasn't about to show him and give him an excuse to stay awake for me. He was exhausted, and it was better for both of us if he got some sleep.

Jude rubbed the back of his neck as we stepped into his room. It was just as bare as the rest of the house, but with a large, comfy bed, a dresser, and not much else. "It's—"

I turned to him. "Jude. There's no reason to be embarrassed because your house isn't as over the top as mine."

"That's an understatement." He glanced around the space. "If your house is over the top, mine is a prison."

Laughing, I rose up on my tiptoes to pull him down and kiss him. "I'm not with you because of how you decorate your bedroom. You could live in a tent, and I wouldn't care."

He smiled, but it didn't fully reach his eyes. I didn't think it was actually the bedroom he was nervous about, but I didn't press him. I already knew he was tired, and I knew when I was overtired, everything felt like *more* and too much.

Quickly, I slipped into my shorts and too-big T-shirt, in time to see Jude put on sweats…and nothing else. I was committed to getting this man some rest, but being exposed to his body for any length of time was a dangerous thing.

He caught me looking. "As you know, I usually sleep naked."

It was true; every night he'd been at my house, he hadn't had a stitch on him. I assumed it was because he'd had his way with me. "Why not tonight?"

"I know myself, and if you get into my bed with me and I'm naked? There will be very little sleep happening."

I fought the blush that rose. We'd agreed he ruled in the bedroom, and so far, it had been…amazing. The handcuffs he used on me made everything brighter and wilder, and I barely recognized myself in this person who loved surrendering to his control.

Or rather, I wondered why I hadn't found this version of myself earlier.

"That's fair." I waited until he pulled back the blankets to get in, not wanting to mess up any system he had for his bed. But as soon as we were both under the blankets, Jude pulled me to him, settling me against his chest. It was my favorite place to be. Here, I felt entirely safe, and I couldn't imagine ever feeling otherwise.

He was holding me too tightly for me to look up at him, so I whispered the words into his chest. "You're going to sleep, right?"

One deep breath in and out. "Yes. I'm going to sleep."

"Good." Those were the last words we said, and I drifted off in comforting warmth.

The noise ripped me from sleep, and I didn't know where I was. Everything was dark, and it took me a second to remember I was at Jude's house. In his bed. And he was screaming.

On the other side of the bed, he was thrashing. Shouting while he fought an invisible enemy, and it was clear he was not showing them any mercy. There was just enough light for me to see the shape of him and the lines of his face.

My stomach sank. This. This was what he was afraid of. It was why he didn't want to go to sleep and why he looked haunted. Only one thing he didn't realize—this didn't scare me. I had my own nightmares, and I understood what they could do to you.

Plus, I knew Jude would never hurt me.

He moved again with another shout, and I moved too. Toward him. Reaching past his arms, I took his face in my hands. "Jude."

His head jerked, trying to get away from me, but I held on. "Jude, it's Lena. You need to wake up."

Jude's face twisted into a snarl, and he moved so fast I couldn't track it. One moment, I was leaning over him, and the next, I was on my back with him looking down at me. This was Jude the warrior. The face he wore now was not one many saw, and if they did, they didn't live to tell the tale.

But he didn't do anything but pin me down. I reached out again, touching his face. "Jude, it's me."

All at once, he came awake. I saw the difference and watched him take in where he was and what he was doing. "Oh fuck." He scrambled away from me, the bedside lamp coming on before he dropped his face into his hands.

"Jude—"

"Did I hurt you?" He was back with me in a second, checking me, running his hands over me to see if I was hurt. "This is exactly what I didn't want to happen."

"You didn't hurt me. You barely even touched me."

"Are you sure?"

He was still bleary with sleep and the adrenaline of the nightmare, and I recognized panic was still flowing under his skin. "I'm very sure. I'm fine."

"Good," he said. "That's good."

Moving away from me again, he sat on the edge of the bed and shuddered. I reached out and touched his back, but he shrugged off the touch. Even with him facing away from me, I felt him collapsing and pulling away. This was something he'd hoped no one would see, and now I had.

"I'll go sleep on the couch."

"What?"

He just stood and started to move.

"Jude, look at me. Right now." It felt strange to give him orders, especially in his bedroom, but this couldn't happen. Slowly, he turned and looked at me, his eyes bleak with shame and grief. "You are not going to sleep on the couch like you did something wrong or shameful. You are going to come back here and talk to me. I'm not afraid of you, you didn't hurt me, and I don't want you anywhere else but here."

It was easy to see he didn't believe me.

"Don't make me get out of bed and pull you back here. I might not be strong enough to actually move you, but bet your ass, I will try." A flicker of a smile, there and gone.

Jude sat on the edge of the bed, far enough away so he could leave quickly if he needed to. That wasn't going to work for me. I wasn't going to let him think he was broken or like he needed to feel dangerous. I scooted over to him and climbed into his lap, straddling him and forcing him to hold on to me so I wouldn't slide off the bed.

His hands were too gentle where he held me. "You shouldn't be so close, Lena."

"Why?" The way his shoulders drooped broke my heart. I wrapped myself entirely around him, until he stopped resisting and his arms finally came around me in the hug I wanted and he needed.

"I understand this," I whispered. "I get it. It doesn't scare me. I told you I have my own nightmares, but we've never gotten around to talking about that. I dream about Nathan and what he did to Evelyn and me. It's why I had a panic attack in the car the night I kissed you. It's why I called *you*, Jude. Because you make me feel safer than anyone else in my life. Ever."

"Why?" It was like he reflected my previous question back at me.

"Because you found me. They told me you wouldn't let anyone touch me until you got to the hospital. That you were…almost feral until you knew I was okay."

He bumped his forehead against mine. "I needed you to be okay."

"I am okay," I said. "Because *you* saved my life. Because *you* showed up that night when I called. *You* pulled me out of my own head on Thanksgiving and showed me everything would work out, and you didn't make me feel like an idiot for feeling like I did. If there's anything I know about you, Jude, it's that you would never hurt me. Not by choice."

I didn't bother mentioning the painful week when I thought I'd lost him. Even then, he'd been doing it because he'd thought I'd be better off without him. He didn't need to be reminded of it.

Jude began to move his hands over my back, a sign he was coming back to himself. He loved touching me whenever he could, and his hands were rarely still. "Your nightmares still happen?"

"Not since you." I was glad we were too close for him to see my expression. "But, yes. They happen all the time. And when I wake up, it's not so different from what I just saw." I paused, steeling myself. "I never told anyone."

He searched my face. "Did you feel like you couldn't?"

"I don't know." I looked away, but with the hand in my hair, he guided my gaze back. "Everyone was dealing with their own stuff, and I've always been the one who makes people feel better, so I didn't bother anyone about it."

"Lena—"

I kept talking in case I lost my nerve to say it at all. "I don't like the dark. Not the complete dark or being alone in it. It reminds me of that night. When I have to stay late at Deja Brew, especially in the wintertime, closing up is really hard because I have to turn off all the lights, and I just…panic. I was already primed to freak out when Bessie broke down, and it just made everything worse. I couldn't stop seeing Nathan appearing out of the darkness with his gun and—" My breath shuddered. "I can still hear her screaming."

The hand in my hair made sure I kept looking at him and wasn't able to look away. There was no judgment in his expression, just sadness and understanding. "I had no idea it was so bad—that you were going through all of it."

"Of course it's bad. What happened was terrible. Just like what happened to you was terrible. But it doesn't mean I don't want you or don't see who you truly are. And it damn well doesn't mean I don't know the difference between you when you're dreaming and you when you're awake."

Jude's expression hardened. "And you bringing happiness to people doesn't mean you're unable to feel trauma. Nor does it mean you should hide it. Pushing it down doesn't make it better. I would know."

I blinked, my breath shaky. He was right, of course, but those thoughts still swirled in my head as I was sure his awful thoughts about him hurting me were still there. But away from him, especially now, was not where I wanted to be. "Please don't go," I whispered. "Don't leave me alone."

In that moment, I meant leaving to sleep on the couch. But I couldn't help but feel the words meant something greater than that.

The air between us tightened, a spark finally entering Jude's eyes again. He released my hair and eased his hold on me. "Take off your shirt."

Heat dropped through me as I recognized the tone. I pulled the T-shirt up and over my head before tossing it aside. The casual way he looked over me, like I was his for the taking, had an even hotter fire burning under my skin.

Pulling me against him once more, Jude kissed me.

Hard. It felt like the most natural shift in the world to suddenly be yielding as he took control.

Rolling us together, he pinned me to the bed again, just like he had in his dream. But this time, he was wide awake, and violence was the last thing on his mind. "If you're afraid of the dark in the shop, I want you to call me," he said. "If you ever have a moment when you're about to panic? Call me. There's no reason you need to go through any of this alone, Lena."

I swallowed, feeling a little raw from finally admitting everything. It was a relief to know he was feeling the same. "If it goes for me, then it should go for you too. We can both help each other."

He smiled, soft and sure. "All right. Deal." Then he leaned down and brushed his lips over my chest. "But let's let it go for the rest of the night. I think we both need it."

Yes. I agreed, so I nodded.

"And until we both come, the only thing you're allowed to say is my name. And 'please.'"

My body arched in response to his command, subconsciously reacting to it. He was leaving me with only one option—to beg. "Jude."

His smirk was back, and fuck if it wasn't the sexiest thing I'd ever seen. "Remember, I said until we *both* come. So, this might take a while."

I bit my lip to keep from speaking, because I knew now, not obeying would only make him more determined, and I would already be a limp, writhing mess by the end of it. "Please."

Jude's eyes lit with pleasure, and he returned to my skin, slowly continuing the trail he was blazing across it. "Good girl."

Chapter 19

Lena

Mountain Jewels Coffee.

Jude told me about the place after he discovered it, but I admitted to avoiding it until Deja Brew was open again. That was the most important thing to me. That, and regaining the trust of my customers.

But though we'd opened again, Deja Brew had been distinctly emptier than before. Part of me expected it, and the other part was still saddened so many people stayed away even after I'd done what I could to make amends.

But this certainly showed why my business had been slow. My regulars were here at Mountain Jewels. They were here, and one of them came out as I was standing on the sidewalk, intentionally not meeting my eyes.

It wasn't like I had a right to everyone in town. Business was business. However, in a town this size, and with what I did, everything felt a little more personal. I couldn't help that it felt like a betrayal for customers who had been coming to Deja Brew every day like clockwork for *years* to be coming here instead.

Ben, the mechanic and the guy who saved my ass with the ventilation system the other day, exited the shop and gave me a wary smile. I smiled back as best I could. Being upset was one thing. Letting everyone know I was upset was another. This wasn't the same as my nightmares. I needed to stay professional in this as much as possible.

And while it was true, I couldn't stop myself from going inside to check it out, just like Jude had. He told me the coffee was average, but I needed to see for myself and either make myself feel better or accept the truth.

The inside was well designed. Sunny and bright with jeweled accents to reference the name. It was a good branding choice. Everything smelled good, and there were a few bonus items on the menu besides just coffee, but mostly, it was just drinks. That was reassuring. At least I was only competing with them on one front.

I soundly pushed aside the nasty little voice that told me I wasn't competing with *anything* if I couldn't figure out what had gone wrong with the baking.

The menu here had a lot more drinks than I served. Variations on variations of drinks. But it made sense since it was the main product. I was considering which beverage I'd grudgingly try when a blond woman came out of the back. "Oh." She startled for a second before she smiled. "I'll be honest, I was kind of hoping you'd come by."

I blinked at her. "You know who I am?"

"Of course. The famous Lena Mitchell. When I first came to town and started asking about coffee, your name was the only name anyone mentioned. I came by a few months ago, but there's no reason you should remember. I've been meaning to come by again, but everything's just gotten away from me. I'm sure you understand. I'm Allison."

Automatically, I reached out to shake her hand. In the last few days, my mind had created an image of the owner of this place. It was a hag-like creature with long nails and an evil smile. Not this pretty, bubbly woman who seemed genuinely friendly. "Of course." I did understand that. Running a business was hectic at the best of times.

"Can I get you something?"

I hadn't decided yet, so I managed to form the words for something basic. "I'll have a latte, please."

"Coming right up." She turned and started making it with quick efficiency. "I'm sorry, by the way. I feel like I should have given you a heads-up about opening the store. One more thing that kind of dropped off my list. But I really should have come by and said something. If I were the only coffee shop in town and someone showed up as a surprise, I'm not so sure I would take it as well as you are."

She had no idea how I was taking it, and I didn't think I was being particularly gracious in my head. Because everything here seemed good and fine and nice, and I desperately, *desperately* wanted to find something wrong with it, even if that made me a shitty person. "It's all right," I said. "You don't owe me anything."

"Still." She slid the coffee across the counter with a smile. "I hope we can be friends even though we're technically competition. Women in business need to stick together."

I needed to smile and be nice. There was no proof of what Jude had suggested, which was that the timing of her opening the store was suspicious. If anything, she was kind and sweet and supportive. But my smile was forced. "Of course. Come by any time."

As I reached for my wallet, she held out a hand. "On the house. I insist."

"That's kind of you."

"Not a problem at all. I hope to see you around." The bell she had over her door rang, and it gave me an opportunity to slip away as she focused on the next customer.

I tried the coffee as I started my cold walk back across town. Jude was right. It wasn't bad, but it wasn't the best coffee I'd ever had. Though, it was good enough, I understood why people were coming back.

Allison didn't seem like the kind of person to sabotage someone else. It was hard to envision her that way. But as I well knew, people who could be charming and sweet could also be ruthless and vile. Hadn't Nathan—Evie's handsome and charming and completely evil ex—taught us that?

Granted, I didn't think Allison was going to come after me and scar me for life, even if she was at the heart of my troubles. All in all, I didn't feel relieved, just unsettled and unsure of what I really thought.

I was grateful for the walk to clear my thoughts, let them settle. At least the coffee was warm and a decent way to fight off the November wind. Almost December now. Holy crap, Christmas was coming up, and with everything going on, I hadn't bought presents for anyone.

I needed to have Evelyn take over one day so I could drive down to Missoula and do some serious shopping. With how empty the store had been, it likely wasn't going to be a problem.

"You're never going to guess who I just got off the phone with," Evie trilled when I pushed through the door.

"Santa Claus? He's bringing you coal in your stocking this year?"

She gave me a look. "Very funny. No, it was Principal

Walker over at the high school. She wants a metric ton of cupcakes for the Christmas dance next week."

My knees wobbled in relief. That was really, really good news. At least someone in Garnet Bend still trusted I could bake something and it would taste good. "That's amazing."

"It is. And I told you so."

Evie had said from the very start of cleaning up the kitchen that everything would be fine. I wasn't as convinced, but I hoped she was right in the end.

I smiled at her and took a sip of the coffee in my hand to push off the nerves in my stomach. After talking with Jude about my nightmares, I'd agreed to tell Evie. It was her ordeal too, and he didn't believe I should keep it from her. She was my friend, he argued, and she would want to support me.

"I need to tell you something."

Her face dropped. "Are you okay?" She pointed to the cup. "I haven't had a chance to go over there yet. Please tell me it's just a craphole we can ignore."

Shaking my head, I laughed. "Not a craphole we can ignore. Not something I think will threaten the shop if I can get people to trust us again."

"Okay, what's up?"

I glanced toward the door to make sure we weren't going to get any customers before I nodded over to our couch and chairs. "I promise it's nothing bad. Well, it is, but it's to do with me and not you."

Evie settled on the couch and blinked. "Please spit it out so I realize it's not as bad as you're making it sound."

Yeah, I wasn't doing a good job right now. "I hadn't told anyone this until Jude a couple of nights ago. But… I've been struggling with what happened to us."

"With Nathan?" Evie went entirely still. My friend was pretty good about the whole ordeal, but I knew she struggled with it too. Arguably more than I did since she was the one who was tortured and who had scars all over her body.

"Yeah." My voice sounded raspy. "I've been having nightmares, and the night I first kissed Jude, I'd been having a panic attack when Bessie died because it was so similar. When I'm here alone and it's dark, I freak out. I just… I'm not handling it well."

Her face softened, and she took a minute to absorb it all. "I honestly had no idea," she said. "You've been hiding it really well."

"I've been trying to."

"Why? Why didn't you say anything? I would have understood."

I squeezed my hands together, fidgeting with the discomfort. "I didn't want to bother anyone with it. Everyone else has gone through something worse. I was *with you*. I know what he did to you was ten times worse than what he did to me."

Sitting forward, Evie pinned me with a stare. "I don't buy that. Not for a second. The things he did to us were different, not better or worse. Nathan tried to kill you too. And having to watch someone tortured is a form of torture in itself."

She was right, of course, but it still didn't feel comparable to me. "He buried you alive. I think that's a bit more intense than an overdose."

"Lena, it's not a competition." I opened my mouth to say I knew, but she stopped me. "Hold on, let me finish. What happened to me was awful. Life-altering and shitty. I'm not going to pretend it wasn't. But just because it happened to me does not somehow invalidate what happened to you. There's not an invisible measuring stick you have to line up your trauma with in order to see if you deserve to feel badly about it."

When she put it like that, then yes, of course. I had no argument to make there.

"Just because someone could look at our two experiences and think one is objectively 'worse,' doesn't mean it wasn't the worst thing to ever happen to you. Pretending it's not won't help."

"That's for sure," I said with a sigh. "I just wanted to keep being the person everyone thought was okay. You know? Everyone comes in here and feels better—or at least, they used to—because what doesn't make you feel better than coffee and sugar? I didn't want to mess that up by suddenly being this person who wears her trauma on her sleeve."

Evelyn tilted her head when she looked at me. "Is that how you feel about me?"

"What? God, no. Of course not." I shook my head. "Never."

She smiled like she knew she'd get that response and had planned it. "Good. Because I *actually* wear my trauma on my sleeve." Lifting her scarred arm, she underscored her point. "But if you don't think of me only in the context of my trauma with a fucking visible reminder every day, why would you assume people would do it to you?"

"You're making too much sense," I grumbled.

"It happens when you're always right."

I stuck out my tongue but ended up smiling. "Yeah, I know. And I know everything you've said is right… It just feels different."

Evie nodded, standing and stretching before grabbing the rival coffee and tasting it. "I know. Being inside your own head can be a total trip. But you can get the hang of it. This is not good." She made a face.

"It's fine."

"Ours is better."

I tried desperately not to laugh. Both she and Jude had said the same. Sure, they were biased, but I still loved to hear it. "Thanks."

"On the previous topic, I think you should make an appointment with Rayne."

Dr. Rayne was the therapist in town who worked with Resting Warrior. Jude saw her; Evie saw her. Basically, everyone at the ranch did. So it wasn't like she would be unfamiliar with the situation. Still, my stomach twisted at the thought.

Taking a breath, I tried to step back mentally. Of all the things I shouldn't be wary of after knowing and loving Resting Warrior for so long, it was going to therapy. And it wasn't therapy itself that made me pause. No, it was the idea that going meant admitting there was something wrong. Which was equally nonsensical, but still the way I felt.

"You don't have to keep going if you don't like it," Evie called as she poured the rest of the Mountain Jewels coffee down the sink. "But I think trying it once will help."

"You're right. It probably would." It wouldn't be easy, but in the end, it would likely be worth it. "I'll look into it."

"Awesome." She grabbed two cups and filled them with *our* coffee and handed one to me as she sat back down. "Now, we need a plan to win the town back over, because we can totally do it. We just need to be strategic. The cupcakes for the dance will definitely help, and we'll do a bunch of tests to make sure everything is fine. But I have ideas."

"Tell me." I guessed that was the one thing about having a slow day. We had plenty of time to make new plans.

Chapter 20

Jude

The screens blurred in front of my eyes as I dug through page after page of information, trying to find something. Anything.

But my mind was elsewhere. Spinning back on itself and retracing paths I'd gone down a hundred times before. It was tiring, but at the very least, I was sleeping. Fitfully, since I kept waking up to make sure I hadn't lost my shit and hurt Lena, but it was better than nothing.

My appointment with Dr. Rayne this morning had gone well, but I was still raw from what happened the other night. Lena didn't care that it had happened, but I still did. The terror I felt in those moments when I woke up and was pinning her down—

I wouldn't forget the feeling for a long fucking time. And yet, I knew it was nothing in comparison to what I would feel if I *actually* hurt her. Even by accident.

No part of me regretted finally taking my shot with

Lena. The past few weeks had been the best in my life by far. But waking up and finding I'd bloodied her nose, blackened her eye—or worse—was still one of my greatest fears.

It wasn't just that I was afraid of hurting Lena either. I couldn't let another person get hurt because of me. Ever. Once was enough, and I would never be able to take it back, because Isaac was already gone.

If I'd been stronger. Better. Maybe I could have helped him. If I'd been able to hold on a little longer and insist they get him out with me and not left him behind, then maybe he'd still be here.

Rayne insisted, and logically I knew I wasn't responsible. I'd been barely conscious when they carried me out of those caves. But still, even if I hadn't been able to get him out, there must be something I could have done to keep him from taking his own life. Been there for him more, checked in more, made sure he was getting the help he needed.

The guilt telling me Isaac might still be alive if I'd done *something* was too big, and even after all this time, I didn't know how to deal with it.

But I was newly determined not to let my guilt get in the way of my relationship with Lena. It had delayed it long enough; I wasn't going to spoil the best thing to ever happen to me. She was right. We were both having nightmares, and we could help each other. I simply had to take it one day at a time.

In an attempt to distract myself and also do something worthwhile, I was digging into Allison DeVries, the owner of the new coffee shop. My instincts were still telling me something wasn't right, but in looking for some proof she was the source of Lena's troubles, I'd come up empty so far.

Allison was clean as a whistle. All the proper business permits were filed. She didn't have any outrageous debt, and there were no signs the business was a front for something more nefarious. If this woman was actually the source of the problem, then it was a professional job, and that created an entirely new set of issues.

Sighing, I pulled out my phone and called Jenna Franklin. I was good, but she was better. If something was up, she'd be the one to find it.

She answered on the third ring, sounding like I'd woken her out of a dead sleep. "Hello?"

"Hello to you too."

"Who is this?"

"It's Jude at Resting Warrior."

Some rustling on the other end of the line. "Fuck. What time is it?"

"About three in the afternoon." I tried to suppress my chuckle.

"Shut up," she said, but it didn't sound angry. "Had a couple all-nighters. They really took it out of me, and now I'm completely out of whack."

"I can call back later."

"No." She spoke through a yawn. "I'm up now, and I already should be anyway. What can I do for you?"

I gathered what I had so far on Allison's file and sent it to the encrypted email she usually used. "I'm doing some digging on a person and just wanted to double-check I'm not missing anything."

"Missing, huh? What kind of stuff are you looking for?"

"Anything which might make it seem like she's not legit. Or has a motive to hurt someone. Anything."

I heard the distinct sound of typing. "The owner of a

coffee shop? Doesn't exactly seem like a hardened criminal."

"I know."

Along the way, I wasn't sure when the theory of Lena being sabotaged popped into my head instead of it being some kind of accident, but the idea wouldn't leave me alone. Three years of perfect business and perfect baking, and suddenly two incidents within weeks that struck at the heart of her business? There was every chance I was being overly paranoid. But being overly paranoid had saved lives in the past, so I wasn't going to let the bone I was digging for go until I was one hundred percent sure there wasn't anything to it.

"You were thorough," Jenna said. "Are you really thinking there's something else to find?"

"Hoping, but not optimistic."

She made a noncommittal sound. "Okay, tell me why you suspect her of anything, and maybe I can look at something more targeted."

I gave a quick explanation of what had happened with Lena and how the timeline matched up suspiciously, to the massive benefit of this new store.

Jenna was smiling; I could hear it. "While I admit it looks funny, have you considered it could just be bad timing?"

"Yes. And for Lena's sake, I'm hoping it's not."

"It's sweet you're doing this for her," she said. "And I'll do a little more digging to make sure, but I don't see signs she's falsified anything or that there are more layers to dig through. If you think there's something wrong, I'd look in a different direction."

Frustration rose, sure and true. That was the thing. Something was *wrong*, but I couldn't pinpoint what. Where else was there to look when there were no signs anything had been tampered with, no bad ingredients, no equipment malfunction, and even Ben said the HVAC system looked as good as new.

So where could I look?

"Thanks, Jenna. If you find anything else, let me know."

"Will do."

The call ended, and I stared at the ceiling for long minutes, going over everything. Was I digging for nothing? Maybe it was just a fluke. A bad batch of flour we couldn't catch because it went sour in the oven or something.

I hated seeing Lena in pain. She was hiding it well, but Deja Brew being empty was hurting her. Now I knew how well she could hide things she didn't want people to see, and I knew what to look for. She was panicking, and I understood why. Right now, she was watching a thing she'd built start to crumble in front of her eyes, and she was trying to hold it together with both hands.

No matter if I was chasing wild geese, I wasn't going to stop until we knew for sure. Because it felt like something was wrong, and my instincts told me it didn't have anything to do with Lena's baking.

Chapter 21

Lena

My body ached. The last two days had been a whirlwind for both Evie and me, making a mountain of cupcakes for the dance. Not just cupcakes, but more than we needed. We tasted every portion of every batch of cupcakes from batter to baked, the fillings on the ones which were filled, and every batch of frosting we made.

They were officially delicious.

No bad bakes in sight here. Just pure, unadulterated sugar. I didn't envy the parents of the kids, but at the same time, I was happy to be able to give the kids something great to remember this dance by.

Principal Walker specifically asked the cupcakes be left unassembled so the kids could make their own, which we thought was an amazing idea.

Evie was sitting in Bessie's passenger seat, glaring at the stacks of cupcake boxes in the back seat, making sure none of them fell over. "They're fine."

"I am taking no chances." She didn't even take her eyes off the boxes as I pulled into the high school parking lot.

On the floor of the back seat were a couple huge bowls of frosting, another one in the trunk, along with the cupcake stands, and we'd brought so many decorations, I wasn't sure how any of the kids were going to choose.

I pulled up to the curb and got out. We weren't late, but I wanted to get these set up quickly so it was a surprise. The dance would start shortly, and it took longer than we expected to get all the moving pieces together.

"I'd know the sound of that engine anywhere," a voice called from the parking lot.

I popped the trunk as I looked up and found Ben standing in front of a car with an open hood. "You would know it," I said with a laugh. "She's been in your garage practically more than with me."

He shook his head. "Isn't that the truth." Leaning down, he reached into the car he was working on. "How's she running?"

"Fine, so far. Maybe you fixed her for good this time."

He adjusted something and dropped the hood. "As much as I'd like to agree, I very much doubt it. She's beautiful, but she needs to retire soon."

"Shh. She can hear you." I grabbed the cupcake stands and a bowl out of the back. "I didn't know you made house calls. Or…school calls."

"I don't. I'm not here as a mechanic. Just peeking under the hood while I have a second since she doesn't let me toy with her car."

I opened my mouth to ask who "she" was, when I heard a new voice. "Okay, Ben, I have the table set up. We can start bringing in the dispensers."

Evie was stock-still on the sidewalk, staring at Allison as she came out of the school, and I was staring too. What was she doing here? Tension wiggled in my gut, nerves that had been a million miles away suddenly alive and well.

"Oh hey, Lena." Allison smiled and waved. "Good to see you again."

"You too." My voice sounded like a robot. Get it together, Lena. "Let's go, Evie. Cupcakes won't set up themselves."

It shook her out of her startled state, and we walked in together. At the last second, I peeked back and saw Ben draw Allison into his arms and kiss her. Well, that explained why I'd seen him at the coffee shop when I stopped by.

"What the fuck?" Evie asked. "She better not be serving rival cupcakes."

"I doubt it. I didn't see cupcakes on her menu."

"Still," my friend scoffed. "What the fuck?"

I swallowed. "It's fine. Let's just do this."

The school gym was decorated exactly the way you might expect for a Christmas dance. Streamers and sparkling snowflakes hung from the ceiling. Balloons were everywhere, some already scattered on the floor, and there was a healthy dose of confetti. I didn't envy whoever had to clean it up.

"Oh, there you are!" Principal Walker waved us over to a long table covered in a snowy-looking tablecloth. "The secret of make-your-own cupcakes got out, and everyone's really excited."

"I'm glad." I smiled. The principal was a tall woman, even taller in the heels she was wearing. She looked like she'd be more at home in a city than in Garnet Bend, but she was incredibly kind, and I'd never heard anyone speak poorly of her—not even the students. "Hopefully they live up to the expectations."

"I'm sure they will. This looks fantastic." She was pointing to the bowl of metallic-silver frosting in my arms.

I set down one of the stands. "We thought they might like a little shine. Here is fine?"

"Yes, this half of the table is yours. The other half is going to be a hot chocolate bar. I assume you already know you have some competition in town?"

"I do." I had to be careful here. "I'm sure it's lovely."

Her phone rang in her hand, and she glanced down at the screen before back up at me. "I have to take this. Let me know if you need anything?"

"I will."

She walked away, already answering the person on the other end of the line. Evie had a box of the cupcakes open and was already lining them up on the multitiered stand. "A hot chocolate bar? We could have done that."

"It's okay," I said, though my stomach was sinking. "After Thanksgiving, she didn't have to order with me at all, and she did. She's doing us a favor already. I don't blame her for hedging her bets. Let's get everything inside."

We passed Ben and Allison on the way back to the car, the two of them rolling a cart with two giant kegs of what must have been hot chocolate. "I won't lie." I grabbed the other bowls of frosting and decorations. "When I was in high school, I would have loved a hot chocolate bar."

"Me too." Evie's voice was grudging. "Still don't like that she's doing it, though."

I smiled. My friend was loyal through and through. "I appreciate it. But let's give her a chance. She's only been nice to me so far, and there's no real reason to dislike her for opening a business."

She sighed dramatically. "Ugh. Fine. For you."

Between the two of us, we were able to carry in all the

rest of the supplies in one go and start truly setting up our half of the table while Allison and Ben worked on their half.

I had to admit, between the two, it was an impressive display. And ours was done first since the hot chocolate bar had what looked like a complicated refill system. "Looks like you might have to stay here," I joked.

Allison smiled and snuck a glance at Ben, who had ducked beneath the table. "Maybe. But there are worse ways to spend a night."

"Going to relive days beneath the bleachers?"

"Maybe." She winked, and we both pretended nothing was said as Ben reappeared.

Evie arranged the last of the bowls of sprinkles. We had everything from rainbow to chocolate to the little crystal sparkles, which fit with the theme perfectly. "I think that's it."

Allison stepped up and looked too. "I think it's great. The kids are going to love it."

"Thanks." Between the sparkles, blue and silver colors, and the mountains of cupcakes that looked like Christmas trees, I hoped it would be everything they wanted. "Good luck with the refill system."

She sighed. "Yeah. I might have gotten in over my head with this one. But it should be all right."

There was an awkward moment where neither of us really knew what to say. Thankfully, Evie saved me. "Come on, girl. Lucas is begging me to come home."

"Sounds good." I waved to Allison and Ben, though he couldn't see me since his head was back under the table. "Have a good night, guys."

"You too."

"Hold on a second," Ben called, ducking out from under the table. "I think this got dropped. Rolled under the table. Where should it go?" He held out a container of silver decorating powder we'd brought to let the kids dust the cupcakes if they wanted. Sure enough, the little pyramid of decoration containers looked like it had been bumped.

"Sorry," he said. "It was probably me moving around back there."

"No worries." I laughed. "No harm done."

Allison touched me on the arm. "Do you think there's enough stuff for the two of us to make a cupcake before the kids get here?"

"There's plenty. Come to think of it, I should make one and bring it to Jude. You want one, Evie? For Lucas?"

"Sure."

I made short work of two cupcakes, keeping Jude's simple. He liked chocolate, and a lot of it—he didn't need the frills and decorations. Me, on the other hand, I loved every bit of the decorating. I put sprinkles and sparkles and even dusted some of the silver *and* shimmering blue on top.

"Let me have that." Evie took the silver dust from me, shaking it over her cupcake. Lucas's looked more like Jude's.

Allison and Ben chose sprinkles, and the frosting was a mess, but she was grinning. "It makes me glad I only sell things which come prepackaged. Honestly, Lena, I don't think I could make anything as pretty as that."

"That's nice of you to say."

She looked behind me. "I think things might be starting up. I'm going to stash these for when we're dealing with teenagers and can't take it anymore."

I waved and grabbed my two cupcakes before joining Evie. We pushed out into the chilly early evening. "Is Lucas actually begging you to get home?"

"No." She snorted. "But I wasn't about to get stuck in

an awkward circle for half an hour while we all paddled around one another. Cupcakes aside."

"I appreciate it. And," I added, "Jude isn't begging for me to get home, but he did pick up Chinese takeout, and I'm dying to eat so much of it I'm no longer able to move."

"Sounds like an evening I can get behind."

I dropped Evie off at her car and headed straight back to my house. Even with Allison's appearance, I was feeling great. She was nice, and there wasn't any reason for me to feel threatened or even that my toes were being stepped on. The combination of cupcakes and hot chocolate was sure to be a big hit.

"Hello?" I was careful with the cupcakes as I opened the door, making sure not to smush any of the frosting. "I'm here."

God, I could already smell the Chinese, and my mouth was watering.

"Welcome home." Jude was there, stepping close to help me with my coat before kissing me while I juggled both cupcakes in one hand.

"I like the sound of that. And I brought you sugar."

He smiled against my lips. "I'm going to need to up my gym time if you keep bringing me extra baked goods."

"I've seen every inch of your body now, sir, and I don't think a cupcake is going to make a dent in your fine ass."

Jude raised an eyebrow, but he took a bite of his cupcake when I held it out for him. "Mmm. See? Nothing wrong with your baking. Before dinner?"

I licked some of the frosting off mine, savoring the melting chocolate and the tart, semi-sweet bitterness of the decorations. That was the key to baked goods not everyone realized. Sweetness was the real killer. Too much, and you couldn't enjoy it. There had to be balance, and *this* was a cupcake. I was back, baby.

That cupcake was a goner. I devoured the rest of it.

Walking into the kitchen, I brushed the crumbs off my fingers. The food was all set out on the counter, still in the takeout containers.

"I didn't dish it up yet since I wasn't sure when you were coming back."

"That's perfect. Because I was thinking..."

Jude smirked as I crossed to him, wrapping my arms around his waist and looking up at him. "You were thinking?"

"Maybe we could eat a little later. Because once I do, I plan on eating so much of it, I'll be nothing more than a ball afterward. And I think I'd like something else before I turn into a pumpkin."

I saw a twinkle in his eye I'd missed before. "I thought you might say that."

I narrowed my eyes. "No, you didn't. You couldn't have."

He reached behind him, and I heard the clink of metal a second before he moved, spinning me and pinning my back to his chest while he took my hands. They were caught by one of his big ones easily, the movement of clasping the handcuffs around my wrists more natural than breathing to him.

It shouldn't have been nearly as hot as it was.

"It's funny." His breath warmed my cheek as he leaned around to kiss me there. "If I didn't know, then how come I had these ready?"

"I don't know." It was hard to get air in my lungs. Warmth spread through me, my heart pounding in my ears and between my legs. I was a living pulse the second this man touched me. "Maybe you were just hopeful."

"Or maybe..." I felt him smile. "Maybe I knew you'd be feeling a little victorious and want to play first."

"You're wrong." It was a lie. He was right on the fucking money.

Jude drew his lips across my neck, and I gave up any pretense of not wanting this. My hands were off-limits now, and though I still struggled with the fact that I enjoyed it, I wasn't about to let my brain ruin this. Teeth met my skin, a gentle bite where my neck joined my shoulder, drawing a moan from me.

"Do you like being at my mercy, Lena?" The words were low and soft. In another context, they could be deadly, and that was the beautiful heart of it. To surrender to someone who had every bit of power to hurt you, but they never would.

"Yes."

"I could bend you over the sofa and take you here." He wove his hand into my hair, pulling my head back so more of my neck was exposed, and I was pretty sure I was going to pass out from arousal before we got anywhere.

"As much as I like the idea, I'm not cleaning up the velvet."

He laughed, spinning me and bending to toss me over his shoulder, careful to situate me gently because of the handcuffs.

"Jude!" My voice was nothing but a shriek that turned into a moan as he swatted my ass. But he didn't stop, carrying me up the stairs to my room—though I thought of it as more of our room now. We were here more often than not.

He placed me on the bed and smiled. Playful, but completely in control. Breathing into it, I felt myself relax. The more we did this, the more comfortable it became—the more I started to value not having to think, knowing we would both have pleasure in the end.

I didn't have to worry where to move or whether Jude

liked anything I did, because he was in charge. If he didn't like something, he changed it. And there was not a second in which Jude took control when I felt anything less than whole and cherished. He never made me feel small or let me second-guess myself.

My breath left me, thinking about the three words I'd dreamed about for more than three years, but it was so soon, and I wasn't sure I was ready. But god, I was definitely falling in love with him. Truly and completely.

"What are you thinking about?" he asked softly. In those moments, he'd been studying my face. Jude knew how to read me so well; who knew what he might have seen?

But there was another thought too—a curiosity we hadn't yet tried, and the adrenaline rush of victory and the sugar rush of the cupcake made me brave enough to ask. "By now, I'm sure you've seen enough to know I read a lot of books."

He leaned forward, placing a hand on either side of me on the bed, caging me in. "Mm-hmm."

It was hard to think when he was so close and looking at me like that. "Some of them had…what we do. And I never thought I'd like it, but I do, and—"

"You can say it, sweetheart. Don't be nervous."

I took a shaky breath. I *was* nervous. "I just wanted to try something, and it's easier to show you."

Jude looked curious, but he didn't say anything or move as I scooted myself to the side of the bed, wiggled off…

Then dropped onto my knees in front of him.

His eyebrows rose into his hairline, but he didn't look upset. No, he looked *hungry*. Looking up at Jude from down here was like looking up at a skyscraper. He went on forever, and every inch of him was mine.

Jude reached for me like it was an instinct, hand

cradling my face and tucking his fingers under my chin to make sure I was looking straight at him. "What are you doing down there?"

My whole body flushed pink. His attention, the way he looked down at me, even his hand on my face while I was down here on my knees, hands locked behind my back…

The rightness of it made me shake. It felt like my whole body was glowing under Jude's sun and I was a flower blooming solely for him.

"I see." He brushed my bottom lip with his thumb slowly, sensually.

"I don't understand it."

"Do you need to?"

I swallowed and leaned into his hand. "I don't know."

Jude looked at me for long moments. "Stay there, and don't move."

He went downstairs and was back in less than two minutes with a bag in his hands. "Close your eyes. I brought something, but I wasn't planning on it tonight. It'll only take a couple minutes. Are you comfortable?"

"Yes."

I closed my eyes, listening to the vague sound of shuffling and plastic being unwrapped. Not a condom, though, something else. The bed moved a little, and there was a clinking and rustling, but whatever he'd just done, I had no idea.

"You can open your eyes."

He was in the middle of pulling off his shirt when I did, drawing my attention to all of him. Watching Jude was like watching a masterpiece being unveiled piece by piece. He even put on a condom while I watched, still kneeling.

Fully naked now, he helped me up, making sure I was steady. He unlocked one of my hands and not the other before peeling layers off me. My shirt, bra, and jeans all hit the floor, and with every movement, he touched me. Brushing across my skin, making me jump. "You're still nervous?"

"I don't know."

"Don't be. Hands?" Jude locked them in front of me this time, pushing my underwear off my hips and lifting me out of them. He laid me in the middle of the bed, and I had a wash of déjà vu from when we first did this, my hands above my head. We'd used handcuffs before, but not quite like this.

There was a soft *click*, and suddenly I couldn't move my hands from where they were stretched above me. My eyes went wide. "What?"

"You don't have an easy place to attach my favorite accessory," Jude said with a grin. "So, I bought one. It's a set of straps that go under the mattress. I can put you anywhere I like."

I shuddered, relaxing into the feeling. This, I liked. The last time he'd told me to keep my hands above my head, it was all I could think about, trying not to move them. If I didn't have to think about it, I could focus on nothing but him.

Jude placed a kiss directly in the center of my chest, easing himself between my hips and entering me slowly. So slowly, it was deliciously agonizing, until he was settled deep inside, pinning me down with his body. He brushed the hair off my face. "Let's talk."

"Now?" I blinked at him, not fully coherent when I was surrounded and impaled by him.

"Now. When I can keep you right here, see your face, and feel your reactions." He moved his hips and kissed me slowly, melting any tension I had left. I curled my legs around his hips, savoring the feeling of being tangled with him. If I didn't know how much pleasure could come after this, I would happily stay here forever, wrapped up in everything that was Jude.

"You're happy?" he asked. "With how this is going?"

"Yes," I breathed, startled. "Of course. Are you not—"

He covered my mouth with his, silencing me and my spike of panic. "Sweetheart, I am beyond happy. I meant here, in the bedroom, under my control."

Biting my lip, I nodded. I'd never thought I could be happy as I was now. This man had me in *handcuffs*, tied to my bed to have his way with me, and I felt like I was bathing in perfumed sunlight. "More than I ever thought I could be."

Jude rocked his hips again, the movement grinding against my clit and shooting sparks of pleasure up behind my eyes. "I hope you know I'm not the kind of man who needs you on your knees to be happy." His face was serious.

"I know."

He slipped one hand under my head, and then the other, so I was cradled by him. "Do you want that because you think it would make me happy? Or do you want it for you?"

My body reacted before I could speak, everything in me tightening and squeezing down on him. "I—" I swallowed, my mouth suddenly dry. "I wanted to try it. Never thought it would feel like that."

"Anything you want to try, I'll try it with you," he said. "This isn't a one-way street. Just because I want to be in control here, and you like it, doesn't mean you have no say." The kiss he placed under my jaw had goose bumps running across my skin. "That being said, you look fucking beautiful on your knees."

"Oh?" The sound was more a moan than anything else.

"And I'll happily have you kneel for me if you want to be there. The *fantasies* I have about your mouth…"

My hips arched against his, the images flooding my mind instantly making me so much more desperate for him to move and fuck me. "Please, Jude."

He grinned like he didn't know exactly what he was doing to me. "It could be fun."

I didn't know what he meant. All I knew was I was using my legs to try to make him move, and it was about as effective as kicking a mountain.

Jude moved, lifting himself off me just to drive home again. Stars exploded behind my eyes, and I nearly came. Everything inside me was so aroused and alert, I knew I wasn't going to last.

Hooking his hands under my knees, he lifted them, pressing my legs until I was bent nearly in half, stretched for him. I felt even more vulnerable, and my mind switched to the blissfully blank place where it was only the two of us and our pleasure.

Easing out and in, Jude groaned, his grip on my legs telling me he was holding himself back too. "Ask me again."

"Please." It was automatic. I would do whatever he wanted now. I was putty in his hands. He rolled his hips, and they didn't stop moving. Pleasure was already building in my core, and I sank into it.

His arms came down around me, bracing him as he fucked me harder. Words whispered in my ear. "Good girls beg for what they want. As long as you don't stop begging, I won't stop fucking you, but I need to hear your pretty voice."

"Please." He stopped mid-stroke. The man had the self-control of a warrior, and I searched for my words, trying to find what I needed. "Don't stop. Please don't stop." I put the words on a loop in my mind.

I didn't stop, and neither did he. I begged Jude to take me until my voice ran into nothing but a single, moaning sound. The world went white, and I shattered. Pleasure raked through me like lightning, twisting through me and making me dizzy.

"Did I say you could stop?" he teased. "I don't think you've quite earned your Chinese."

There was no way I was coherent, but I let Jude hear me until he kissed me quiet and we both went over the edge together.

Chapter 22

Jude

Lena was fast asleep when my cell rang. It was late, but not so late a call meant an emergency. I'd worn Lena out with sex and then Chinese food, and the way she was curled around her pillow like it was the only thing in the world was adorable.

I silenced the ring and eased out of bed, moving downstairs to take the call. But the name on the phone stopped me in my tracks. "Ellen?"

"Jude, hi." She sounded shaky. "I'm sorry to be calling so late. I've been making calls all day, and I literally just realized what time it is. I'm sorry, I'll call back later."

"No, it's okay. Are you okay?"

Ellen Ackerman was someone I hadn't seen in a long time. Not since her husband's funeral, when she was so distraught I didn't know if she even remembered my being there.

"I'm fine," she said and sighed. "Well, I'm okay. You know how it is."

"I do."

"But…it's the five-year anniversary of Isaac's death soon. I'm having a little memorial. I mean, not like another funeral. More of a get-together just to remember him and for people who loved him to reconnect. That kind of thing."

The fact that she thought of me was both touching and brought my guilt freshly to the surface. While I was helping Lena with the bakery, and getting lost in her, Isaac hadn't been in the forefront of my thoughts for the last few days. I usually thought about him every day.

I wasn't sure if it was a good thing or a bad one.

"Idaho Falls?"

"Yeah. Next week. I'll email you the address if you can make it. I didn't book the same place as the funeral. It felt a little macabre."

I laughed but didn't quite feel it. "Send me the details. I'd like to make it if I can."

"Thank you. I know it's pretty last minute, so I understand if you can't, but it would be good to see you. See everyone who can make it. I spoke to Noah, and he told me he couldn't." Given that he and Kate were barely recovered from their ordeal, it made sense. "How are you doing?"

"Right now, I'm good." I was glad to be able to say it truthfully. "Better than I've been in a long time. But it comes and goes. You know how that is."

"Yeah. I do."

"I think about him a lot, you know. All the time."

Ellen laughed once. "I'm not sure he'd want you to. But I'm glad you do. As long as it's not holding you back."

That, I couldn't respond to. Not now, at least. "I'll look

at my schedule if you send me the details. I'd love to make it. I just have to make sure I'm clear first."

"Of course. Same email?"

I chuckled. "Same one."

"I'll send it right over. Sorry again for calling so late."

"Not a problem. I'll be in touch."

"Goodnight, Jude."

I ended the call and blew out a breath. Five years was a long time. Of course I wanted to go, but I wondered if going would send me spiraling backward. Or maybe it would provide me with the closure I was lacking.

Lena stirred when I reached the bedroom, rolling over to face me when I lay back down. "Everything okay?"

God, I was addicted to the sound of her voice. Sleepy, with a hint of rasp from screaming my name, her voice made the sexiest sounds in the world. "I don't know. I think so."

She blinked her eyes open and cuddled a bit closer. "Do you need to talk about it?"

One deep breath in, and one deep breath out. My natural instinct was to bury it. But with Lena, I couldn't do that. As hard as it was, I wanted to hide nothing. "I told you about Isaac. My teammate who killed himself."

"Yeah."

"That was his widow, Ellen."

Lena's eyebrows rose. "Is she okay?"

"As well as she can be, I think. It's the five-year anniversary, and she's inviting people to go for a kind of memorial."

"That could be nice."

"Maybe," I admit. "But I'm just unsure about it."

Lena rolled toward me, fitting her back to my chest with an ease that made me ache. We fit together perfectly, and I was getting to the point where I couldn't hold it in anymore.

She was sleepy but still paying attention. "Why unsure?"

"Don't know if it will make the nightmares worse."

"You should ask Dr. Rayne. See what she thinks."

I wrapped an arm around her waist. "Not a bad idea. But I also don't want to leave you, in case anything happens."

She made a little sound. "I'll be okay. Those cupcakes were great, things are open, and you being gone for a day won't change anything. So if you think it will help, then you should go."

"I'll think about it."

"Good."

Would it help? That was the question. But Lena saying I should go eased a little worry I had. I still didn't think things at Deja Brew were an accident, but she was right too. My being gone for a day or two wouldn't make much difference. Especially if I could ask Daniel to keep an eye out.

Regardless, I didn't have to think about it now. Now, all I wanted to do was hold Lena and sleep.

The sound tore me from sleep, and I sat straight up, looking for the source. The attacker. It took long seconds to realize I wasn't dreaming. This wasn't a nightmare. I was perfectly clear and in Lena's bedroom.

The sound was coming from her. She was curled in on herself, nearly fetal, moaning. Was she having a nightmare?

I knelt on the bed, turning her over. "Lena? Wake up for me, sweetheart."

Another keening sound came out of her, and her eyes flew open. She lunged, pushing past me and off the bed, running for the bathroom. "Lena?"

The porcelain clank of the toilet seat echoed, followed by the sound of vomiting. Holy shit.

I counted the days in my head. We hadn't been together long enough for Lena to be pregnant. It wouldn't be a problem if she was, but we'd been careful, and I didn't think this was it. I followed her into the bathroom where she'd collapsed, head over the toilet. She made a sound of regret. "Ugh. It's okay. You don't need to see this."

"Sweetheart, I've seen worse things in my day than some puking."

As if my words conjured more, she heaved into the toilet again. I grabbed a washcloth and soaked it with cool water before lifting her hair off her neck and placing it there. Then I turned on the shower. "Maybe it was the orange chicken," I said quietly, keeping my voice soothing. "You ate all of it before I had a chance to."

"Maybe." She sounded miserable. I flushed the toilet before lifting her off the floor. "No, Jude, I don't think I can move. It's not done. I can tell."

"I'm not taking you back to bed. I'm just moving you into the shower. It may sound strange, but it will help."

"Okay."

She didn't fight me as I stripped her out of my shirt she was wearing and her underwear. The water in the shower wasn't hot or cold; it was perfectly in the middle. I nudged the temperature a little toward the warm side. Lena moaned. "I don't want to throw up in the shower."

"It's all going to the same drain, baby." I lifted her under the spray with me. "Don't worry, I've got you."

I did have her, and I would always have her.

It occurred to me these were the moments wedding

vows referred to. Sickness and health. My nightmares and hers, whatever this was. I didn't need a vow to know I would happily do this for her forever.

The clock read a little after three, and we stayed there on the floor of the shower until well past five, when Lena finally collapsed against me after another round of heaving. "I think that's it," she said. "I can't explain it. It just feels like whatever it was is gone."

"Okay. Stay here in the water for a second, okay?" I stepped out and grabbed a towel before I brought her out and dried her. Normally, Lena would joke with me or laugh and push me away if I tried to do things like this. Right now, she was barely moving.

I dried her as best I could before putting her back into bed, not bothering to dress her just in case she needed to get back in the shower fast. "I'm going to get you some water, and I'm going to call Evelyn and tell her you're not coming in."

Lena simply nodded. It was a testament to how badly she felt that she wasn't trying to force herself to go in. Her skin was nearly as pale as her sheets. I took her phone from the nightstand and found Evelyn's number while I filled a glass of water.

But it wasn't the voice I was expecting that answered. It was Lucas. "Lena?"

"It's Jude, actually."

"Oh." He chuckled once. "What's up?"

My instincts began to tingle. "I was calling to let Evelyn know Lena can't come in to the shop today. She's sick. Been throwing up for a few hours and didn't even fight me when I said she couldn't go."

Lucas swore under his breath. "Yeah. Sounds familiar."

I froze. "What?"

"Evelyn's had her head in the toilet going on four hours now. I was going to tell Lena the same thing."

"Fuck." I rubbed a hand over my face. "We had Chinese takeout last night, so I assumed it was that. But if Evelyn has it too, it has to be something they both ate."

There was a long silence before Lucas spoke again. "I hope you know I'm the last person who wants to point this out, and it's the last thing I want to say…" I already knew what was coming. "But you know where they came from last night."

"The school." Where they dropped off cupcakes for everyone and even brought some home. "But Lena brought a cupcake home for me, and I ate it. I'm not sick."

Lucas sighed. "Maybe it was something at the bakery, then. But given what happened at Thanksgiving…"

At this moment, I was glad Lena was upstairs and couldn't hear me. "I'm not crazy, right? This stuff with her seems targeted and intentional?"

"It does. But I don't have a clue why anyone would target Lena. I think she's the only person in the town who's universally liked. Or she was, before all this started."

"That's a motive in itself," I grumbled.

Lena's phone buzzed in my hand, and I glanced at it. "Fuck." It was a number I knew too well from our time living here. We all had it memorized in case of an emergency. "Lucas, I have to go."

"Keep me posted. And when I'm out grabbing some sick supplies, I'll drop some by if you want."

"That would be great, thanks."

I ended the call and took a deep breath before answering the next one from the sheriff. "Hello, Charlie."

"Who is this?"

"Jude Williams."

He grunted. "I guess that makes sense. About time, too. But I called for Lena."

"Unfortunately, she's sick at the moment, but I can take the message."

"Throwing up?"

I closed my eyes. This was bad. Dread curled along my spine, along with my every instinct screaming a storm was coming I wouldn't be able to protect her from. "Yes. For several hours."

"Well, I'm sorry about that. But we have a situation. I've got sick kids. A *lot* of sick kids. Some are like Lena, just throwing up, and some are in the hospital now. I heard about what's already happened with her, and I'm going to need to talk to her."

I shook my head even though he couldn't see me. "She didn't do this, Charlie."

"I don't want to think so, but right now, the common factor is the cupcakes at the dance. And with this many people sick, the parents want heads to roll."

"Can you come here to talk to her? I don't want to take her through town, you know how people can get. And all things aside, I'm not entirely sure she can stand up right now."

"This evening," he said. "Around dinnertime? I need more time to talk to everyone."

"That's fine. It'll give her some time to recover, too."

"See you then."

I took the water to Lena and left it on the bedside table. She was fast asleep again, and I wasn't going to wake her up to tell her this. If I had to be the one to tell her something bad had happened, *again*, I wanted her to feel a little better first.

It was a good decision. Her phone was buzzing constantly. Voice mails from the school principal and plenty of parents. I deleted most of them—Lena didn't need to hear the kind of hate people were hurling at her. I understood it. These were parents afraid for their kids, and that kind of love made you lash out. But she would suffer enough without their words.

It was midafternoon before I heard any movement. I had a knot in my gut the size of a baseball as I went upstairs to find Lena finally awake and sitting up. She had a little color back, but she still looked sick. Her phone was in the pocket of my sweatpants, and I could still feel it vibrating against my leg.

I sat down on the edge of the bed. "How do you feel?"

"Better. I don't think I'm going to hurl up my guts again, so that's good. But I'm shaky."

Lucas had dropped off some electrolyte drinks. I would get one of those for her now in case her stomach wasn't able to handle real food yet. "Good."

She turned a cute shade of pink. "Thank you for what you did. It can't have been fun."

"The last thing I was thinking about was whether it was fun."

"Still."

I took her hand and wove our fingers together. "I just want you to feel better." Although I knew the conversation we were about to have was going to tear her apart.

"I do. Hopefully I'll be back on my feet tomorrow. Have you seen my phone? I'd like to check on Evie."

Squeezing her hand, I nodded. "I have seen it. But I have to tell you something first."

Her face fell, and I saw fear enter her eyes. Every part of me *hated* that look on her face. I wanted to pin her to the bed and tell her she was safe and love her until she knew she didn't have to be afraid of anything. But I also had to tell her the truth.

"When I called Evie, Lucas answered. She's sick too."

"What?" She blinked, and I saw her go through the same thought process I had about the takeout. "No. Please don't say it." Her eyes filled with tears. "Please."

I pulled her to me and into my lap, holding her tightly against me. "I got a call from Charlie. There are a lot of sick kids right now. Some the same as you, some worse." Her sob broke through my words, and fuck if my eyes didn't start to water at the sound. "He needs to talk to you, and he'll be here in a few hours."

"Are they going to be okay?"

"I think so. A few are in the hospital, but it didn't sound life-threatening."

She sagged in my arms, giving in to the tears she couldn't hold back anymore. "I hurt kids." The small words were broken. "I poisoned them."

"No, you didn't."

"What else is there?" She pulled away from me, crawling back to the center of the bed. She wasn't strong enough to do anything but lie there, but her shoulders shook. "No one will ever come back to Deja Brew. My reputation is gone, and now I poisoned children. What am I going to do?"

I wiped the mist from my eyes. She sounded devastated, and I wanted to cry for her. But this was exactly the kind of situation where my control reached beyond sex. Lena needed someone to give her a safe place in this storm, and that was me.

Lying down beside her, I tugged her against my chest. "You didn't do this, Lena."

She tucked her face down into the pillow away from me, and I couldn't have that. I needed her to know she wasn't alone in this. "Look at me, sweetheart." Lena shook her head. "It wasn't a suggestion." The words were gentle, but they held the command she needed.

Slowly, she turned over, but she didn't meet my eyes. Better than nothing. "I don't believe for one second this was your fault. I ate the cupcake you brought me, and I'm not sick. Not *all* the kids are sick, so there could be another explanation. And I'm still not convinced this isn't targeted harassment."

She still didn't look at me, and it was clear she didn't believe me. Gently, I slid my hand up her spine until it was buried in her hair, guiding her face to look at mine. Immediately, she closed her eyes.

I tightened my fingers a fraction. "Look at me."

When she did, I recognized what I saw there. Desolation. It was the same look I'd had when I came back from those caves. Nothing was right and nothing was the same, and everything I'd thought I'd had was gone. This was Lena losing everything.

"I know you," I said. "I see you. You would never hurt anyone on purpose. Especially children, Lena. You *did not* do this."

The tears welled up again, and she let them spill over silently.

"We're going to talk to Charlie and figure it out. I'm going to figure out who's done this, and we're going to fix it. But no matter what, I've got you, okay?" I pulled her to my chest and kept her there. "You can let go, I've got you."

She did let go; sobs wrenched from her body out of a place so deep it made me ache. Her fingers dug into my shirt, clinging to me, the only anchor she had, and I didn't let her go—not even for a fucking second—while she cried.

Chapter 23

Jude

I left Lena to get dressed when I heard Charlie pull up outside and went out to meet him. He was a good man, but he took his job seriously, and right now, his face was grave.

He sighed as he approached. "You know I wish I didn't have to be here."

"I know."

"I won't lie, though. This is serious. I've had parents at the police station, screaming about pressing charges. After the pies, and I heard something about some cookies? It's starting to look intentional."

Crossing my arms, I stared at him. "Or someone has been very careful to make it look that way."

Charlie held up his hands. "I know Lena, and I can't imagine her doing this, but I still have to do my job and follow wherever this leads. Unfortunately, it leads straight to her right now."

"Yeah." I gestured to the stairs. "She's changing, and she'll be down in a second."

In the living room, Charlie sat in the armchair facing the couch, and he looked so out of place I could have laughed if this wasn't so serious. The police uniform and Lena's decor didn't mix.

"Hi, Charlie." Lena appeared at the bend in the stairs, and I took her hand as she came down and led her to the couch. She needed to answer the questions, but I was going to hold her while she did it. Even without words, I wanted her to know I was with her one hundred percent.

"Lena." The police chief leaned forward on his knees. "I'm sorry about this."

"Probably not as much as I am," she said as she settled on the couch and let me pull her back against me with an arm around her waist.

It made him smile. He pulled out a small notebook and a pen. "Probably not, no. But I do need to ask you questions, and I want to say up front that I know you, and despite that, I have to ask everything. It's not meant to be offensive."

"I understand."

He asked her to walk him through the process of making and delivering the cupcakes, which she did. Everything from how she and Evie tested each ingredient, to dropping them off and setting them up next to the hot chocolate display.

That perked my interest. "Allison was there?"

Lena nodded. "They hired her for it. Evie was bummed we hadn't been asked to do both, but I thought it was a good mix. She was nice. Made cupcakes with us before we left. She was with Ben, and he made a cupcake too."

"The mechanic?" Charlie asked. "Did you see them eat those cupcakes?"

Lena shook her head. "Yes, the mechanic. They're dating now, from what I gather. And no, I didn't watch them eat them. Allison said she was going to stash them for later in the evening. Their display had to be monitored."

The story then brought us to her own sickness.

"Honestly," Charlie said, "the fact that you were sick, *and* Evelyn was sick, is a point in your favor. It doesn't seem likely you'd poison yourself on purpose."

There were plenty of psychopaths who would do just that in order to throw someone like Charlie off the trail, but I kept the thought to myself.

"However, three of the kids are still in the hospital, and they're no closer to finding out what it is. No conclusive tests yet."

Lena shuddered. "I'm sorry."

"Was it for insurance money? After the business with the Pearson farm, it wouldn't surprise me."

"No. Of course not." Her spine straightened against me. "I would never do this, and I would never hurt children on purpose." The waver in her voice told me she was close to breaking again, and I tightened my hold on her.

Charlie fixed on me. "You ate one too?"

"I did. But no sickness here. And there are kids who didn't get sick either, right?"

He nodded. "Right. But the only common denominator is the cupcakes and the hot chocolate. I'll be speaking to the owner over there too. But given the incidents at Thanksgiving…"

"I know it looks bad," Lena whispered. "I know."

The man stood, closing his notepad and putting it away. "I don't have anything to arrest you on, but I need to ask you not to go anywhere. I've put off the parents pressing charges since we don't have proof, but it's the best I can do."

Lena wasn't even breathing, but she nodded. "I understand."

"I also can't allow you to open Deja Brew. I'll need full access to it so we can sweep for evidence. You haven't been there since you left?"

"She hasn't," I answered. "She's been with me the entire time."

She stood, pulling away from my hold. "I'll get you an extra key to the front door."

"Appreciated."

I stood too. "I looked into Allison DeVries, and I didn't find anything. But I'm going to look again, and I might take a look through the town's security footage if Jerry will let me."

"Let me know if you find anything." He looked toward the kitchen where Lena had gone. "But I don't need to tell you this is bad, right?"

It was. Even if we could fully and completely prove Lena's innocence, her business was likely finished. That kind of broken trust didn't just heal, even with proof. "You don't have to tell me, no."

"Here you go." Lena handed Charlie a small silver key. She looked…tiny. The weight of the world was on her shoulders, and there was nothing I could do to lift it.

"Thanks, Lena. I'll be in touch soon."

I walked him out and watched him drive away. My phone buzzed in my pocket, and I answered without even looking. "Hello?"

"Hey," Daniel said. "I've heard. Through the grapevine. You guys okay?"

"Lena is very much not okay. I'm going to be MIA for

a few days to stay with her. Until we figure out what the hell is going on."

"Understood. Tell me if you need anything. We all know Lena would never do this, and whatever we can do to clear her name? We'll do it."

"Thanks, Daniel."

Lena was on the couch when I came back inside. "I guess that went about as well as it could have, huh?"

"I'm glad it didn't end with you in handcuffs that aren't mine."

That, at least, drew a tiny smile from her. But it was gone as quickly as it came, replaced by the despondent blankness which had been on her face since she'd stopped crying.

"We're going to figure it out," I said, sitting down and pulling her to me again. I couldn't stop touching her, and I was glad she didn't seem to mind. If anything, she melted into me, accepting my hold. "I promise."

Lena sighed. "Yeah. But we both know it's already too late."

She meant for her business and reputation. I didn't fully agree, but I wasn't going to argue. Not when she felt like this. I just tucked her in closer to my side and kissed her hair. Together, we would get through this. And when I found out who was targeting her, there would be hell to pay.

Chapter 24

Lena

Jude and I spent an entire day in my house doing nothing but watching movies, avoiding calls, and pretending the rest of the world didn't exist. He made love to me slowly. No handcuffs or begging. Just him taking control and loving me in the way only he could do.

I wished I could say it all made me feel better, but I felt like I was walking around with a hole blasted in my chest. This morning, he woke me, saying he had some quick things to do at the ranch he wasn't able to avoid, and he'd be back later.

But I couldn't just stay in my house. Charlie had given me the all clear on Deja Brew. Not to open, but at least to go inside. I guess the crime scene team had scoured every inch of the place and taken everything they needed. And I just...needed to see it.

Not like it would make it better. I would need a time machine to do that. Every time I thought about it, I felt like I was going to be sick again. Who knew? Maybe I'd carry this feeling with me for eternity.

I texted Jude before I left so he wouldn't go back to my house and panic when I wasn't there, but I needed to do this. He'd been amazing and perfect, but I wanted to see this on my own.

I noticed the writing before I even got out and had to sit for a minute to gather myself. The graffiti hit me in the chest. Red and black paint covering nearly the whole window and door. *POISON.* A skull and crossbones.

Tears pricked at my eyes, but I clenched my teeth and held them back. I'd cried enough, and it wasn't like the statement wasn't true. Things I'd made for joy had put people in the hospital. Only one kid was still there now, and hopefully they would figure out what it was, but just because I'd gotten lucky enough not to kill someone didn't mean shit.

I locked the door behind me. Even if I were permitted to open right now, no one would come. That ship had long since sailed.

Aside from the front being extra dark due to the graffiti blocking all the natural light, everything was as I'd left it. Mostly. Things were moved and put back slightly off from being searched by the police and tested by the crime scene unit. Watching crime scene technicians on TV was a lot more fun than being the one having your home ripped apart and put back together.

Deja Brew wasn't my house, but it was definitely part of my home.

Familiar frustration bubbled up, and I let out a scream of rage in the kitchen and kicked one of the stools over.

Evie and I had checked *everything*. It all tasted fine. It was great. But apparently not. Something we'd both eaten was bad, and I'd paid for it in more than just a night of throwing up.

Every hour that passed brought me closer to believing Jude was right and this was intentional. There was no way this could have happened three times in a row. Not after I'd cleaned everything and ordered new supplies. I'd been baking for a long fucking time, and while I wasn't perfect, I hadn't poisoned anyone before.

I wasn't sure if it made the most sense, but believing someone else was to blame at least brought some relief.

As nice as she'd been, the only person who would have an obvious motive to do this was Allison, the owner of the new coffee shop. Maybe Jude was right, and the timing of the business was too convenient to be ignored. She seemed sweet, but I was willing to bet if I went across town right now, business would be booming.

What I needed was proof and peace of mind. If she was targeting me, there had to be proof somewhere, right? If I watched her, maybe I'd see something that could help me. It wasn't like I had anything better to do, and I'd been around the Resting Warrior guys enough that I knew following someone was a decent way to get information.

My phone rang with the specific tone I'd picked out for Jude. There were really no other calls I wanted to answer right now, so I ignored every other tone but his. "Hey."

"Hey," he said gently. "I got your text."

"I just needed to…do something. Came over to look around."

"You doing okay?"

I grabbed my keys from where I'd tossed them on the counter. "I'm not sure anything can make this okay."

"Are you coming home?"

"No," I hedged. "I thought I'd just…stay here a while and wallow in misery."

Jude was silent for a beat. "All right, we both know that's not the truth, so why don't you try again?"

I made a face he obviously couldn't see. He knew me too well, and it had its drawbacks for things like this, even if it made everything else amazing. "I'm going to follow Allison DeVries. I think you're right. She's the only one who has a reason to have done this, and I need to do something."

"You're at the bakery?" I heard the sound of him moving around.

"Yeah."

"Wait for me there. I'm on my way."

Already walking for the door, I didn't want to. "Jude, I—"

"Wait for me, Lena." His voice was steeped in the command I couldn't say no to, and the line went dead. I nearly growled in frustration. If I were a better liar, I'd probably be getting in Bessie and starting to drive right now. But if I didn't wait, Jude would worry. At this moment, I didn't care about following his order, but I also didn't want to make him panic.

Soon enough, I heard the sound of his truck pull up to the curb and turn off. I met him at the door, and he pushed inside, locking the door behind him, just as I'd done.

"Hey." I was in his arms in seconds, Jude pulling me close. "God, I'm sorry about all this."

Over the last few days, he'd been with me so much—held me so much—this felt more natural than being away from him. Even in my frustration, I felt my body relax next to his.

"I looked into Allison again. That's one of the reasons I went over to the ranch this morning. Jerry also sent me the town security footage, and there's nothing obvious on there pointing to Allison having anything to do with this."

"But you said..."

"I know," he agreed. "And I still think this is someone coming after you. But I can't let you do this, especially not alone. Charlie is watching you, sweetheart. Getting caught following your rival through town wouldn't help things."

Anger flared in my chest, and I pushed away from him. It was a valid point, but my bruised heart wasn't interested in logic right now. "You're not *letting* me do anything, Jude. I wasn't asking your permission. We're not in bed right now."

The blow struck, and his face fell for a moment before he closed his eyes. "I phrased that badly."

"I'm woman enough to own that I like it when you control things in bed. I love it, and I don't want it to stop." The words felt wild in my chest. They were things I probably shouldn't say, and yet I couldn't seem to stop the train already on those tracks. "But you don't get to dictate what I do and where I go. That's not something I'll tolerate, and if you think I will—"

Jude stepped to me, taking my face in his hands and kissing me hard. I wanted to be angry at him for interrupting, but this wasn't a kiss trying to take over or shut me up. This was a kiss meant to soothe and calm. To break through what he saw was taking me over. I hated him for it just as much as I loved that he could see it and find a way to reach me.

"I'm not trying to do that. I don't want to keep you locked away or make you feel you can't do things, and I'm sorry I gave you that impression. But I also really don't want you to end up in jail." He smiled, rubbing his thumb across my cheek. "I've grown too used to being in your bed to settle for conjugal visits."

That drew a smile from me, but only for a second, and he saw it. "But also, I didn't say I wasn't going to let you do it. I said I wasn't going to let you do it *alone*."

Something desperate in my soul eased.

"I know the power of instincts, and I wouldn't be here with you without them. If you think something is wrong? We're going to check it out, and I'm going to be with you. Not only because you and me driving around together is a bit less suspicious, but because I am here for you." He kissed my forehead. "Always."

Closing my eyes, I settled into the moment, trying not to think about how Jude had basically just declared us forever. Of course, that was what I wanted, but we hadn't talked about it. Too many other things had gotten in the way. "Thank you."

"I even brought some things to help." He took my hand and kept me close under his arm as we left the bakery. It was a pity I couldn't leave everything else spinning around in my brain behind, too.

Chapter 25

Jude

I watched Lena from Bessie's passenger seat. Her teeth worried her bottom lip, her hands shifted on the steering wheel, and she was distracted. It wasn't a lie that I was worried about her. I recognized desperation, and god, I understood it. But desperation could lead to disaster, and I didn't want to see Lena go through more than she already had.

That being said, whatever she went through, I would be with her. No matter what.

I'd told her the truth in the bakery—I didn't want or need to control her life. When we went to bed was a different story, but if I wanted to keep dominating this gorgeous woman in our bed, turning her into nothing but a collection of breath, sighs, and pleasure, I had to make sure she stayed out of jail. I hadn't thought it would be an issue until earlier today.

Lena had been quiet since we'd parked down the street

from Mountain Jewels Coffee, waiting for them to close. The shop itself shut down relatively early, as Deja Brew had done back when it was only Lena working there with no other employees.

Reaching over, I picked her hand up off the steering wheel and held it. I didn't say anything, but I wanted to touch her. Most people knew I was quiet, and with Lena, I already spoke more than I did with everyone else. Right now, words weren't needed. If we weren't sitting in the car, I'd be holding her.

Earlier, I'd told her I'd always be there for her, and I hoped she knew it was true. Right now, in the middle of so much chaos, I didn't think the time was right to tell her how deeply in love with her I was, or how I didn't need any more time to know she was mine.

But as soon as we figured this out, I was going to tell her. Maybe take her out to Resting Warrior's second property and make love to her under the stars first. I wanted to ask her to move to my house and make it exactly everything she wanted. Or, if she didn't want that, I'd ask if I could install some better security at her house.

I didn't care where we lived, as long as it was together.

"There she is," Lena said, moving to pull her hand from mine, but I held it.

"Wait. Don't start the car until she's starting to pull away."

She looked at me, still nervous. "Are you sure?"

"Very. We're not in a city. We need to be careful if we're following her, so she doesn't notice. We're also less likely to lose her out here."

"Right." Lena blew out a long breath. "Sorry."

Lifting her hand, I kissed the back of it. "You don't have to apologize for not being an expert in espionage."

She smiled faintly, still watching our mark through the

windshield. I was going to figure out all of this, if only so I could make my girl smile again. A real smile, and not only the ones that managed to break through everything going on in her head.

"Now we can go." Allison had started her car and was pulling out. "But slowly."

Lena obeyed, starting Bessie and following Allison at a good distance. We would have to be careful, but thankfully, most people weren't as aware of their surroundings as they should be. It was unlikely our target would notice us following her unless we were right on her back bumper.

"This is probably stupid," Lena said quietly. "What if she just goes home?"

"It's not stupid if it makes you feel better."

She didn't say anything to that.

We followed Allison's truck west out of town, keeping at least two blocks behind her while we were still within its limits. "She's really dating Ben?" I asked. Because I was curious, but I also wanted to lighten the mood.

"Seems that way." Lena shrugged. "When I went to check out the coffee shop, he was there, and when we were at the school, he was with her helping her set up all the hot chocolate. It seemed like he was going to stay with her the rest of the night too. I saw them kiss in the parking lot."

"He was there when I stopped by the first time, too. Guess I know why now." Allison turned left in front of us, heading south. "She's not heading home."

Lena looked at me. "How do you know?"

"When I looked into her, I found her address. To get there, she'd keep heading straight."

"Still doesn't mean she's doing anything wrong." Despite her denial, Lena's voice had more energy in it now. I knew what it was like to hope for something you shouldn't, and this was it. Neither of us should be *hoping* this woman poisoned a bunch of teenagers, but if she did, the relief would be huge.

Out here, it was mostly ranches and farms. Very few people, with huge swaths of land blocked off. If you were flying over it, the ground would look like a patchwork quilt. In winter, as we were now, it was even less populated, as any cattle spent most of their time indoors and the few trees were stripped bare.

"This is something," I said.

Ahead of us, Allison had put on her brakes and was turning into a drive to a farm. Two barns and a small house were visible. We were still far enough back that we couldn't see all the details, but I knew where we were, and this wasn't anything I'd seen connected to the woman. Maybe we'd hit the jackpot after all.

"Pull over there." I pointed to a spot near a fence that had some cover. We still might not see much, but it was better than nothing.

Through the sparse leaves and branches of some brush, we watched Allison get out of her car and wave to a man approaching her. It seemed clear both that he was expecting her and that they knew each other.

To people outside of Resting Warrior, having surveillance equipment in your truck might seem strange. But all of us kept some basic things in case of emergencies. Radios, flashlights, spare clothes, and binoculars. I'd grabbed those before we left the bakery, and I pulled out a pair of binoculars now.

"You brought those?"

I smiled as I focused them on Allison and the man. "Told you I brought some things to help."

The man—who I presumed was the owner of the farm—was all smiles with Allison. Especially when she dug into her bag and pulled out a stack of money and handed it to him.

"What was that?" Lena placed a hand on my arm.

"Money," I murmured.

"Okay, that's weird, right?"

I nodded. "Very weird."

The man headed back to the house, and Allison walked toward one of the barns. I followed her with the binoculars until she went inside. "Okay, let's go past the farm and turn around. She's gone into the barn. Once she leaves, we'll see if we can find our way inside and figure out what the hell is going on in there."

"Okay."

Lena started the car, and just in time, too. Allison was already pushing out of the barn and heading back to her car. "Quickly," I said. "Over this rise to turn around, and give it a couple minutes."

She did as I instructed, and when we finally drove forward enough to see, Allison was pulling out and heading back in the direction we'd come from. Perfect.

Beneath my feet, the car bucked.

"No, not now." Lena pressed the gas pedal, and Bessie shot forward just before she sputtered and died. "*Shit.*" I could see the frustration building in her. "Of course this would happen right now."

I reached over and rubbed the back of her neck. "I'll call Ben and see if he can get a tow to us. If we don't call now, it will be too late. And I'll call Daniel to come pick us up."

Her face fell. "But the barn?"

There was nothing I wanted more than to barge on to the property and find out what was in there. But we couldn't be foolish about this either. I was still dedicated to keeping Lena out of jail. "We know it's here now, and we'll come back to it. Find a way to see what's inside. It's better this way. We'll be better prepared."

Maybe I could even find a way to point Charlie in this direction and take Lena out of it altogether. That would be the ideal situation.

"If you're sure," Lena's voice was low with disappointment. I couldn't pull her over into my lap in this car, but I wasn't about to let that stop me from touching her. Leaning over, I caught her lips with mine, kissing her until I felt her body relax.

"I'm sure," I told her when I pulled back. "We're going to figure this out. I promise."

Pulling out my phone, I looked up the number for the mechanic.

Chapter 26

Lena

Ben shut Bessie's hood with a sigh, wiping his hands on a rag. "Remember that time a few days ago when I told you Bessie needed to retire soon?"

It had only taken a day for him to get her working again. Which was good, so Jude didn't have to drive me everywhere. But at the same time, it felt strange to be doing this—something which had become commonplace and normal—when everything was as far from normal as possible.

I smiled at him, but I didn't have anything to say about Bessie's retirement. Of course I knew he was right. Bessie was a classic car, and both the repairs and replacement parts were getting more expensive and difficult to find. Every time she shuddered and died was a time my heart fell, knowing everyone would look at me *again* and internally roll their eyes.

And yet, I couldn't do it. Maybe I was just too overly

sentimental, but this car had seen me through everything. Through college and moving to Garnet Bend. Through opening up a coffee shop even though my family had said I was crazy for wanting to live in a town this small. Through meeting Jude and everything with Evelyn. Right now, besides Jude, Bessie was the only thing I had.

The idea of getting rid of her was like a knife in my heart.

Just a little while longer. Then maybe I could stomach it. After we figured out who was coming after me, and I got any shred of my life back.

"Lena?"

"Sorry." I shook my head. "Got lost in my thoughts there for a second. You might be right, but for right now, just hit me with the damage. There're only so many fires I can fight at once, you know?"

Ben smiled. "I understand. Give me a few minutes, and I'll be back with the paperwork."

"Hey, Ben?"

"Yeah." His voice was muffled in his office.

"Did Charlie come talk to you?"

He stuck his head out the door. "He did, yes. I'm really sorry about what happened. I told him I was there when you set up and I hadn't seen anything strange. For what it's worth, most people don't think you did it."

It wasn't worth much, honestly. There were enough who did believe it, and that wasn't something I could just wave a wand and fix.

Biting my lip, I wondered if I could push him to admit anything about Allison. Or maybe he didn't know. "Did you guys eat the cupcakes you made?"

"Yeah. They were good, too."

My phone rang in my pocket before I could ask him anything else, and I looked down at the screen. "Speak of the devil," I muttered. "Ben, I have to take a call. I'm stepping outside." It was cold, but I pulled my coat closer. If it went badly, I didn't want this call overheard. "Hey, Charlie."

"Lena, how are you?"

I laughed once. "I think that's largely going to depend on why you're calling."

"I'll put you out of your misery, then. It's good news. Or at least, better news."

Blowing out a breath, I felt my whole body sag. "Really?"

"The lab down in Missoula finished going through every sample we took and compared it to what was found in the kids and in the cupcakes. There's no evidence of it anywhere in your store or workspace."

Of course there wasn't, because I didn't do this. I didn't say it out loud, though, instead waiting for him to continue.

"Personally, I find it unlikely if you poisoned your own baked goods, there would be no sign of it where you made them."

"Yeah."

"I can't say you're off the hook entirely," he sighed. "We still don't have an answer about who did this or why, and parents are still banging down my door, coming for your head. But I'm lifting the restriction on Deja Brew. You can open the store if you want."

I spun in a circle, letting my joy overwhelm me just for a moment. "I'm not sure opening it is a good idea, but thank you."

"Yeah. I'd wait if I were you."

"What was it?"

Charlie cleared his throat. "What was what?"

"What was it that made everyone sick? I was never

told." And of course, I wouldn't already know since I wasn't the one who put it there, I added silently.

"Oh." The sound of shuffling papers came through the phone. "Funnily enough, it was metal."

I stopped my pacing in front of the garage. "Metal? What kind of metal?"

"It was a mixture of a few, but mainly copper. Doctors told me it's 'acute copper poisoning.' Obviously worse in the kids who ate a lot more. Those are the ones who ended up in the hospital. But the last one should be going home tomorrow."

That was a relief, at least. No one died. That was good. But copper? Weird. "Thanks, Charlie. If you learn anything else, let me know?"

"Will do."

The line went dead, and I stared at the phone. Copper poisoning. I didn't even know such a thing existed, and yet something tickled in the back of my mind. I couldn't put my finger on it, but it was like déjà vu without the actual original.

Ben was waiting with my bill when I went inside. I took out my wallet, prepared to wince at whatever was on the paper. "Good news?" he asked. "I saw you dancing around for a second there."

"Partially. I'm allowed to open the bakery again if I want."

He smiled. "That is good news. Congratulations."

I signed the bill and swiped my credit card. "Thanks. It's good, but it doesn't change the fact that at least half the town thinks I tried to poison their kids."

"No, it doesn't," he chuckled. "But once they find the asshole who did it, I'm sure people will come around."

"One can only hope. She's ready?"

He handed me the keys. "She is. And if you ever do

decide to retire her, I will happily come help you put her up on display somehow so you can still have her but not drive her."

"Noted." The throaty purr of Bessie's engine was soothing. I pulled out of the garage and waved to Ben, resisting the urge to test her speed on the way back home.

Worry still clung to every part of me, but this was better. For the first time in days, it felt something like hope. The fact that Jude was waiting on the other end of the drive only made it better.

~

"You're sure?"

"I'm sure," Jude said, pulling me to him and wrapping his arms around me. He was tall enough he had to lean down a little bit to rest his chin on my head, but I loved when he did it. It made me feel small and protected.

"I've followed her, and she hasn't gone back to the farm. Nothing she's done has been remotely suspicious. Believe me, I wish it had been. It would be easier."

Two more days had passed since Charlie cleared me to open Deja Brew, and there'd been no more news. Jude had been watching Allison DeVries, but apparently, he'd found nothing. Which was frustrating.

We hadn't gone back to the farm either, because barging on to that farmer's property without Charlie, or a warrant, would backfire. Before he cleared me, we would have done it anyway, but we didn't want to give him any reason to look at me again, or Resting Warrior.

Between what had happened at the Pearsons with Cori, the gang Noah had tried to take down, and me, Charlie, though good-natured most of the time, was sick of seeing our faces. I didn't blame him in the slightest.

"I've handed it off to Daniel and Lucas. They're going to watch her while I'm gone. They'll have eyes on her the whole time, and if she does something, we'll know."

"Okay."

He squeezed me tighter. "I don't want to leave you right now."

The memorial for his teammate was tonight, and Jude was driving to Idaho for it. He'd be gone overnight. Since we'd finally gotten together, it would be the longest we'd been apart. I didn't want him to leave either, but I also knew this was important for Jude. He needed the closure it could give him to see Isaac's widow and hear she was doing well. Maybe seeing some of Isaac's other friends would help him too.

"You need to go," I whispered. "You want to, and there's nothing here I can't handle for a night."

He wove a hand through my hair, guided my face back so I was looking at him, and smirked. "Sure about that? The way you begged last night, I'm not sure you can last that long."

I blushed even though he was teasing. It would be hard not to come home tonight and find him ready to take me upstairs and have his way with me. But I had other things I could do. They wouldn't be nearly as satisfying, but I could take care of it. "I'll be fine."

"I saw that."

Curling my fingers into his shirt, I pulled him closer, aiming for distraction. "Saw what?"

"The thought. You're an open book, and you don't have permission to do that."

I slipped out of his arms. "I don't know what you're talking about."

"Oh, I think you do." He pulled me to him, guiding me until my back was against the wall and I had nowhere to go. Jude was fully hard pressed up against me, and if he didn't have a long drive ahead of him, I might have begged him again.

Jude lowered his mouth to my ear. "No orgasms while I'm gone."

"That's not fair."

He shrugged. "I never claimed this was fair. You can if you want."

"What's the 'but' there?"

"Whatever you use, whether it's a hand or a toy, I'll use it on you too." A sly smile crept onto his lips. "And I'll give you so many orgasms, you'll beg me to stop. So, you choose."

I shuddered, imagining that. A punishment, but part of me wanted to see what it was like. I wouldn't decide now—tonight when I got home, I would see how I felt. After a day of cleaning and washing things, I wasn't sure I'd have the energy to be rebellious.

"I'll think about it."

"I'm sure you will." He kissed me, pressing me into the wall with his body until all I could feel was him. I never got tired of kissing him or touching him. Jude was almost always touching me if we were in the same space, and I didn't mind. After three years of *wanting* to touch him and not being able to, I savored every second.

When we broke apart for breath, he pressed his forehead against mine. "I'll check in later, okay?"

"Okay."

Tension hung in the air between us, the shape of three little words. I saw it in his eyes, and I felt it on my tongue. But I held myself back.

I loved Jude. I'd loved him for a long time, and I didn't want the first time I told him to be before him leaving. Instead, I'd keep it for when we had all the time in the world. Because I knew as soon as I said it, he wasn't letting me leave his sight. My stomach flip-flopped at the thought.

"Call me if you need me." I felt the effort it took for him to step back and grab his overnight bag before heading to his truck, and I stood on the porch waving goodbye like some kind of war bride in an old movie.

When he was gone, I sighed. I hadn't quite decided when to reopen Deja Brew, but I needed to clean it up a bit. The lab techs had moved the kitchen all around and put it back, but I noticed where things were slightly off.

Plus, I needed to wash the graffiti off the front of the building. That alone was going to take a while.

I didn't know if I'd be able to do it in one go without Jude. The chances of someone stopping to yell at me or shame me were high.

Tossing my phone on Bessie's passenger seat, I rolled my eyes. I was still getting texts and voice mails from people. Some friendly, and some…not so much. Today, I didn't want to see any of them. Jude would check in later, and that was the only thing I'd answer. Otherwise, I didn't even want to look at the thing.

I left it in the car. By the time I was finished here and heading home, Jude would be in Idaho Falls.

Evie would probably scold me too if she knew I was doing this alone, but I felt like being alone right now. I needed to figure out a way to win the town back over once they caught Allison. Since spotting her at the barn, I was completely sure it was she who'd done this.

Maybe I could do a grand reopening? All new recipes and plenty of things to eat. But even if people *knew* I didn't put copper in my baked goods, if the positions were reversed, I'd be wary too.

No, this was going to take some thought and some effort. I didn't have any ideas at the moment, but I was already closed. Might as well take the time I needed to build back trust. The savings I had would tide me over for a while.

A *bang!* sound came from the back in the kitchen. That was weird. "Hello?"

Nobody should be in here, but a few people did have keys. I wouldn't put it past Evie to sneak in the back and try to clean things up without my knowing.

No one was in the kitchen, and none of the equipment was running. The only sound now was the gentle hum of the refrigerator. The door to the patio was shut, and it didn't look like anything had slipped onto the floor.

But there was a piece of paper on the back worktable. I didn't remember it being there, but I could have missed it the last time I was here. Maybe it was a note saying the lab techs had finished.

It wasn't that. I picked it up, staring at the handwritten words, in handwriting that wasn't mine.

I can't take the guilt and the hate. I think everyone is better off if I'm not here anymore. I'm sorry if you're hurt by this decision, but trust me, it's better this way.

-Lena

My stomach dropped. What the hell *was* this? I didn't write it, and it was a sick joke. I wasn't killing myself. If this was the same person…

Someone had to have left it here. The banging must have been the back door. They were in here while I was here? Panic started to rise, and I held it back. They weren't here now. Maybe they'd left some sign behind.

Breathe, Lena.

I grabbed the handle of the back door, and it only moved an inch. I heard a scraping metal sound as I pushed. The door wasn't jammed… There was something blocking it.

Our back door was a fire exit. It should never be blocked. Ever.

Another *bang!* sounded—this one louder. Another one and another one. Six in total. I couldn't pinpoint the source of that sound, but it felt final. Too big to be ignored. Jude told me to go with my instincts, and they were telling me to get out now.

I couldn't push down the panic anymore, and I sprinted for the front door. Jude was already gone, but I'd go to Resting Warrior. There, I'd be safe while I called Charlie and told him about the note.

My hands shook as I tried to unlock the door, adrenaline pulsing through me, but I managed to get the lock turned on the second try.

The door didn't open. I pushed, and it wasn't moving an inch.

"Shit."

Something rattled, but the door wouldn't budge. The graffiti on the outside blocked nearly everything. The small spaces I could see through told me there was something in front of the door. And a chain. Someone had moved it there once I came inside, trapped me in here, and chained the doors shut.

Which meant they were watching.

The graffiti also meant no one could see inside. There was no way for me to wave down someone on the street or to get anyone's attention.

My phone was still sitting on Bessie's passenger seat where I'd left it, like an idiot. I'd have to call from the land-line in my tiny office in the back in a hurry.

I needed to get out of here, because if someone went to all this trouble, they would go all the way.

What was that smell?

I ran back to the kitchen, which was getting cloudy, the room filling with…exhaust.

Chapter 27

Jude

I passed Deja Brew on my way through town. Lena wouldn't be there yet, but she wouldn't be far behind me. The front of the building still made me see red, the giant word "*POISON*" in red and black. If I found out who did it, I would report it to the sheriff, because I didn't know if I could trust myself confronting them.

As much as I was committed to keeping Lena out of jail, I had to keep myself out of there too. The idea of being without her for any length of time was unthinkable.

When I came home tomorrow, I was telling Lena I loved her. This morning, it was there between us as it always had been. But I found I couldn't say the words and then walk out the front door like it was nothing. When I told her, I wanted to be able to carry her to bed and illustrate those words on her skin while I loved her.

But it felt good to feel it in my chest. I loved her, and I was going to make sure she knew. Tomorrow.

Grabbing my phone, I found the call from Ellen last week and dialed. When I'd responded to her email, I'd told her I'd call her when I was on my way, just to confirm. Now that I was well out of town, I figured it was a good time.

"Hello?"

"Hey, Ellen. Jude Williams. Just calling to let you know I'm on my way. I'll be there in a few hours and check in to the hotel in plenty of time for the memorial."

"Oh, good." I heard the relief in her voice. "How far are you out of Garnet Bend?"

"Fifteen, maybe twenty minutes. Why?"

Ellen paused and then sighed. "If it's not too much trouble to go back, would you stop by and see if you can convince Isaac's brother to come? He said no, but I'd really like to see him."

It felt like lightning was about to strike me. My hairs rose on end, the sudden, urgent feeling of *wrong* hitting me more strongly than in weeks. "What are you talking about, Ellen?"

"What am I— You didn't know?"

"Know what?" I tried to keep the growl out of my voice and wasn't successful.

"Isaac's brother lives close to you. In Garnet Bend or just outside of it? I'm not sure. I don't know his exact address. Moved there over a year ago now. We're not exactly close, so I assumed he moved out there to be near you and maybe do some stuff with Resting Warrior. But he's been cagey about coming to this, and if anyone might be able to convince him, it's you."

"I didn't even know Isaac had a brother, Ellen."

"Oh." The silence was full. "Well, they're half brothers. They had a hard time with each other. I mean, they loved each other, but it wasn't always smooth sailing. He didn't come to Isaac's funeral, and I think he regretted it. This would be a perfect opportunity for him to fix that."

My instincts were screaming. Isaac and I had been friends, and I thought I'd known most people in his life before I cut everything off after his death. If he and his brother were close at all, then his brother would have known who I was. Isaac lived and breathed the unit. We were his friends, and even when we were all together, he was the one constantly telling stories about what idiots we'd been or bringing up inside jokes.

If his brother moved this close to Resting Warrior and didn't reach out, there was a good chance it was because he didn't want me to know he was here.

"What's his name?"

"Benjamin Phipps. I can give you his address if you want."

The world narrowed, everything suddenly making sense and relieving the constant *itch* I'd been feeling these past weeks. Fucking Ben. He'd always been around, conveniently everywhere Lena was. He even helped with the ventilation, and he was the one doing this to her? I didn't know why, but I was going to find out. I needed to turn the hell around.

This wasn't about Lena. This was about me. He'd lost Isaac, and—

"No need. Ellen, I need to call you back."

"But—"

I ended the call, glad the highway was empty because I pulled an incredibly illegal U-turn before I dialed Lena. No answer. I tried to swallow down my fear. She wasn't expecting a call from me for hours, and she could have put her phone down and walked away.

It was fine. She was fine.

Dialing Daniel, I kept the phone on speaker so I could focus on driving faster.

"Jude?"

"It's not Allison."

A beat of silence. "What?"

"It's Ben. Aka Benjamin Phipps. He's Isaac's half brother."

Daniel swore. "Where are you now?"

"Twenty-five minutes out. Fifteen if I break a whole bunch of laws. You?"

"About the same to the west. We're following her."

Probably to the farm, which likely had nothing to do with this. "He knew," I said. "If he's gunning for me, Lena's the perfect target for it. And he knew I'd go to Isaac's memorial. A sure way to know I'd be gone and she'd be alone. Fuck."

"We're turning around now. You called her?"

"No answer."

Daniel blew out a breath. "Keep trying. He didn't know you'd find out this quickly. She's probably fine. If he's smart, he'd wait until he knew you couldn't get back."

That was true, and yet I felt in my bones it wasn't right. "I don't think so. We need to get to her, Daniel."

"Call Charlie and drive. We're moving as fast as we can."

Terror, true and deep, struck me in the chest. I should have said I loved her. What did it matter *when* I said as long as I got to do it at all? If I didn't—

I cut off that thought.

Every inch of my body was drenched in icy fear. And it was the worst I'd ever felt in my life. Worse than waking up from nightmares, worse than being tortured. Those things were pain. And I would go to my grave knowing that fear was a thousand times worse than any pain.

I'd wasted so much time with Lena, thinking I knew what was best for both of us, and now I could have lost her before I got nearly enough time with her. Now, it was my worst fear come true. Lena would be hurt because of me. That man wouldn't be near her if it weren't for me. If I kept thinking about the possibility we'd be too late, I'd have to throw up on the seat of the truck, because I wasn't stopping.

My phone shook in my hand. I glanced down, trying to focus more on the road than on the phone. But if Charlie was at the police station, he could get to Deja Brew faster than I could.

His phone rang out. No answer. Fuck it. I was truly speeding now, the road disappearing beneath my wheels too fast. I'd never been more grateful to live here, where there weren't many cars even on a busy day. If there was traffic…

No. I would make it. Everything in me sharpened and focused, the way it did before a mission. The way it had when we'd gone in to rescue Noah. My instincts weren't on the outskirts now. They were resting easy, knowing the truth.

I wasn't a religious man, but right now, I was praying to God I wasn't too late. So I could tell her I loved her, that I was sorry I ever brought this kind of danger and pain into her life, and make sure she was mine forever.

First, I had to save her life.

Chapter 28

Lena

I was going to die.

That was the first thought I had.

I was going to die. The exhaust was spilling through the vents and coating everything in a brownish haze. Call for help—the office. There was a phone in my office.

The air was cleaner in here, but that wasn't the only thing that was clean. My desk was cleared of nearly everything, including the phone and the computer. I hadn't come in here when I visited; there'd been no reason to. Would I have noticed?

I shut the door to block the smoke and went to the window. It opened onto the patio, and I could figure out the rest after.

It wouldn't open. I shoved against the pane, trying to force it up, but there was no give. What the hell? I opened this window all the time in summer. Panic was clouding my brain faster than the exhaust. Something hard and dry coated the bottom of the window, completely solid. They'd sealed the window.

This was the only window that opened in the building. The other ones were out front, giant plate glass. The doors were blocked. The window was sealed, and I had no way to call for help.

Think, Lena.

If I was going to go down, then I was going down fighting. This wasn't going to be the end of me.

I could try to block the flow of exhaust. Slow it down long enough for me to figure something out. We had towels and aprons here; those might work. I'd have to hold my breath and go in stages.

Already, the exhaust was curling in under the door, and I was starting to smell it. Fighting the urge to cough, I took a big breath of the cleaner air and opened the office door, shutting it behind me. I might be able to keep that air purer longer. Not much, but it would have to work.

I grabbed whatever cloth I could find from the closet and tossed it onto the table, trying to get up onto the counter without breathing. Already, my lungs were screaming, but I could do this. I *would* do this.

The grate clattered to the floor, and I shoved a rolled-up towel inside it. Another one, and another one, slowing the flood of exhaust. There were other vents, and it wasn't perfect, but it was better.

I dropped to the floor, barely making it out of the kitchen before gasping. The air in the front wasn't much better, and I was starting to lose my sight. This was a city's worth of smog in a single room.

For one second, I let myself think about Jude. He had no idea what was happening, and if he came back and found me like this, it would be Isaac all over again. He wouldn't believe the note, nor the way I died—he knew me too well for that—but it wouldn't matter. I would already be gone, and everything I'd been dreaming about would be gone with me.

I was trying to live in the moment with Jude, but it would be a lie to say I hadn't thought about our life together in the future. After the moments we said *I love you*. I'd imagined us making it official and moving in together. Deciding whether to have a family. Growing old with that family and our friends by our side.

None of that would happen if I didn't get out of here.

Hauling in another breath, I ran back into the kitchen, grabbing more towels and trying to block another vent. But the other ones were hidden behind things I couldn't move while holding my breath. I shoved a towel into the crack behind the oven before escaping into the office. It was so cloudy in the kitchen, I couldn't stay there. I needed to get out.

My eyes watered from the exhaust and the fear creeping in. I didn't want to die. Not like this. Knowing Jude would take the brunt of it only made it worse. The person who'd locked me in here was shoving a knife in Jude's heart, and I couldn't stand it.

There was no way for me to break the window out front. I didn't have anything heavy enough to do that kind of damage that I could also lift. Even if I could, I didn't know if I was strong enough to make the glass break.

The front door was chained. No way through that either. The back was blocked, but it didn't seem chained. If I had any chance of getting out of here, it was through the back door.

Okay. I could do this.

I grabbed a pen off the desk and pulled my shirt over my nose. Holding my breath was only going to work for so long. The paper was still on the counter. I grabbed it and scrawled a giant X over the words written there, and in the clean space, I simply wrote *I love you.*

If the worst happened, he would have that. I may not have been able to say it in person, but at least I would have said it.

Placing my hands on the back door, I pushed as hard as I could. The door moved, but not enough. Whatever had been put behind it was fucking heavy. The only thing I could think to do was to slam into it. I could do that. Then at least he'd know I tried to get back to him.

Backing up, I used the last of my held breath to run, turning my shoulder to shove into the door. It moved an extra inch before rebounding. But it did move. I had a chance.

I was out of air, and in my rush, I left the office door open. I felt in front of me for the door of the kitchen that led into the front. It was just a little clearer near the doors where all the exhaust hadn't managed to build up. I took another choking breath. This was probably my last chance.

By the time I was running at the door again, I was already out of breath, but I threw myself against it anyway, praying I was somehow strong enough.

I wasn't.

My body inhaled, forcing me to let go, and I choked on sickening, awful smoke. Dizziness drove me to my knees, limbs unable to hold their strength. I'd tried and failed. The tile of the floor was cold on my cheek. When did I lie down on the floor?

Nausea washed over me, my body seizing tight and trying to force out the exhaust. Dizziness pulled me down into nothing. This was what happened to people who shut themselves into garages, wasn't it?

Something sparked. A garage…

I couldn't open my eyes, and I was so tired. It wouldn't hurt to sleep for a little bit, would it? I would try to open the door after I rested. That was all I needed.

A rest.

Chapter 29

Jude

I hurtled through town too fast, nearly hitting at least three cars and a couple of people, too. Every fucking traffic law in existence? I broke it. There wasn't a damn thing that would stop me from getting to Lena *right now*.

Sirens popped up behind, following me. Good. I needed them to follow me and help.

I grabbed my phone. "9-1-1, what's your emergency?"

"I need an ambulance sent to Deja Brew right now."

"Sir, what's the emergency?"

"I'm on my way there now, and it's very possible someone will need medical attention. This is Jude Williams with Resting Warrior. *Do it now*." I didn't wait to hear if she obeyed. I was only a few blocks away now. "I'm coming, Lena."

There. I saw the building. Bessie was parked out front, and smoke was seeping out from under the front door, which was *blocked*. Fucking air conditioners stacked on top of one another in front of the door, two wide. And not the small ones. Those were heavy on a good day. Six of them in front of the door?

I jerked the truck to a stop on the sidewalk. "*Lena!*"

The sirens were still going, and the cops were yelling at me until they saw what I saw. The blocked door, the chained handles, and smoke seeping from every crack. "Help me, please."

They started moving the air conditioners, but it wasn't fast enough. Could I ram the truck through the front window? No. If she was just inside the window, trying to get out, I could kill her. What did I have?

I looked over. Well, I had air conditioners.

Heaving one up, I stepped to the window and slammed the metal against the glass. It cracked, but it wasn't enough.

"Hey, we're almost there," one of the cops said. I wasn't waiting. They would need to find bolt cutters for the chains—she could be dead by then. Another slam against the glass and the corner went through it, sending the spiderweb cracking further. Smoke—no, *exhaust* poured out from the hole. The fucker was suffocating her.

I saw the barest glimpse of carpet. It was clear. I took a single step back and hurled the air conditioner right at that spot, arms screaming with the effort. The window shattered, and I held up my arms to protect myself from raining glass.

An explosion of exhaust rolled into the sky, but it was so thick I still couldn't see. "Lena!" I called her name. She was in there somewhere.

I took the biggest breath of my life and leaped through the window. They were calling after me. Car doors were slamming, and I heard Daniel's voice yelling something. I didn't register any of it. I was looking for her. Where was she? The smog was so thick I could have tripped over her, but I didn't see or feel her anywhere.

Come on, sweetheart.

My eyes watered, and my lungs began to burn. The smog was thinning thanks to the broken window. It was just enough. There she was. Her body was crumpled by the back door. She'd been trying to get out. Fuck.

I pushed back the rush of emotion at seeing her. Get her out. Get her out. Get her out. She was so light in my arms when I scooped her up. Far too light. She didn't feel right.

No. Please.

"Here," Daniel called to me as I stepped out of the window. He had a coat on the ground covering the glass so I could lay her down. Lena was too pale, and she wasn't breathing.

The world was crumbling beneath me, but I forced myself to move. I knew CPR. Every man at Resting Warrior did, and we renewed our certifications whenever we needed to. Not yet. She wasn't gone yet.

A hand touched my shoulder, and I shrugged it off, checking Lena's airway. Clear. I locked my elbows and placed the heels of my hands over her sternum, starting compressions. The ambulance wasn't here. Why wasn't it here?

"I called an ambulance. I don't think she believed me."

"It's on its way."

Lena's body jerked under the compressions, lifeless. My vision blurred, and I blinked the emotion away. I wasn't too late. Wasn't too late.

"Come on, Lena." I gritted the words through my teeth, forcing every ounce of strength into her heart. "We're not done. Hear me? I have things I need to tell you, and you have to be awake for them. Come on."

The silence around me was brutal. I didn't stop except for one second to blow into her lungs. She needed to live. I didn't know if I would survive this.

Lena's whole body spasmed, jerking and coughing. I swore I saw exhaust come out of her mouth. "Lena."

Her eyes whirled, finally landing on me. "Jude."

I placed my fingers on her wrist, feeling the beat of her heart. It was there, low and steady. She was here. "Hey, baby." I leaned down close so she could see me. "You're going to be okay."

She reached up for me and didn't quite make it. I wrapped my hand around hers, and with the other, I brushed the hair back from her face. I wanted nothing more in the world than to kiss her, but I wasn't going to deprive her of any more air. "I love you."

The words settled easily in the space between us, as if they were always meant to be there. "I'd planned to tell you tomorrow when I came back, but I never should have waited. I love you, and I've loved you for a long time, Lena."

"I love you too." She was smiling, eyes watering, but she was still groggy. Who knew how much of that stuff was still inside her and what it would do? "Of course I love you. I tried to tell you, just in case."

"No just in case. You're still here. You're with me." The ambulance siren reached me, coming toward us fast. "You're going to be just fine."

I didn't look away from her eyes even as the paramedics came and I had to move aside as they checked her heart and lifted her onto the stretcher. An oxygen mask appeared, but Lena didn't look away either. I was her anchor.

Someone waved, and I flicked my eyes up to Charlie. He raised his eyebrows in question, and I nodded.

"They're going to take you to the hospital." I pressed a kiss to her forehead. "I'm going to be right behind you, okay? Just going to talk to Charlie, and I'm driving to you. You're not going to be alone for a second."

"Okay."

She closed her eyes, and I looked at the paramedics. "Is she okay?"

"She will be. You did well bringing her back. Now we need to get her in the ambulance."

I squeezed her hand, and it took every bit of my will to release it. "Daniel?"

"Lucas is going," he answered. "Evie and Grace are already on the way. They'll probably be there before you will."

Hauling in a breath, I let myself fall into a crouch and scrub my hands through my hair. She was alive. I wanted to throw up all over the sidewalk. If I'd called Ellen even a minute later, I might have been too late, and she would have been gone.

Daniel's hand touched my shoulder again. "You made it," he said quietly. "You got to her. She's safe. Don't dwell on the almosts."

"Yeah. Easier said than done."

"Don't I know it."

Charlie came and stood in front of me, hands on his hips. He gestured to the cops who'd followed me through town. "They told me what they saw, but I need to hear from you because it's definitely not the whole picture. What the hell is going on?"

I told him about Ben and his connection to me. I was still trying to wrap my head around it and force my mind to release the terror and adrenaline still soaking my system.

"You're sure it's him?" Charlie asked.

I blew out a breath. "As sure as I can be. I think I can

get a confession out of him. Especially if we don't let on that Lena survived."

He blinked in shock. "You want to fake her death?"

"Of course not. But I want him to think he won. If he thinks he did, then he has no reason to run."

"If he finds out on his own?"

"Then it doesn't matter." I shook my head. "It's just a precaution. He wants me to know who did this. One way or another, I'll be talking to him. Let him enjoy his last night of freedom, and tomorrow, I'll get you everything you need to put him away."

Charlie looked at me until I sighed. "I'm not going to kill him, Charlie. But at least allow me the grace of saying I want to."

A smirk appeared and disappeared in a moment. "Fair enough. Let me know what you need. I'm going to get this area cleared and taken care of. There was a generator around back, but it's off now. It was hooked up to the ventilation and blocking the back door. Very cleverly done and fucking heavy too. Given the air conditioners and that, Ben makes sense. We'll want to look for physical evidence to back up the confession when you get it."

"Of course." There was one more thing. Lena had said she tried to tell me she loved me. "Just one second."

I pulled my shirt up over my nose and ducked back into the bakery through the broken window. The air was clearer now, the remaining smoke hovering near the ceiling, though things were still hazy.

Looking around the kitchen, I saw the vent near the ceiling. Things were shoved into it. Towels, and what looked like the string of an apron.

Fuck. The deep terror of almost losing her came roaring back to the surface. She'd been in here, knowing she might die, and she'd tried everything she could think of. It cracked something in my chest.

Focus, Jude. Get what you need so you can go to her.

On the worktable near the back, I found a piece of paper and a pen. I approached it but didn't touch it. I already knew they were going to dust this place for prints, and maybe Ben had touched this?

Words written on the paper were crossed out, and a frantic *I love you* was written beneath them. One scan of the words she'd tried to get rid of had me seeing red. He was going to make it look like suicide. I didn't think it would have held up, but the reaction I would have had…

I took a picture of the note with my phone before stepping out of the kitchen. "Charlie?" He turned, looking through the window. "You need to see this."

He came through, and I pointed to the paper. "I haven't touched it."

Reading the words, he shook his head. "Jesus. Yeah, that will help. We'll dust it for prints too."

"Do you need anything else from me right now?"

"No. Go see your girl. I know where to find you."

I clapped him on the arm. "Thanks, Charlie."

"But keep me posted on your plan. I want to be there. No false alarms this time."

"No false alarms," I agreed. I sure as fuck wasn't going to let that happen.

The police moved their cars to let me through, and I sped to the hospital. At this point, I didn't care if I was breaking more traffic laws. I needed to see her and hold her. She was everything.

Lucas was waiting for me just inside the doors of the waiting room. "Hey. They moved her upstairs already, and she's sedated. More out of precaution than anything else."

"But she's okay?"

"Doctor wants to monitor her to see if there're any lingering effects, but at first glance, yes. She just needs rest. All the stress, the copper poisoning on top of this, the doc basically said she needed a long-ass vacation."

No arguments from me there. I would happily take Lena to the beach for a few weeks, lay her out on the sand, and make sure she relaxed by fucking her to exhaustion every day and every night.

Evie and Grace sat by her bed. Lena herself was pale, oxygen mask in place, and still as death. Only the steady rise and fall of her chest assured me she was here with me, but my stomach twisted anyway.

God, when she was better, I was going to make her mine. Forever. Lena deserved more than a sickbed proposal, so I would make it perfect. But it was happening. It should have happened long before now, and I wasn't wasting any more time.

"She's okay." Evie was red-eyed with tears. "Or she will be."

I couldn't even speak. Walking to her side, I knelt next to the bed and pulled her into my arms. It didn't matter that she was asleep. I needed to feel her safe and warm and breathing. Whispers echoed behind me, along with the scrape of chairs. I didn't let Lena go.

It wasn't clear how long I stayed there with her in my arms, listening to her heart beating steadily on the monitor.

"I'm just going to check on her, okay?" A nurse stood on the other side of the bed, smiling sympathetically.

"Yeah." I laid her back, dropping a kiss on her forehead. "Yeah, okay."

"The doctor will be back around to talk to you shortly."

I nodded, standing, and heading out into the hall.

There were so many more people here, the nurses at the station were wide-eyed. Everyone from Resting Warrior, come to make sure one of their own was okay.

"Noah?" I pinched the bridge of my nose between my fingers. "Can you call Ellen? About the memorial?"

He cursed. "Shit. Yeah. I'm sure she'll understand."

"Thank you." I looked at Daniel. "I don't know how long she'll be under, and I don't want to wait. Someone stays with her, and we go. We'll call Charlie on the way."

"You have a plan?"

I sighed. "Since I already promised Charlie I wouldn't bury him, I'm aiming for a confession. But we're going to need a wire and for the rest of you to get comfortable hiding."

My friends just smiled.

Chapter 30

Jude

Charlie wasn't surprised when I called him and told him I wasn't going to wait until the next day. He said he'd figured as much. It only took a couple hours for us to get ready. I had on a wire, and everyone but Lucas was here with me. He stayed with Grace, Evie and Lena, and he'd never know how grateful I was he was there just in case.

After this, it would be a long time before I took anything for granted again. Especially Lena's safety.

Most of our time preparing was everyone getting into position slowly and quietly, making sure they weren't seen. Ben was at the garage. His car was there, and we'd seen him greet a customer once. He hadn't left.

I wasn't armed. This didn't need to escalate, and I didn't trust myself around him. If something happened, I was a good six inches taller and probably thirty pounds of muscle heavier. My chances were good in a fight. If, for some reason, I was getting my ass handed to me, it was one more reason I wasn't here alone.

All of them could hear me, but it was one-way. I didn't need a distraction; they just needed the signal. "Ready," I said under my breath as I turned the corner. There was no point in knocking. Shoving through the door, I saw Ben standing in front of the open hood of a car, his back to me. There was one beer bottle on the floor, empty, and another on a worktable. It was barely afternoon, but that wasn't a good sign.

"I'm surprised it took you this long to get here, honestly."

"You knew I'd come?"

He huffed out a breath and turned, wiping his hands on a cloth. "Of course. You're not stupid. If I'd been able to finish the job, you might have been more distracted. I don't know what tipped you off about Deja Brew, but you got fucking lucky."

I blinked. That was easier than I expected. At the very least, I'd thought he would deny it at first. And of course, he'd been watching to make sure she died. "So you did all this to get at me?"

"Yes."

My hands curled into fists, and I forced myself still. "Why?"

"Because you got out. You're still alive, and when you had the chance to save Isaac, you didn't." He shook his head and smirked. "But when I got here, you were so obviously miserable, it was easier to just leave you alone. You were doing an excellent job of punishing yourself. Better than I could have done."

I swallowed. "But?"

"But then you came here with that *stupid* fucking car, and I heard you ranting about how much you wanted Lena and how you might actually go for it. Then when I was out walking one morning—to get coffee, I might add—I saw you drop her off and kiss her. You had the look on your face Isaac did when he was with Ellen, and he doesn't get to have that anymore because of you. It's not right for you to have it at all."

The pain in his voice was one I recognized. The kind of pain that didn't go away and didn't get easier—you eventually just learned to live with it and tried to deal with it as best you could.

"You could have talked to me," I said. "I could have told you the truth."

"I'm not interested in hearing anything from you."

"Really?" I opened my hands wide to show I had nothing to hide. "Because whether or not you want to, I think you need to. No matter how happy I've been or haven't been, there hasn't been a single day when I haven't thought about Isaac. I feel the guilt about his death and grieve it every *fucking* day."

He opened his mouth, and I kept going. This was my chance to get it all out, even if it didn't end up making a difference. "I could show you my bedroom wall that's made of more spackle and putty than anything else because I have nightmares. Of being tortured, and Isaac screaming. It used to be every night. I tore sheets to shreds and destroyed my house, fighting off enemies I still feel I should have been able to kill.

"And I still get them. It's not every night, thanks to Lena, but I do. And the fact that he's gone still tears me up. I'm never going to get rid of the guilt. Maybe I'll be able to handle it better, but it's never going to leave."

Ben snorted, tossing the rag onto the engine of the car and walking away. "You're still here, and he's not."

"I know, and no one knows more than me that it's

partly my fault. I've never left anyone behind. Not on purpose. And the fact that I didn't have a choice *destroys* me. When they carried me out of that cave, I was barely conscious. If I'd had any piece of my mind free, I would have forced them to go back, and I would have made them carry him out of there with me.

"And believe me, I've wondered whether I could have helped him more once he was home. If I could have reached out more or should have noticed something nobody else did. I'll be asking those questions until the day I die, but those questions are never going to bring Isaac back."

The crash made me jump. Ben grabbed one of the metal tool chests and threw it over, sending tools and bolts everywhere. "Your guilt doesn't do shit. Nothing you do makes any difference because he's still dead and you're still here. I want you to feel what it's like to lose someone like that. And if it weren't for that bitch, you would be in just as much pain. It was her, right? Fucking called and left me a message, begging me to come to the memorial and ride with you if I needed to." He shook his head, looking less and less rational by the second. His hands shook, and he started to pace, agitated. "Didn't get that message until after I got back from starting the generator. I could have saved it for another day, but she had to go and call you. Saved Lena's fucking life."

I needed to be careful here. "And Allison DeVries? How does she play into all this?"

"Convenience. Competition is a good motive, right? You wouldn't believe the amount of research I did to fuck up things for your girl." Ben sounded proud of it, and my stomach rolled. "I made a copy of the bakery keys once when her car was here, and it was easy."

"Tell me." I didn't actually want to hear it, but the

more detailed a confession I got, the more likely it was for him to do time for attempted murder.

"I dehydrated all those cookies." He shrugged. "It was more of an inconvenience than anything else. The pies were vinegar. By that time, I wanted to make things hurt for her. Because it wasn't just his captivity that drove Isaac over the edge, it was the isolation. The way people looked at him like he was crazy and broken. It didn't matter if Ellen was there with him or if I tried to get through, it only mattered what everyone else thought."

Ben's mouth curved into a sneer. "And little Lena Mitchell cares about what everyone thinks about her. It was easy. The cupcakes were easy, too. Just switching out the decorative dust to put on top and mixing some metal shavings into one of the frosting colors, and you've got sick kids. No one forgives that, especially when there's a big sign that says poison on the door."

He'd done it on purpose so no one could see her call for help. Already planning ahead. Every muscle in my body was locked tight, keeping myself from touching him. I would do nothing to damage this confession or argue that it was given under duress. Nothing. Even if it killed me.

There was nothing I could say to his arguments. He was already too far gone, well on his way to drunk, and he wasn't going to listen to reason. But I could give him what I could have given his brother—more than I had. "I can help you, Ben." I swallowed the bitter taste in my mouth. "No matter what you think, I understand your pain. Isaac was my friend and my brother, and I miss him every goddamn day. And if he were here? I would help him too. I would bring him here to the ranch and get him all the help he needed if I could. So I will do that for you. After you serve your time, we'll help you."

He was faster than I thought. From the pile of spilled

tools, Ben grabbed a tire iron and lunged. I jumped back just far enough not to get hit, but I missed on the backstroke. Pain burst through my side, and I shut it down, catching his arm before he could slam the metal into my head.

All the shit on the floor caught me, and I slipped, letting him rush me, and we hit the floor together. I took one hit to the jaw before we were swarmed by people. My friends came from every direction, hauling Ben off me and getting him under control. "Where the *hell* did you all come from!?" he roared, fighting where Noah and Daniel had him pinned facedown on the ground.

Liam helped me up. "You okay?"

"I'll live." A couple bruises, maybe. But they were worth it. Crouching down beside Ben, I made sure he was looking at me before I spoke. "They didn't come from anywhere. They've been here the whole time. Because, like I said, we don't leave people behind."

Charlie had handcuffs in his hand, and I smiled in spite of myself. I didn't think I'd ever look at handcuffs the same way again, knowing how Lena liked them.

"You want to do the honors?" he asked.

"No. I don't. But thank you." No part of me wanted to touch Ben again. Self-defense was one thing, and I was fully in control, but I wasn't going to test it. "I'm going to get back to the hospital."

He opened the cuffs. "I'll keep you posted. And, Jude, I'll do my best to make sure everyone understands that none of this was Lena."

"Thanks, Charlie."

I didn't stick around to watch them take Ben away, instead turning my back and heading toward the woman I loved.

Chapter 31

Lena

My head hurt. It pounded like I'd drunk myself under the table with the girls, but that definitely wasn't what happened. I didn't remember much past…

I opened my eyes, focusing on the dim light in the room and the beeping beside me. Jude was asleep, head on the blankets and arm draped across my lap. The hospital. I had some hazy memories of the ambulance and Jude's desperate face, telling me he loved me, but not much else. Only knowing I was going to die, and wishing I'd told him I loved him.

Had I told him?

I moved, reaching out to touch his arm, and winced. My chest ached like a bowling ball had landed on top of me. "Ow."

Jude jerked up, eyes full of sleep, before he saw me looking at him. Then his face lit up, and he was all smiles. "Hey, sweetheart."

He kissed me, sliding a hand beneath me to cradle my head. "How are you feeling?"

"I seem to be alive."

"You are alive." His voice caught, and he gave me a wavering smile. "It was a close one."

As I reached for his hand, he took mine and held it tight. He was trying not to show me how terrified he'd been, and I loved him more for it. I didn't want him to be terrified or scared to show it. But that would come later, when we were home.

"Why does my chest hurt?"

Jude brushed a strand of hair out of my face and looked at me for a few moments before he started to speak. "You were dead when I got there, sweetheart. Your chest hurts because I did CPR."

I…didn't remember that. Of course I didn't, if I was already gone. I—

Emotion hit me in the chest. All the emotion I'd had to press down and ignore because I was trying to stay alive. It made my chest ache more, but I couldn't stop it.

Jude kicked off his shoes, lifting me up so he could join me on the bed and wrap himself around me, careful of the cords hooking me to the heart monitors. "It's okay," he whispered into my hair. "You're here."

I curled into him and let him hold me. This was my safe space—he always had been, even when we weren't together. Jude saved me and protected me.

"Who did this?" I finally asked, and Jude told me everything. I could tell it was hard for him to say and, even harder, thinking it was his fault. But Ben was arrested now, and Jude and I were still here. I was completely cleared, and Charlie would tell everyone, but this was a small town. It was going to take time for people to trust me again, even after they heard this story and knew I was innocent.

"I'm so sorry, Lena. He never would have come after you if it weren't for me."

"Maybe not," I said quietly. "But he did it because he saw we were happy, and I wouldn't trade the happiness."

"I don't deserve you." He tilted my face up to kiss me, and I wished with everything I had we weren't in the hospital and my head and chest didn't hurt. I wanted him, and I didn't want to wait.

"I told you I love you?" I asked. "Because I do. I always have, and when I was in there, it felt so stupid that I hadn't said it yet."

"You did tell me. And I love you so fucking much, Lena. I was already planning on asking you when everything was settled, but I want us to live together."

My heart went still for a beat. "I thought we basically were?"

"Officially," he clarified. "And I don't care where it is. If you want to move in to my place and do what you said —take the bones and make it exactly the way you want it, I'll paint it and decorate it as many times as you like. If you want to stay in your house, I'll pack up tomorrow and bring my stuff over. All I ask is you let me beef up the security some more."

He was completely serious. Jude didn't mess around when it came to stuff like this, and he didn't say things he didn't mean. Of course I wanted to live with him—I wanted to do everything with him. We'd barely been separated since that first night, and this didn't make me want to change that anytime soon. But which to choose?

I liked my little house, and I'd made it my own. All the furniture and the books, the way it was decorated, I loved all of that. But I loved Jude's house too. I saw potential in it to be something truly amazing. Plus, if we did it together, it would be a house for both of us and not just me. That was aside from the fact that Jude's house was about three times bigger than mine.

"Did I shock your heart into stopping again?"

"No." I laughed. "I was just thinking about both options, and I think I want your house. If we can make it something we both love and I get to keep some of my furniture."

"Done," he said, capturing my lips with his. "You can do whatever you want, as long as I get to keep you." His eyes turned wicked. "And I'm definitely getting a new bed. One that has plenty of places to use restraints. Especially handcuffs."

"Shh." I pressed a finger to his lips. "Not here."

"Yes, here. I almost borrowed Charlie's handcuffs on the way back and locked the door." His mouth was on mine, gently pressing me down into the bed and drowning me in heat.

"Am I interrupting?" an amused voice asked.

We broke apart and found the doctor standing in the doorway, one hand on the door like she was about to knock. "No," I said. "Of course not."

"Thought I'd check on you this morning."

"What time is it?"

Jude smirked. "It's early. Maybe eight?"

"Oh." I'd slept the whole night? I glanced down at the tubes in my arm. They'd kept me that way. It made sense, I guess.

"How are you feeling?"

I winced. "My chest hurts and my head aches, but I'll take it since I'm, you know, not dead."

She smiled. "That's a good thing. And everything looks good for me too. I want to keep you one more night for observation and make sure you don't have any lingering effects from the exhaust inhalation or resuscitation, but if everything's fine tomorrow morning, you're clear to go home."

"Thank you."

She smiled at us both before she left, not even scolding us for Jude being in the bed with me. Of course, she was probably used to it by now. The Resting Warrior men protected their women, and I was one of those now. My face went hot.

"What was that thought?"

"Nothing."

"Hmm." That sound did things to me. "I'll get it out of you later."

He probably would, and I didn't argue with him.

"Everyone's going to want to visit today. I'm pretty sure Evie's been working on the biggest bouquet of flowers Garnet Bend has ever seen. You okay with that?"

The thought of seeing everyone… I wanted to, but it was also overwhelming. I'd pretty much been hiding since everything had happened at the school. None of our friends had thought I'd done it, but I was still raw.

I wasn't quite over the need for people to see me as the sunshine girl, and I never wanted to be seen as a victim. Sighing, I made a mental note to call Dr. Rayne as soon as I was out of the hospital. Evie was right; I needed to talk to someone about that. About everything, really. I already had nightmares, and another near-death experience wasn't going to make them easier.

Still, I wanted to see my friends. "As long as you stay with me, I'll be okay."

"I'm not going anywhere, Lena." He leaned forward and whispered the words in my ear. "Ever. I promise. I'm staying with you forever."

Epilogue

Lena

Five Months Later

My stomach was filled with butterflies. Everything was shining and new, and the smell of fresh paint hadn't quite faded from the interior of Deja Brew.

The day was absolutely perfect, and people were lined up outside, but I was still more nervous than I could ever voice out loud.

The grand reopening had been a long time coming and had taken a lot of planning. But that was after Jude swept me away for a New Year's vacation on the beach, then moving in to his house and starting to turn it into a home we both adored. It wasn't a place with bare white walls anymore, and Jude had built a new bed for us with everything he'd promised.

I'd never really taken a vacation, and almost being

murdered seemed like a good excuse to take one. It had done me good, taking time to breathe, plan, have sessions with Dr. Rayne, and go home to Jude every night, ready for him to leave me breathless.

When I'd finally had the window in Deja Brew replaced earlier in the spring and began rebuilding, people had started to reach out. Time had cooled passions, and both Charlie and the local news had done a good job repairing my reputation.

Of course, hearing it all from Ben's lips and exactly how he'd sabotaged everything did wonders. The town was down a mechanic, but that was a solvable problem.

Even Allison DeVries was on my side. As soon as everything about Ben came out, she'd begged Charlie for my number and apologized. She saw how everything looked, and ruefully admitted how easy it was for Ben to charm her into letting him close to her. It made it all too simple.

She didn't even blink when I asked her about the barn, and then I felt a little foolish—though nothing had felt foolish in my desperation. Allison was growing her own coffee plants. They took years to mature, and they were just starting out, but she had dreams of starting her own coffee line. The farmer had the extra room to help and was a family friend. In spite of everything, we'd started chatting, and I had hopes she could be my friend too.

Lucas and Evelyn's wedding next month would help in the rebuilding process, but right now, I was only thinking about the people outside who were waiting to come in and try the veritable *mountain* of baked goods Evie and I had made over the last couple of days. Jude and every other person in the Resting Warrior family had been in and out, testing the food and making sure I wasn't going crazy when I wondered if it was good.

"Lena, stop pacing. You're going to make people think

something's wrong." Evie stood in the door to the kitchen with one brow raised. "Do I need to send you out back to run around the block?"

I shook my head. "No. I just—"

"If you tell me you're worried one more time, woman, I am going to smack you. Everything is perfect, and everyone is *excited*. Do you see that crowd?"

"They could be here to throw tomatoes at me," I muttered.

That wasn't true, and I knew it, but I couldn't shake the fear that gripped my stomach. Until I saw people's reactions, I wouldn't be calm.

"Hey." Arms came around me from behind, pulling me against him. "Everything is beautiful, and everything tastes amazing. I definitely did *not* just sneak some more of the chocolate frosting." Jude leaned down and kissed my cheek. "Breathe for me, sweetheart."

"I'll try."

If anything, everything had simply gotten better between us. With Ben gone and us living together, we were making up for lost time. Not once had I gotten tired of being close to Jude, and I knew he felt the same.

Even now, his holding me was easing my nerves and making me feel better. I could stand here forever and forget about the people outside. That would be fine with me.

"How long are you going to make them stand out there?" he asked, though I could feel him smiling.

"Forever. Let's cancel it."

"Stop stalling."

"But—"

"Lena." Jude's voice dropped into the register that made my hair stand on end and heat sink down into my bones. "Do I need to handcuff you to the worktable in the back and let them in myself?"

I managed to take a breath. "No."

"Good girl."

It was good they weren't in here yet, because the soft sound that came out was definitely not something I needed customers to hear. "You can't say that to me in public."

"You realize that only makes me want to do it more, right? I like the idea of you being wet for me under your pretty dress."

I was wearing a dress he loved—deep green and with a fifties-style skirt and high heels he'd already declared would stay on after we got home tonight.

"You're evil."

He squeezed me one more time. "And you like it."

I groaned. "Fine, let's get this over with."

People perked up as I approached the front, and when I opened the door, I was shocked. People poured inside so quickly I had to step back and simply get out of the way. I hadn't looked, but it seemed like the entire town was here. People were standing on the sidewalk in both directions, around one corner and down the street the other way. "What is going on…?"

"What's going on," Jude whispered, "is you underestimated how much the people of Garnet Bend care about you. They're fickle as hell, but they're ready to be here and support you."

I was speechless. Already, the line was out the door, and Evie was in over her head. "Get over there," Jude said with a wink. "I'll manage the line."

"Okay."

I couldn't even handle the emotion clogging my throat. Everyone was here, and they were smiling. Every customer who made a purchase said something kind or apologized. They really were happy I was back.

My heart may have jumped in my chest every time

someone took a bite of a pastry, but there were only smiles and compliments. Hours felt like minutes, and by the time we closed the doors behind the last customer, I was exhausted, my feet aching.

"Go home," Evie said. "I will clean up. Enjoy your victorious return as Garnet Bend's favorite businesswoman."

"Don't be silly." I reached for an apron on the hook. "It'll go faster with two."

She caught my hand. "Lena, I've got it. Jude is waiting for you on the patio."

I blinked at her. "Out back?"

"Out back."

My stomach did a little flip. I hadn't gone out back much—I was still dealing with the memories of hurling myself at the door and it not opening—but when I opened the back door, my jaw dropped.

The lights that hung over the space were all lit. The tables held glasses of champagne and candles, music was playing from somewhere, and Jude was dressed in a suit he had *not* been wearing earlier. "What's going on?"

He held out a hand to me. "Just a little congratulations for you. You did it."

I took a sip of the champagne he gave me. "Thank you."

"Okay," he said. "It's a little more than congratulations."

My heart stopped. Literally stopped. And I wasn't worried—I already knew Jude would start it again for me as many times as he needed to. "Oh my god."

He pulled me closer, putting down the glass on the table. "We have a lot of things happening soon. You'll be busy here with the reopening, plus Lucas and Evie's wedding, finishing the house. But do you remember what I said to you in the hospital?"

My whole body was tingling. I didn't know if this was all a dream or not, but I wasn't sure I was comprehending all this. Panic and joy and everything else tumbled around in my chest, and I couldn't breathe. "You were staying with me forever?"

"I'm staying with you forever." Taking my face in his hands, he looked at me. In that one look, Jude Williams saw all of me. My flaws and imperfections. My struggles. My joys and my fears. He looked at each piece of me, and he didn't run away. And in turn, I saw every bit of him. "Three years is more than enough time to know, don't you think?"

Tears were already blurring him in front of me as I nodded, and I couldn't stop them from coming faster as he sank to one knee in front of me. They were happy tears. I wasn't sure I would ever be happier than I was in this moment right now.

"Will you marry me, Lena? And stay with me forever?"

"Of course I will." I managed to hurl myself at him before I fell apart completely. Jude kissed me, lifting me up as he stood and spinning me around.

It was a long time before he set me back on my feet, and longer still before we broke apart, both breathless and nearly sparkling with joy.

"I love you."

I leaned my head on his chest. "I love you too."

"Here." He pulled a small black box out of his pocket. The ring was white gold, tiny diamonds twisting around the band and swirling around a larger center one, and it fit perfectly.

"I'm never going to take it off."

"I like the sound of that. And I already know it's the

only thing I want you wearing when we get home." He smirked, leaning down to kiss me one more time. "Well, that, and the high heels."

•••

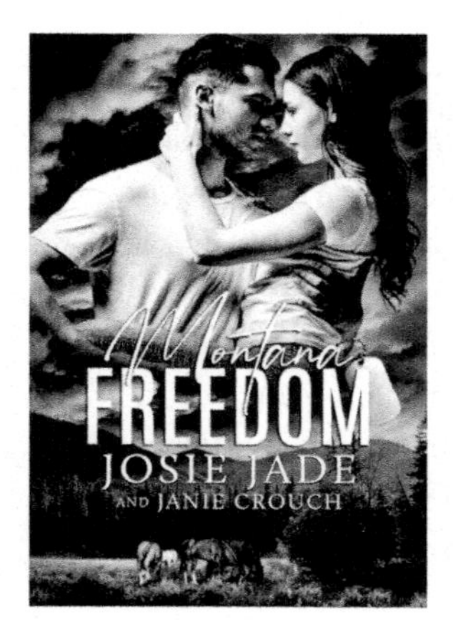

Thank you for reading MONTANA STORM! The Resting Warrior Ranch series continues with MONTANA FREEDOM, the story of Daniel and the woman in the cage. Grab it **HERE**.

And…

Click here to join Josie's VIP reader email group and as a special gift to you, you'll receive free ebooks each month. Plus, updates on Josie & Janie's new releases, sales, and specials.

Acknowledgments

A very special thanks to the Calamittie Jane Publishing editing and proofreading team:

Denise Hendrickson
Susan Greenbank
Chasidy Brooks
Tesh Elborne
Marilize Roos
Lisa at Silently Correcting Your Grammar
Elizabeth at Razor Sharp Editing

Thank you for your ongoing dedication for making these romantic suspense books the best they can be.

And to the creative minds at Deranged Doctor Designs who fashioned all the covers for this series and made the books so beautiful—thank you!

About the Author (Janie Crouch)

"Passion that leaps right off the page." - Romantic Times Book Reviews

USA Today and Publishers Weekly bestselling author Janie Crouch writes what she loves to read: passionate romantic suspense featuring protective heroes. Her books have won multiple awards, including the Romance Writers of America's coveted Vivian® Award, the National Readers Choice Award, and the Booksellers' Best.

After a lifetime on the East Coast, and a six-year stint in Germany due to her husband's job as support for the U.S. Military, Janie has settled into her dream home in Front Range of the Colorado Rockies.

When she's not listening to the voices in her head—and even when she is—she enjoys engaging in all sorts of crazy adventures (200-mile relay races; Ironman Triathlons, treks to Mt. Everest Base Camp...), traveling, and hanging out with her four kids.

Her favorite quote: "Life is a daring adventure or nothing." ~ Helen Keller.

facebook.com/janiecrouch
amazon.com/author/janiecrouch
instagram.com/janiecrouch
bookbub.com/authors/janie-crouch

About the Author (Josie Jade)

Josie Jade is the pen name of an avid romantic suspense reader who had so many stories bubbling up inside her she had to write them!

Her passion is protective heroes and books about healing...broken men and women who find love—and themselves—again.

Two truths and a lie:

• Josie lives in the mountains of Montana with her husband and three dogs, and is out skiing as much as possible

• Josie loves chocolate of all kinds—from deep & dark to painfully sweet

• Josie worked for years as an elementary school teacher before finally becoming a full time author

Josie's books will always be about fighting danger and standing shoulder-to-shoulder with the family you've chosen and the people you love.

Heroes exist. Let a Josie Jade book prove it to you.

Printed in Great Britain
by Amazon